W9-CLP-520

DECENT PEOPLE

DECENT PEOPLE

A NOVEL

DE'SHAWN CHARLES WINSLOW

BLOOMSBURY PUBLISHING

NEW YORK · LONDON · OXFORD · NEW DELHI · SYDNEY

BLOOMSBURY PUBLISHING
Bloomsbury Publishing Inc.
1385 Broadway, New York, NY 10018, USA

BLOOMSBURY, BLOOMSBURY PUBLISHING, and the Diana logo
are trademarks of Bloomsbury Publishing Plc

First published in the United States 2023

ISBN: HB: 978-1-63557-532-3; EBOOK: 978-1-63557-533-0

LIBRARY OF CONGRESS CATALOGING-IN-PUBLICATION DATA IS AVAILABLE

2 4 6 8 10 9 7 5 3 1

Typeset by Westchester Publishing Services
Printed and bound in the U.S.A.

To find out more about our authors and books visit
www.bloomsbury.com
and sign up for our newsletters.

Bloomsbury books may be purchased for business or promotional use. For
information on bulk purchases please contact Macmillan Corporate and
Premium Sales Department at specialmarkets@macmillan.com.

To the reader

DECENT PEOPLE

ONE

JO

March 1976

Josephine Wright could have kissed the ground, she was so glad to arrive back at her house in West Mills, North Carolina. She looked at her watch. It was seven o'clock. She had been on the road from Harlem since eight o'clock that morning. Typically, the drive took only eight hours. And that allowed for congestion on the George Washington Bridge and the bumper-to-bumper traffic one could count on while passing through D.C. But today there had been a bad automobile accident as Jo entered Delaware. She had crept at a snail's pace for nearly an hour. And there was that longer-than-usual break she'd taken at a rest stop in Maryland.

"Home at last," Jo said, allowing herself to enjoy the stillness in her car. For a moment, she sat looking at the shrub-lined, redbrick cottage she had purchased three years ago. Jo had bought it in preparation for her retirement in West Mills—the town where she had been born. It was also where, as a child, she had met Olympus "Lymp" Seymore—the man she had waited so long to find, the man she was soon to marry.

Now that Jo lived in the New Land Lane cottage full-time, it and West Mills felt more like home—no longer just a once-a-month refuge from New York City.

Jo could hardly believe she'd lived in New York for forty-eight years. It was even harder to fathom that she'd survived thirty-five years of secretarial work in the English Department at Flatbush College. She missed neither. But she did miss having her older brother, Herschel, nearby. Her most recent trip to New York had been to visit him. He had collapsed—dehydration, his doctor said—and Jo, fearing it was a heart attack or stroke, had rushed to Harlem to be by his side. She had been there for just under two weeks.

Herschel was sixty-five—only five years older than Jo—but she wished he would take better care of himself. He and his companion, Dean—they had been together twelve happy years, a relationship Jo sometimes envied—sat in their apartment almost all day, every day. The two of them got very little exercise, and they ate and drank whatever they wanted. Whatever they wanted included lots of cakes, muffins, cookies, salted peanuts, cola, and not nearly enough water.

"For the life of me, I *still* can't understand why you want to live in the South," Herschel had said as she was leaving his and Dean's 128th Street apartment earlier that morning. Though he had nowhere to be, he woke up most weekday mornings at six o'clock, showered, shaved his head, and dressed in slacks and a heavily starched white shirt. "I still think it'll prove too slow for a busybody like you down there."

He was right about one thing: Jo was a busybody. She had volunteered at community centers in Brooklyn and Harlem. She was often called on to be the president of this board, vice president of that one. And she was a meticulous bookkeeper.

Some of the other volunteers started calling her Miss IRS. Whenever she discovered embezzlement, she called the thieves to account. In response, they called her every name in the book. Jo didn't enjoy taking people down. But she had enjoyed finding the culprits.

"Even if I were to grow tired of West Mills, I won't be coming back to New York, brother," she'd told him. "And my offer still stands." If he and Dean wanted to move south, she would help them find a place of their own. They could even stay with her for a couple of months while they looked. Herschel had scratched his gray goatee.

"No, thanks. The South's no place for me, and you know why." He often said he would die and go to hell before he ever took up residence anywhere below D.C. He and Jo had both attended and graduated from Howard University. Herschel had provided janitorial services to cover his tuition. Jo had gone on a partial scholarship. The money she made from cleaning houses had covered the balance.

Jo had not forgotten how most of the men and boys in West Mills treated Herschel. She was only a young girl then, but she remembered. And though that had all happened decades ago, she could not blame him for not wanting to go back.

"Well, big brother, the two of you always have a room there." She had to stand on her tippy-toes to kiss his cheek.

"You know that man of yours wouldn't want us around. I appreciate it, though."

Jo had not yet told Herschel that Lymp was actually her fiancé. Given her history with men, she was afraid of jinxing it. She and Lymp were planning to elope in June. Vegas, probably. Maybe Miami. They didn't really know when or where they would marry. Sometime in '76, they imagined. Jo would tell her brother when their plans were solid—when she felt certain her fiancé wouldn't get cold feet.

Jo got out of her silver '75 Plymouth Duster—another pre-retirement gift to herself—and began to gather the trash that had accumulated during her drive. A Pepsi bottle here, a Lance nabs wrapper there, and pieces of dried leaves from the rest stop seemed to be everywhere. The smell of a neighbor's two horses wafted up her nose. While his property was large enough for them to roam behind his house, Jo felt certain the horses would be happier if they had more room to run.

Jo looked forward to seeing Lymp. It had been two weeks since she felt his strong-from-thirty-push-ups-a-day arms wrapped around her. And she missed those deep dimples of his. Jo even longed to smell the Old Spice she sometimes wished he'd stop using.

They had spoken on the phone earlier that morning, before getting on the road. She had tried to call him again at the rest stop, but there had been no answer. It wasn't a workday for him. His part-time job at the filling station was Tuesdays through Thursdays. He could have gone out to run errands or been outside working on some old car part with his son, she figured.

Having taken a quick shower in her olive-green tub, which matched the sink, which matched the tiles—Jo had been procrastinating with redecorating—she was ready to go and see Lymp, who lived across the road and a few houses to the right. As she was locking her door, she heard a vehicle turn into her driveway. It was Nate Seymore, Lymp's son, who lived just a handful of houses to the left with his mother.

It was just like Nate to stop and say hello. A southern gentleman, like his father. But when he got out of his brown pickup truck, he did not greet Jo with the cheerful, dimple-showing smile he usually donned—the smile he had inherited from Lymp. Nate looked solemn and exhausted.

Hellos exchanged and cheeks kissed, Jo asked, "What's wrong?"

"A whole lot happened today, Ms. Jo," Nate said, hands stuffed into his butterscotch leather jacket's pockets. "Can we go inside and talk?"

"What is it, Nate?" Jo asked, alarmed. "Is Lymp all right?"

"Well, that's what I want to talk to you about."

"If something's happened to your father, tell me now," Jo demanded. "Where is he, Nathaniel?"

"He's home. But I wouldn't say he's all right." He gestured toward her front door and they went inside, where Jo refused Nate's recommendation that she sit.

"Talk to me, Nate."

"Marian, Marva, and Laz are gone," he announced.

"What do you mean?"

"They're dead. Somebody shot 'em in their house."

Nate had just delivered the news as though telling her what he'd had for breakfast.

"Dead?" Jo shouted. "The Harmons?"

"Yes, ma'am. And that's only half of it. People trying to pin it on Lymp."

"Jesus Christ!"

Jo was not religious. But who else do you call on when you hear that your fiancé is suspected of murdering all three of his half-siblings?

"Yeah," Nate said. "With him not gettin' along with them too well, folks' imaginations running wild. Their mouths are, too." Jo brought both hands to her temples. "You all right, Ms. Jo? I think you oughta sit?"

5

"Yes, I think I should," she said, lowering herself into the floral-print, Victorian-style couch the previous owner had left behind. A housewarming gift, she'd said.

Nate went to the kitchen to get her a glass of water. If Jo had kept alcohol in the house, she would have requested something much stronger.

If Lymp was home, it meant the authorities suspected someone else. There was nothing to worry about. Still, she couldn't imagine what he was going through. Jo decided that she'd have the glass of water and collect her thoughts. Then she would go and be by her man's side.

MY MAN IS *my best friend*, Jo often heard women at the office say about their husbands and fiancés. Though Jo had been married before, it wasn't until '73, when she started seeing Lymp, that she understood what her colleagues meant. And she loved it. One moment Lymp might be flirting with her, the next he was asking her to tell him, in detail, about her day. He also offered opinions—solicited or otherwise. Jo enjoyed it all. Lymp was unlike any man she had ever dated.

Soon after Jo's twenty-fifth birthday, she had married Garrett—an amazing lover who would turn out to be Flatbush's most notorious womanizer. They were married for just one year. Jo wrote it off as a live-and-learn experience.

At thirty, Jo met Timothy. They had embarked on a one-year courtship and a one-year engagement before he revealed a change of heart.

"I love you, Jo. I really do." They were standing outside of a brownstone in Harlem where Billie Holiday had just performed. It was December and freezing. "But not the way

I ought to love someone I'm about to walk down the aisle with. Please forgive me."

When Jo broke the news to her brother, he said, "I've said it once and I'll say it again. Take a break." They were having drinks together at an underground gay bar in a Negro section of Queens. "You don't *need* a man to be happy. Mama's been just fine with just us."

"I know that, Herschel. I don't look to men to make me whole or any of that. I should slap you for even suggesting I'm that kind of lady. I can make my own money and put a roof over my own head. Just like Mama has. But that doesn't mean I want to be lonely."

"Like Mama?"

"That's not what I said," Jo asserted. On some level, he was right. Jo didn't want to be lonely like their mother, who never remarried after their father died. He had passed away when she was only three years old. "I just think everyone deserves a special someone."

"I won't argue with that, sis. Cheers." They raised their glasses.

Reed, a neighbor's nephew, was Jo's next gentleman caller. He was a Southerner—born and raised in Birmingham, Alabama. He had moved to New York to become what he often referred to as a *serious writer.* And he taught at a grade school in Harlem. After nine months of dating, he proposed, Jo accepted, and they were married two months later.

All seemed well. But after the first year of marriage, Jo noticed that Reed became withdrawn, increasingly obsessed with the Civil War novel he'd been writing since before she'd met him. He would stay up late, night after night, scribbling in notebooks, reading passages aloud as though auditioning for a role in a play. Then, after a month or so, he'd burn the manuscript in their bathroom sink, smoke filling their Crown Heights apartment.

Romance between the two of them became a thing of the past, but he still treated her kindly. Jo thought his disinterest in lovemaking would pass if he would just finish the book and try to get it published. But month after month, she woke to clumps of burned paper in the basin.

Jo stayed with Reed for seventeen long years. Why? There were four reasons. First, he was the only man who didn't seem to mind her straight-up-and-down figure or her refusal to relax her hair (though, now, she got a perm every six weeks—no dyes). Second, Reed didn't pressure her to give him children. That was his biggest gift to her. Jo had never been one of those girls who fantasized about being a mother. She enjoyed babysitting neighbors' children every blue moon. But full-time parenting? No, thank you, she'd once said to her mother on the topic.

Third, Jo's mother, Susan, adored Reed, mostly because he always kept a job. "No marriage is just right, JoJo," her mother said to her at year five with Reed. "As long as he gets up and goes to work, let him fuss with that book all he wants. Reed'll either finish it or he won't. Either way, he's your husband. And he loves ya. He's a keeper. Reminds me of yo' father. A good man. You stay put. You don't wanna grow old without a husband like me and my sisters, baby girl. Trust me." Despite her frustrations, Jo took her mother's advice and stayed with Reed awhile longer.

But as Jo approached her fifties, and realized that to Reed, she was only the woman he lived with, ate dinner with, kissed on the cheek before bed, she knew it was time to go. So, in the fall of '61, she filed for divorce. Reed did not fight it.

Unexpectedly, after that Jo found herself in a workplace affair with Benjamin, a white English professor at Flatbush College. Jo knew what they were. Or, she thought she knew. It had to be secret, which she enjoyed for about a year. But once Jo began thinking about Ben all day, hoping he'd come into the department's office to check his mailbox or to ask for a piece of chalk, she knew something would have to change. So she told Ben that she loved him and wanted more than a weekly rendezvous at her apartment or his. And though she was prepared to let Ben go, she hoped he'd say, "Then let's be together, Jo. Fuck what people will say." But he didn't. He was grateful for their fun time together, he said. And he wished her the very best of luck. The following semester, Ben moved to Boston. A professorship at Emerson. She missed him, but she was proud of herself for telling him how she felt and for letting him go. She grew accustomed to his absence quicker than she had expected.

Jo wanted love. True love. And once she was well into her late fifties, she felt less sure it would come her way. So, after her mother passed and Herschel fell in love, Jo began planning for a quiet life in the South, in West Mills—the place from which she had been torn as a twelve-year-old girl. When she traveled down to look at homes in '73, two days after her fifty-seventh birthday, she found that some of the west-side corn and cotton fields she used to play in were now dirt roads lined with houses, mobile homes, and auto repair shops. And lots of pine trees. It seemed as though everyone had pine trees in their yards. Jo hadn't remembered those from her childhood.

Jo fell in love with Mrs. Gyther's cottage, which, in many ways, reminded her of a prewar NYC apartment. A living room just the right size for entertaining four or five people; two bedrooms separated by a full-size bathroom. And when Jo learned that there were sturdy hardwood floors under the carpet, she could have picked up the Realtor and spun her around. All Jo would have to do is have them buffed and shined a bit. The yard, though small, was just another bonus. Jo would be able to mow the lawn herself. Mrs. Gyther's cottage was the second property she had viewed. Now, she could barely remember the six that followed.

On Jo's second weekend visit to her cottage, Lymp came over to say hello. When she saw him, she remembered that they had gone to school together before she moved to New York.

"Didn't you throw a pinecone and hit me in my forehead one time?" Lymp asked as they stood on her front lawn.

"It's possible. But you must've thrown one at me first." They laughed like schoolchildren. Jo also remembered that Lymp had never been anything but sweet to her. Never called her Stick, like most of the other children had.

Jo believed their reunion was a good sign. She needed for it to be a good sign. If finding the cottage was an ice-cream sundae, having Lymp as a neighbor was the cherry on top.

"I've been married twice," she nervously announced to him on their first date, which was dinner at the cottage. Fried trout with hush puppies. It was on that night that Jo knew she'd have to get rid of the electric stove and buy one operated by gas. Frying with electric did something to the oil, though she couldn't put her finger on the difference to save her life.

"Oh yeah? Twice, huh? Me, too."

"Really?" Jo asked.

"Nah, I'm just jokin'. I ain't been married yet. Got a son, though. My pride and joy and my best buddy. You a widow?" He bit into a golden hush puppy. Jo hoped she'd left them in the oil long enough.

"No," she said, stealing glances at him to try and gauge his reaction to her answer. There wasn't much of one.

"Well, maybe the next time'll be the right time. Ain't that how the saying goes?" He winked.

"So they say, Mr. Seymore." Jo fought back a smile. "But that's the last thing on my mind right now."

After a handful of outings with Lymp, it was plain to see that people in West Mills respected him. When she accompanied him to Manning Grocery, there were some who wanted to stop him for ten-minute conversations. There were some who only nodded, but Jo could tell that he got along with most. It was a shame he didn't get along as well with his two sisters and brother: Dr. Marian Harmon, Marva Harmon, and Lazarus Harmon.

WHEN NATE RETURNED from the kitchen, he said, "Lymp'll be happy to see you, Ms. Jo. It's been a bad day for him. For all of us."

"Nate, tell me all that's happened. Don't leave anything out. Then I want to see your father."

Angela Glasper, Marian's receptionist—she was also one of Nate's closest friends—had found the Harmons' bodies in their large home. When they hadn't shown up at Marian's clinic, Angela knew something was wrong, and she went looking for them, Nate explained. Their bodies were at the foot of their staircase when Angela spotted them. Lazarus had been shot in the head. Marian and Marva were both shot in the chest. The coroner believed they'd been dead for nearly two days—killed on Saturday night.

"My God, my God, my God," Jo whispered. And without trying, she remembered, as if it were only days ago, playing hide-and-seek with Marian and Marva. The memory made it nearly impossible to swallow.

Found dead at the foot of the staircase. The image made Jo shudder. She remembered the Harmons' grand staircase. As a young girl she sometimes sat on that staircase and eavesdropped on her mother and Louise Harmon as they spoke about ways to help feed the less fortunate. Jo remembered the entire house quite well. Some referred to it as a mansion. It sat off in a remote corner of West Mills, near the Virginia line. It was large, white, with columns and a balcony on the second level. The Harmons had always been the most monied family on the west side of the canal—the Black side. Jo recalled hearing grown people speak about how strange it was for a colored family to live in a house of that size—and not be working in it.

Jo and Marian were the same age, Marva a couple of years younger. Lymp was three years Jo's junior. Jo barely knew Lazarus. When she moved away from West Mills at the age of twelve, Lazarus—most people called him Laz—was only two, maybe three years old.

"Nate, I don't even know what to say. I'm at a loss for words."

"I know what you mean. I can't believe it, either. It just don't seem real."

Lymp must be beside himself. For people to assume the worst of him just because he had a strained relationship with the Harmons was ridiculous. It was outright offensive. Jo knew people who hadn't spoken to their siblings in decades. That didn't mean they'd kill them.

Were the Harmons at the top of Lymp's Christmas gift list? No. But they were his sisters and brother, flesh and blood.

THE FOUR OF them shared a father—the late Mr. Jessie Earl Harmon, a pillar of the Black community. Lymp had been quite close to his father, he had shared with Jo. And she found that to be endearing, having lost her own father to pneumonia long before she was old enough to even remember.

One evening in '73—it was their seventh or eighth date—Jo and Lymp went out to the Elks Lodge for dinner. It was a long, rectangular brick building with a cobblestone parking lot. Apparently, the land had once been the home of a small Baptist church that mysteriously burned down before electricity had even been installed.

That night in '73, in what was considered the nonsmoking section—the partition was invisible—Lymp told Jo all about his relationship with his father. Jessie Earl had wanted all four of his children to be close-knit, since he had been an only child.

"If I was any more different from them, I'd be a cow, or a bird or somethin'. I don't have a thing in common with those three," Lymp said. "I stayed here. They all moved away. Hell, I can count on one hand how many times I've even traveled outside of Carolina and Virginia. Marian and them been to other countries. All three of 'em been to college and so forth. Only time I've been on a college campus was to go looking with Nate when he was thinkin' about enrolling. That was ten, eleven years ago. Before that, I never stepped foot on a campus. Jessie Earl was always real proud of Marian, you know."

Lymp never referred to his father with a common title such as *Pop* or *Pa* or *Dad*. He always called Jessie Earl by his name.

"Well, I imagine so," Jo said. "What about Marva and Lazarus, though?"

"Seemed like he was always irritated with those two. Marian was the favorite. Then me, maybe." He chuckled.

"Maybe *you* were his favorite," Jo offered.

"Nope," he said. "Marian, for sure. Did you know she was one of the first Black girls to get in at that medical school she went to?"

"Which one was it again?"

"Damn if I know. One of them schools in New York City. You'd know of 'em better than I would. I was proud of her, too. My big sister. A doctor. That made me feel good, Jo. You know what I'm sayin'? I stopped goin' to school after tenth grade. Never was all that great at it. Made more sense for me to go to work. Help my momma."

"Is that when you started welding?"

"Yep," Lymp said, smiling. He loved it. His father hadn't liked that Lymp never finished school, but he hadn't harped on it for long. Jessie Earl bought Lymp a truck so he could drive himself to work in Newport News, Virginia. "I had to pay him back. But guess what he did."

"Tell me."

"A week after I made the last payment, he wrote me a check for all the money I'd been givin' him that couple of years. He was a good father, Jo."

"That was really nice of him." Jo remembered Lymp's father fairly well. He was a nice-enough man, most of the time, to most people. But Jo also recalled seeing a darker side of Jessie Earl Harmon. On a few occasions, when she was at the Harmons' to play with Marian and Marva, she'd seen him push his wife, Louise, out of his way. Once, Jo saw him slap the woman across the face because Laz's nose needed wiping.

"I did welding for thirty-some years before I got hurt. Ever since I was eighteen years old. Before that, I worked odd jobs doing this and that right here in West Mills—on the east side, mostly."

Lymp asked Jo if she had ever run into Marian, Marva, and Lazarus in the North. She explained to him that while New Jersey and New York were neighbors, the two states could feel worlds apart if a person never had a reason to go to the other state.

Somberly, Lymp shared with Jo that it wasn't until Marian, Marva, and Lazarus were all moved away that he and Jessie Earl truly formed a father-son bond. He said that Louise Harmon had, just months before she died, become kinder to him, which he had found nice and strange. "She'd always hated me," Lymp said. "No wonder her children didn't like me."

That night at the lodge, Jo found herself taken by Lymp's vulnerability, his honesty. Garrett and Ben could benefit from just one conversation with a man like Lymp Seymore, she remembered thinking.

"I miss Jessie Earl. You don't get but one father. I ain't care nothin' about his money and land and all that. I didn't want none of it. Not one bit of it. Jo, if I told you how many times I'd even been in his house before Marian and them moved away, you wouldn't believe me."

"How many times?" Jo asked.

"I can count them on one hand." He raised his right hand up as if showing her something on his palm.

"You can't be serious, Lymp!" Jessie Earl must have been far crueler than she had imagined.

"Yeah, I am. Serious as a hard stroke. Not even five times. But I didn't care. I guess he call himself being decent to Louise by not having me there. My momma used to say, 'If he can't invite you to his home, like a father supposed to, you don't need him.' And I'd say, 'It's all right, Mama. I'm just happy he pays me any mind at all.' Lot of folk had daddies living right down the road from 'em, or over on the east side—if you know what I mean—who didn't pay them no attention. And I know a lot of people like that, Jo. I was lucky."

But Lymp eventually found himself in the Harmons' house regularly, he said. Jessie Earl's health began to fail in '64, and in early '65, he was dead. A few mornings after his funeral, Lymp and his mother were sitting at their kitchen table. "Mama said, 'What in the world do *they* want, I wonder?' So, I looked out the window and it was the three of 'em, stepping up on the porch. Anyway, Marian come to ask me if I'd look after the house."

"The house you weren't invited to?" Jo asked. "Some chutzpah, she's got."

"Some what?"

"Never mind," Jo said.

"Well, Marian said, 'I'll pay you.' I told her she ain't have to pay me to look after my own brother and sisters' property. You won't be able to guess what she said to me, Jo. She looked me straight in my face and said, 'Don't be stupid. These two don't own anything. It's *my* property now.'"

Jo dropped the French fry she was holding back onto her plate and said, "What in the . . . when did she get so mean? My God!"

"Crazy, ain't it? I know. Marva was nicer that day, though. She thanked me and all. Laz just stood there looking crazy.

I don't know which one of them is the strangest. Mama used to say all three of 'em is nutty as fruitcakes. God rest her."

In '71, the Harmons moved back into the mansion in West Mills, and Marian opened Friendly Pediatrics in '72. Marian was the only Black physician in the town—likely the only one for at least a hundred miles, maybe more. Marva was the nurse, though there was a rumor that she lacked the credentials. Laz was simply their driver. Some joked that he was also their bodyguard.

"So, Marian hired some guys to do the things I'd had been doing on the property ever since Jessie Earl died. I ain't been in there since. I drive by it sometimes, just to make sure they ain't let the place fall to pieces. Making sure they ain't fallin' to pieces, too."

"What do you mean?"

"Jessie Earl told me to always look out for them, Jo. That was the last thing he said to me. 'Look out for the other three for me,' he told me. Always called them the *other* three."

"See. You *were* his favorite, Lymp." She smiled at him, but he didn't return it. He looked pensive.

"He didn't have to ask me to look out for them, Josephine," Lymp said. "They my flesh and blood. I'd do that either way. And I do try to look out for 'em. I really do. But they grown. And they don't want no parts of me. So, I go on 'bout my business and leave them to theirs. I know they don't give a damn 'bout me. But I care 'bout them."

That was the kind of man Lymp was. And that was the kind of man with whom Jo wanted to spend the rest of her life.

For a couple of minutes, Jo and Lymp ate their burgers and fries without speaking. Just as she was about to ask Lymp a question, she glanced up to find that he was gazing angrily at his plate, his fist clenched, breathing heavily, lips drawn together.

"Lymp, honey. You all right?" She reached across the table and took hold of his wrists. "Lymp?"

"What?" He seemed startled, as if awakened by a loud alarm clock. "I'm sorry. Sorry 'bout that, Josephine. I just—I just get so pissed off just thinkin' 'bout them sometimes. I'm sorry."

She could see in his sad eyes that he meant it. But he hadn't opened his fist, so she gently palmed it, massaged it until he relaxed.

Having sat back down to avoid attracting unwanted attention and eager to end Lymp's discomfort, Jo said. "It's okay, baby. It's just fine. We all get frustrated sometimes."

Lymp didn't eat any more of his food. Nor did Jo. She couldn't eat when she felt nervous. And that was how the episode made her feel. She'd seen rage bubbling just beneath the surface.

But Lymp had not yelled or even raised his voice. He had not displayed any violence—the kind that Jo had once, as a young girl, witnessed from Jessie Earl. If Lymp had a mean streak like his father, he would've hit that table. He might have even flipped it over. Right?

They sat quietly. A couple of people walked by and said hello. They paid the bill and left.

After that evening at the lodge, Jo decided not to mention the Harmons unless Lymp mentioned them first. And whenever he did, she would steer the conversation somewhere else. Jo couldn't bear to see him have another of those episodes. She hadn't liked the glimpse of rage she had seen in him. And she was glad she hadn't seen it again.

TWO

Jo

"Nate, I'm going on over to your father's. Walk with me?"

"Yes, ma'am. Of course. But I think I should fill you in on something else before we go. I don't want to bring it up in front of Lymp."

"What is it?" Jo was growing impatient. But since Nate was calm, Jo figured she should remain calm, too. She sat back down on the couch.

When the news had got around about the Harmons being murdered, someone had called the sheriff's department and reported that Lymp had, in the past week, said awful things about his siblings—Marian, specifically—to a group of men while at Sutton's Petro.

This was surprising to Jo; in the past year or so, Lymp had gotten to a place of rarely mentioning his siblings.

A few weeks ago, Jo and Lymp had, without realizing it, parked next to the trio in the shopping center. When she and Lymp were leaving Aiken's Rx and More, the Harmons were leaving Marian's clinic, Friendly Pediatrics. His sisters were wearing matching polka-dot scarves.

"Ain't they a lil too old for that, Josephine?" he had whispered. "Dressin' alike like children?"

"Hush up. They might hear you."

Lymp had greeted them first. Then Jo. The Harmons replied in kind. Marian had even managed half a smile. And then they all went about their business.

"Maybe you all will turn a corner soon," Jo had said on the drive back to New Land Lane. "Life's too short not to be close to your own siblings."

Lymp had shrugged his shoulders and changed the subject.

"What was he heard saying, Nate?"

"That they stuck-up, don't show people common courtesy. That sort of thing. You'll have to ask Lymp for the particulars."

"Has something happened between him and the Harmons recently, while I was in New York?" Nate averted his eyes. "Nathaniel?"

"He asked Marian for a loan, and she was nasty to him."

"What in hell did he need a loan from *her* for?"

"To finally get that plumbing work done. He needs a new septic tank and the estimates were pretty high." Jo knew Lymp's plumbing needed some updating and that he was getting quotes. But Lymp hadn't told her that the costs were over his head. Jo would have gladly helped, but maybe his pride got in the way or he needed more than she had to offer. And while she understood him seeking an interest-free loan, she had no idea he would ask Marian. No wonder he hadn't mentioned the needed repairs recently. "Evidently, he got fired up talking about it all at Sutton's. Kicked a gas can around and beat his fist on the hood of somebody's car."

Jo remembered Lymp's clenched fist that night at the lodge. *What's wrong with you, Jo? You know Lymp. You know he's a good person. Someone you can trust.*

"Well, Nate, he's home. The authorities know he's innocent," Jo said. It was more of a reminder to herself than it was to Nate. "Otherwise, he'd be *under* the jail. Who cares what people think? I certainly don't give a damn."

Nate shot Jo an expression that made her uncomfortable.

"You been in the big city too long, Ms. Jo," he said firmly. "'Round here, we care what our neighbors and folk think about us. Not everything they think 'bout us. But we care when somebody thinks ill of us. Ain't but a thousand or so people in West Mills. Matters a whole lot that we can halfway trust one another." Nate was right: Jo had grown accustomed to living in a place where most barely knew their next-door neighbors. If one had committed a crime, it might be years before you knew it.

"Of course," Jo said, embarrassed. "I'm sorry."

"Folks callin' Lymp's house and telling him he oughta show some dignity and gon' and confess. And that if he won't, they won't let up until he moves away from here. Sayin' mean shit to him and hanging up."

"All of this has been going on since the Harmons were found this morning?"

"Yeah," Nate said. He was clearly annoyed at her surprise. "Like I said, in this lil town, shit gets around faster than you can eat an apple. Folk driving by Lymp's house slow and honking their horns. And Jacob Sutton already fired him from that run-down, shithole filling station, Ms. Jo. Treating Lymp like some kind of damn criminal. Like he's a stranger that ain't lived around here his whole life. Lymp don't even like to kill spiders. Ain't no way he would kill his own sisters and brother."

Jo placed a hand on Nate's shoulder.

"Everything will be fine. Lymp's alibi must've been solid. Who was Lymp with when—"

"Me. He was with me."

"Good!" Jo exclaimed, relieved. "Beers at the lodge?" It was something they did together some weekends. Quality time between father and son. Beers, burgers, and arguments over which basketball players should be fired for mediocre performances.

"Yes, ma'am," he said. "I mean, yes, we had some beers, but not at the lodge. At Lymp's. He passed out and I was there watching TV 'til late."

"I see," Jo said.

"I know how it sounds, Miss Jo. Me being my father's only alibi. But it's the God's honest truth."

"I know, Nate. You know I believe you."

But a familiar feeling washed over her. She was reminded of learning that Garrett had cheated on her. Nearly a week had passed before she allowed herself to believe it. *But come on now, Jo. You know Lymp wouldn't kill anyone. And Nate has never given you a reason to doubt his word. An honest young fellow.*

"I need to get over there to him. But you mark my words, Nate. As soon as they catch whoever did this, everyone who's bad-mouthing Lymp will have to eat dirt. Just watch and see. Once the investigation is underway, they'll—"

"I don't think there'll be much more investigating," Nate cut in. Nate's best friend, Percival—he was one of two Black officers at the sheriff's department—had told Nate that he'd overheard Sheriff Horton and the district attorney, Dale Boothe, talking. "They said they won't waste tax dollars trying to find who killed some drug dealers."

"Drug dealers?" Jo exclaimed.

"Yeah. They found a bunch of reefer and sedatives in the house. I was surprised to hear 'bout the pot. Not the pills, though."

"Why not?"

"Just something Angie told me a long time ago," he said. And he didn't seem interested in saying much more about it. Jo would extract it from him later. He went on to say that, according to Percival, Sheriff Horton and the district attorney had made up their minds. "They callin' it a drug deal gone bad."

"The Harmons? Drug dealers?" Jo said. "I don't buy it."

"I don't really think they were, either," Nate said. "But who knows?"

"So, they're just going to close the case? Just like that?"

"Percy said they won't close it right away, but they probably won't be doing much real work on it. Motherfuckers."

Jo wondered why the officers, having seen drugs at the Harmons', had bothered Lymp—regardless of his fiery rant at Sutton's Petro. Who in the world had appointed these clowns to protect the citizens of West Mills, she wondered.

WHEN JO AND Nate arrived at Lymp's front door, she let Nate knock.

"Lymp, Ms. Jo's here!" Nate shouted. "Come to the door!" And after a handful of seconds: "Dad!" Either of them could have used their key, but there seemed to be an unspoken agreement that now wasn't the right time to force themselves in.

"Lymp? Honey?" Jo called. "May we come in?" The space between the cement porch and his house seemed larger than it was the last time she was there. Lymp would have to face facts. The whole house was falling apart and probably needed to be demolished. But she knew he would never commit to such a thing. His mother had inherited the house from her own mother before Lymp was born. He would sooner die than see it knocked down.

Lymp finally opened the door. He was wearing just an A-shirt and a pair of pin-striped pajama pants. It was obvious he'd been crying. The whites of his deep brown eyes looked as though he'd suffered an allergic reaction. And he succumbed again once Jo embraced him.

"It's an evil world, Josephine," he said. "Somebody walked right in their house and killed 'em. They could be mean as rattlers, all three of 'em. But they didn't deserve this. Nobody deserves to be killed like that!"

Jo held Lymp tightly for another minute, then she escorted him to his favorite chair. The black faux-leather recliner where he ate most of his meals and watched TV when he came home from his part-time job at Sutton's Petro. He cried uncontrollably for several minutes. Reed, her second husband, had cried like this when he couldn't get a character to speak to him.

Jo rubbed his back and took his hand. A rerun of *The Honeymooners* was playing on the television.

"And the people turned on me, Josephine," Lymp said then, handkerchief in hand. "Somebody tol' the sheriff they think I did it. You know I wouldn't do nothin' like that. Kill my own sisters and brother? For what? 'Cause Marian wouldn't help me buy a septic tank? That's crazy! I talked some shit about her and the other two, yeah. But I wouldn't k—"

"I know, love," Jo said. Seeing him cry made her heart lurch. "We can talk about all that later. You're home. You're safe. I just want you to try and relax. Just keep holding my hand."

Nate brought in a chair from the kitchen so that Jo could sit next to Lymp, the floor creaking loudly under his feet. In the living room, the only places to sit were Lymp's recliner and his plaid sofa.

"Have you eaten since you got home?" Jo asked Lymp after noticing two untouched Munch bars on the side table. Whenever Lymp bought Munch bars, he usually ate them right away.

"I had a burger at the lodge by myself Saturday evening and came straight here. Then Nate came by with a six-pack of Millers and we drank 'em. Hell, I was knocked out before nine thirty, I believe. Wasn't I, son?"

Nate nodded. "Yeah. I came here with hoagies and beer. But he'd already eaten. I sat here and watched TV and drank beer. Lymp fell asleep and I dozed off, too. Woke up around two o'clock and went home."

"Thank God I got a son who thought to stop by and see 'bout his ol' man. If Nate hadn't come here, I might be locked up, Josephine. Thank God he—" He was unable to finish his sentence. Jo stood, kissed the bald crown of Lymp's head and told him it was okay.

"You don't have a thing to worry about," Jo said as she pressed her cheek against his head.

Jo was relieved that the sheriff appeared to believe Lymp's alibi. Most lawmen might have been suspicious. It was more likely the sheriff simply didn't have evidence to disprove the alibi. Jo would keep that opinion to herself. Now wasn't the time to say it aloud. But for members of the community who had known Lymp all his life to harass him even after the authorities let him go—unconscionable.

"Let it all out, honey. Let it all out," Jo said, dabbing tears from his face. When he'd settled down again, she said, "Let's get you something to eat, sweetheart."

Thirty minutes later, after Lymp was showered and in fresh clothes, Jo and Nate sat with him at his kitchen table while he ate a can of Campbell's tomato soup and a sleeve of saltines. Jo wanted to ask why he'd gone to Marian for money, instead of someone else who might have been able and more willing—his boss, for example. But now wasn't the time.

"A funeral will have to be arranged for them," Lymp said. "I'm the closest kin they had. It should be me, right, Josephine?"

"We'll look into that tomorrow," Nate said. "I know for a fact Edgars & Edgars were Marian's lawyers. I've seen her coming out of their offices a few times since they moved back here. Maybe they had their wishes written up."

"A living will," Jo offered.

"Well, see if they had one of those, Nate," Lymp said. "And Josephine, just so you know, I don't want nothin' they owned. Our father already gave me what he wanted me to have. Years ago. I ain't never been in no wills with them three. So people can go to hell if they want to start that kind of talk." He put his face in his hands and sobbed. Jo felt the urge to pull his head to her chest. Instead, she hooked her right arm with his left and laid her head on his shoulder. After a few moments, he kissed her cheek and went back to eating the soup.

Jo hadn't been in touch with Marian and Marva Harmon since they were girls. And since buying the cottage, she had only run into them a handful of times during her short trips down to West Mills. Marian was polite but indifferent. Marva seemed warmer but hesitant to make any gestures toward a renewed friendship. But Jo hadn't taken it personal. They were all decades older, she and them. People grow up. People change.

"I told Sheriff Horton he could run any kinda lie test he want," Lymp said, silver stubble peeking out through the pores of his chin. She stroked his left jaw with a finger. "I ain't got nothing to hide. Not a thing."

"And I'm sure you passed the polygraph without issue."

"They ain't got one of those machines. Said they'd borrow one from Pasquotank County or somewhere. Then they got to book somebody licensed to work the damn thing. Said they'd call me when they get that sorted out, if need be."

Jo could feel beads of sweat forming on her forehead. *If need be? Of course there's a need! To clear you of all suspicion!*

"Oh," she said. "Maybe you should press the issue a bit. Get that taken care of and shut everyone up. It'll be a load off your mind. Don't you think?"

"I think I'll wait for *them* to call *me*," Lymp said. "Probably not much need for it, really. Nate, did you tell her 'bout the drugs, and 'bout what Percival heard Horton say? I don't know if I believe this drug-sellin' shit. But you just never know what folk got goin'." Jo's face must have betrayed her because Lymp said, "Would it make *you* feel better if I pressed on 'em 'bout the lie detector?"

As much as it pains me to think it, yes, Lymp. It would make me feel more comfortable.

"I don't want the people harassing and accusing you any more than they have. Making life hard for you. That's my concern," Jo replied. A half-truth. "West Mills is your home, and the people here should—"

"I hear what you sayin', Josephine, but I can't think about them right now. People gon' talk one way or another. Don't get me wrong now. It hurts. But if Horton feels like I need to take that test, you can trust and believe he'll send for me. I'm gon' leave that alone."

"Lymp doesn't even know how to hold a gun," Nate said. "Ain't no way he shot three people."

"That's exactly what I told Horton," Lymp said. "He said Marian and them was shot with some kinda small gun. I tol' him I didn't want to hear nothing about how my folks got killed. I don't know much 'bout guns, anyway. Never have."

This was true. Once, when Jo teased about maybe learning to hunt, Lymp made it clear to her that she wouldn't learn it from him. When Lymp was a teenager, Jessie Earl had tried to teach him how to operate a handgun. It was the first and last day Lymp ever touched a gun, he had told Jo.

"Nate, did you tell her about the folk Marian and Marva was havin' trouble with?" Lymp asked, and Nate shook his head. "See, they had all them enemies, but everybody so quick to think *I'd* do something horrible to 'em. Ain't no reason in this world I'd do something so awful, Josephine."

He looked her straight in the eyes in a way that, to Jo, felt like a plea.

"I know, Lymp, honey," she assured him. "It's all right."

"The last thing Jessie Earl said to me was to look out for them. I'm serious when I say that. You know a lot of folk say, 'Such-and-such was the last thing So-and-So said to me.' But that was really the last thing Jessie Earl said to me. I remember like it was yesterday."

"It's all a bunch of bullshit," Nate chimed in. "Folk acting like Lymp's the only one who didn't care for the Harmons."

Exactly a week ago, Eunice Loving, owner of Manning Grocery, and silent partner to many other Black business owners in West Mills and surrounding towns, had marched into Friendly Pediatrics and demanded to speak with Marian.

Angela had been out of the office, on her lunch break, for most of the argument, but she had caught some of it when she returned.

"Angie said Eunice was mad as hell back there in Marian's office. Somethin' to do with her son."

"Was the Loving boy one of Marian's patients?" Jo asked.

"Nope," Nate said. "I asked Angie the same question on the day Marian and Eunice fussed. She said he wasn't a patient there."

"Eunice cussed Marian slam out," Lymp said. He had picked up his spoon again. "And Eunice is a churchgoing woman. Directs the choirs, volunteers at the schools, at the community center, and that kind of thing. A respectable lady with money. She's a lil bit stuck-up, like Marian, to be honest. But I ain't never known her to be *mean*. Her son is a lil funny-actin'. He's a sis—"

"Lymp," Nate interrupted. "No need for all that."

Lymp apologized and went on to share that during his last visit to the barbershop, he'd heard that Lazarus had escorted Eunice Loving out of Friendly Pediatrics. But no one seemed to know what Marian had done to make her so angry.

"Nate, do me a favor and get me a pop from the icebox, son." Jo resisted the urge to tell Lymp that he should have water instead. Like her brother, Lymp consumed a lot of sugar. Jo wanted him healthy. "Then, Marva got to fussin' with the white girl."

"On the same day as Eunice and Marian," Nate added, setting the can of Coke in front of his father.

"I thought Marva and that young lady were best friends," Jo said. On one of Jo's visits to town, about a year and a half ago, she saw Marva and the younger white lady standing in line together at the Dairy Queen. With the smell from the nearby chicken plant whirling around, Jo didn't know how anyone, especially in summer, could enjoy having ice cream outside of that Dairy Queen. She and Lymp went to the one over in Pasquotank.

Marva had introduced them. Jo couldn't remember the young lady's name. It struck her, though, that Marva, who at the time must have been fifty-seven, had such a tight-knit friendship with a white lady in her early thirties. No judgment, just a curious thing.

But the pair had apparently been in a heated argument at the shopping center, just outside the drugstore, Lymp had been told. "Fussin' in that lil alley between the drugstore and the flower shop. They need to close that flower shop. Nobody buyin' them dead flowers. The white girl works at the drugstore, you know."

"Savannah Russet," Nate offered.

"Yeah. That's her name," Lymp said. "She's Ted Temple's girl. Marian had some kind of fallin'-out with him, too. He's the landlord at the shopping center, you know. Probably business-related. But I don't know, the Temples are all bigots."

He went on to explain that the late Adam Temple Sr. had been known to cheat Black farmers out of their land. In college, Jo had read about that kind of land theft, and her mother had once told her about family members who had been victims of it. Sadly, Lymp believed Jessie Earl might have helped Adam Temple Sr. pull it off.

"Adam Sr.'s been dead a long time, but Mrs. Hera Temple's still alive and kickin'. My momma worked in their house for a few months many years ago. She always told me that the Temples would give coloreds a job but wouldn't ever put money directly in our hands. Didn't want to risk touchin' ya."

Jo had met many Adam and Hera Temples over the years in New York City. They were the type of bigots thought exclusive to the South, but they existed in the North, too. They weren't the descendants of plantation owners, as most southern racists were. But as far as Jo was concerned, they may as well have been.

"People saw Marian and Ted Temple fussing in the parking lot 'bout a week and some change ago," Lymp continued. From what he had heard at the barbershop, the argument between Marian and her landlord had been rather intense. Finger-pointing and the like. "You know Temple won't have nothin' to do with his daughter because she married a colored fella. He died. Heart troubles. So young."

Jo didn't remember that, exactly. But she had seen Savannah with her two children. There was no mistaking that the boys weren't completely white. So it was no surprise to Jo to hear that Savannah was estranged from her family.

"Knot and Valley said the white girl threatened—"

"Savannah," Nate interjected.

"Why you keep doing that, Nate?" Lymp snipped.

"Because it doesn't sound nice," Nate replied.

"You think I care how something sound right now? After all's happened to me today? It's a wonder I haven't lost my damn mind already. Shit." He took a couple of deep breaths then a swallow of his soda. "*Savannah* told Marva that she'd kill her *and* Marian if they tried it again. Told Marva not to fuck with her. Excuse my language."

"Just a second," Jo said. "Savannah was heard making a direct threat?"

"Damn right, she was," Lymp replied. "The fellas at the shop didn't know the whole story 'cause it was second-, thirdhand talk. All they knew for sure was that Knot and Valley heard the threat with their own ears. You know who Knot and Val are, don't ya? The winos."

"Don't call 'em that, Lymp," Nate said.

"I don't mean nothin' by it." Lymp waved him off.

"Yes," Jo said. "I know who they are."

"Knot and Val did the right thing today when they heard what happened to Marian and them. They went to see Percival and told him Savannah had issued a threat. They might drink too much, but they got sense in their heads. And they look out for west-side folk."

Jo asked if Lazarus had fussed with anyone lately. Given that he'd been shot in the head, it would seem that he might have been the killer's target. But from what she'd heard Lymp say about him, Laz had had a very limited social life. Jo could relate. She'd never had a wide circle of friends. Her mother had taught her that family were the only friends a person needed. Jo didn't agree with that sentiment, fully. But she had come to live by it.

"Laz didn't have trouble with people," Nate said. "None that we know of, at least. He kinda just went wherever the wind blew him. Seem to me like the wind wouldn't take him far from Marian and Marva."

"Which is *still* a wonder to me," Jo said.

"Some families are just like that, Josephine. The one that's got the most education and the most money just kinda runs things sometimes. That's normal 'round here. And on top of that, Marian was always the leader of that bunch. Ever since we were all children, Marian led. Jessie Earl and Louise was always callin' her the smart one, the sensible one. You grow up hearin' that all your life, it sticks, whether it's true or not.

So, how you think that make the other two feel about they-selves? Small. Make you lose yo' drive, if you ever had any to begin with. You know what I'm saying?" Jo couldn't imagine that sort of life for herself, but she nodded. "Even if Marian had gotten married and had ten children, I believe she still would've had Marva and Laz living with her. That's just how they were."

"Did y'all ever find out who Marian might be dating?" Jo asked. Just a little over a year ago, Nate had heard a rumor that Marian had been seen turning out of a hotel parking lot in Chesapeake on Valentine's night.

Nate shrugged and said, "Never did hear. Probably some man in Virginia, though. She probably wouldn't go for no man 'round here in West Mills." He seemed exhausted. Jo had thought to insist that he go home and get some rest. But Nate was a reliable source of information, and she still had questions. First, if Lymp was hauled into the sheriff's department, surely the others who'd actually argued with Marian and Marva were taken in, too, weren't they?

"No, they were *not*," Lymp declared. "Just me. They—"

"Percival said they were questioned," Nate interjected. "But they weren't brought in. Sheriff and his guys treated them way better than Lymp. If Lymp had a lot of money in the bank, or if he was a white man, the sheriff probably would have just asked him a few questions over the phone and left it at that."

"Is anyone around here telling Eunice Loving and Savannah Russet and her father that *they* need to confess or pack up and move away?" Jo asked. She couldn't stand that Lymp was being singled out. It reminded her of the bullying her brother had endured when they were young.

"Not that we know of," Nate said.

"I feel like I'm in a nightmare, y'all," Lymp said. "I just can't believe folk think *I* did it." He got up and went to his bedroom.

THREE

Jo

The following morning Jo woke up at seven o'clock. She could hear the school bus, its brakes squealing as the driver stopped to pick up the neighbors' children. Lymp lay snuggled next to her, snoring quietly under the navy-blue quilt Jo had bought at the West Mills Flea Market, which was a large barn where vendors set up tables and walked over to McDonald's to use the bathroom.

Jo had talked Lymp into coming home with her. She couldn't let him spend the night alone after having such an unthinkable day. At first he'd resisted. He wouldn't sleep well, he'd said. He believed his tossing and turning would keep her up.

Jo loved that even after all he'd experienced the day before, Lymp still cared so much about her comfort. He was the most selfless of all the men she'd ever been with. She was glad she could be there for him, provide him with some solace. And she was sorry for the hint of doubt she'd felt about his innocence.

Lymp had decided to accompany Nate to Edgars & Edgars to check on the Harmons' wishes for a final service—if such wishes existed in writing. Jo would go along with them but only if they asked her to. So far, Lymp hadn't. And she was glad of it. She would need to drink at least three cups of chamomile before that. She hated funerals and the planning of them. Herschel had handled the majority of their mother's final service.

Jo put water on to boil, and she took a Blue Willow teacup from the cupboard and placed it on the table. The cups, like the Victorian-style couch, had been left by Mrs. Gyther. "Those are a 'welcome back to West Mills' gift," the old woman had said, leaning against one of the cotton-candy-pink kitchen walls. Jo had covered them with yellow, spring-themed wallpaper the first chance she got.

Jo didn't care much for Victorian furniture, and she cared even less for so-called fine china. But why throw out things that work?

It wasn't until the kettle began to whistle that Jo realized she hadn't brought in the bag of teas and coffees she'd purchased while visiting Herschel. She wanted something different from the standard black tea she had already. When she lived in Brooklyn, she'd owned so many different teas her apartment could have doubled as a café.

When Jo opened the front door, she saw a piece of white paper anchored to her car by a windshield wiper. *How can you marry a killer? SHAME*, the note read. It had been written in red ink.

"These people have lost their damned minds," Jo said aloud to herself.

Jo was tired of life pushing her around. She'd been torn from her hometown when her mother decided, with hardly any notice, that she wanted to live in New York City. Jo's mother went to her grave without ever explaining that sudden and urgent decision. And while Herschel had always agreed that it was abrupt, he had never seemed as inconvenienced by it as Jo had. Jo had lost friends and been thrown to the wolves. That was what she thought of the city children and teachers who made fun of her southern drawl.

Then there was the violence. Jo had watched Herschel harassed in the streets of Harlem, then Queens, then Brooklyn. On a handful of occasions, Jo had even had to fight alongside Herschel. She'd held her own, as had he.

Then came the failed relationships. One after another. How Jo made it without turning to liquor or some other vice was a miracle. She wanted more control of her future. Buying the cottage was her first step toward that. Agreeing to marry Lymp was her second. Here might be her third: there was no way she would stand by and watch the man she loved be harassed for something he couldn't have done. He just couldn't have.

"No way in fucking hell," she said to the note. If anyone thought they were going to use her man as a scapegoat, and try to run the two of them off, or do anything that might split the two of them up, they had another thing coming. Jo balled up the note and stuffed it into the pocket of her robe. Lymp had been through enough already.

Back inside the house, Jo settled for a cup of black tea. She was too frustrated to select anything different. She sat in her kitchen's window seat and thought. Given everything Lymp and Nate had told her, it was obvious that the Harmons weren't getting medals for West Mills's Most Loved. But to be murdered?

"I just can't picture it," she whispered to herself, thinking of the sheriff's drug-deal-gone-wrong theory. What sort of drug dealer or addict kills three people and leaves the drugs behind? She took a sip of the hot tea.

"Who you talkin' to, Josephine?" Lymp asked, walking into the kitchen in his birthday suit.

"Just thinking out loud." She gave him a peck on the lips. "Don't worry. I haven't gone crazy." Lymp looked dazed, still half asleep. She glanced at his groin. "It's a good thing no one was here with me."

"Sorry 'bout that, baby," he said. Jo offered him a smile. He turned back toward the hallway. When he returned, clothed, Jo asked, "Lymp, what's that sheriff's name again? I think I need to pay him a visit."

"No the hell you don't! You leave that shit alone. He let me go."

"Right," Jo said. "Because he should have never *taken* you anywhere in the first place. And I think he needs to take a closer—"

"Listen," Lymp said. "I know you sometimes like to help folk with things, and I love that about ya. But I'm telling you not to go bein' a busybody with this, Josephine. You think you on *McMillan & Wife* or something? These lawmen 'round here ain't gon' play with you."

Jo pretended to agree that going to speak to Sheriff Horton would be useless. But when the time was right, she would. She would tell him what she thought of his shoddy work. Maybe he thought he had all the information he needed. But Jo didn't. She was also determined to shame those who were murmuring untruths about Lymp, those who threatened the peace she and Lymp deserved. A simple *Leave us alone, Lymp is innocent* probably wouldn't suffice.

"What time is Nate picking you up?"

"Eleven o'clock."

That was perfect. A more than respectful enough time to go and visit Angela Glasper.

FOUR

Jo

When Jo arrived in front of Angela Glasper's house, two men were sitting on the steps. They were both drinking coffee from Styrofoam cups and smoking cigarettes. A small, cordless radio sat between them, gospel music coming from its one speaker.

A pack of four or five healthy-looking mutts emerged from under the porch, tails wagging. A welcoming committee, it seemed. Not a single one of them barked. They sniffed at her ankles. Their cold noses caused Jo to say, "Okay now. That's enough. Get." And then they turned their attentions to one another.

The men looked to be around Jo's age, but she didn't recognize them. That was for the best. Now wasn't the time for a schoolhouse reunion. Besides, what if they were part of the crew who believed Lymp would commit fratricide?

"If you come for Jane's rolls, she said it's gon' be another fifteen, twenty minutes or so," the slender, gray-Afroed man said. "And we both buying six."

Jo had forgotten that Angela's mother was a baker. Angela had mentioned it long ago, when Nate had first introduced them. But Jo hadn't realized that Angela's mother made the baked goods right there in their home. She had assumed the woman did the baking somewhere else.

"I'm here to see Angela," Jo said to the men.

"She's in there. G'on up and knock," the heavyset bald one suggested, his cigarette dangling from the corner of his mouth.

Evidently, Angela had heard Jo and the men talking. She appeared at the door, wearing jeans, a T-shirt, and a beige bathrobe. By the looks of it, she had been napping with her hand between her right cheek and the pillow. Her shiny hair was brushed back into a loose ponytail. It looked as though she'd recently had a relaxer.

"Hey, Miss Jo," she said, opening the door and inviting Jo in. "I like your suit."

The blue pantsuit was the least wrinkled getup in Jo's closet. She hoped the sneakers she'd thrown on toned things down some. Yes, Jo had every intention to ask prying questions, but she didn't want to *look* like she'd come to ask prying questions.

After taking a seat, Jo thanked Angela again for allowing her to stop by on such short notice. The mouthwatering aroma of baked goods filled the room. She might have come at the right time to buy some of the rolls for Lymp. She knew he was a fan.

"No problem," Angela said. "Well, as you probably figured out, I'm out of work now. It's not like I have much else to do."

Angela's mother, Jane, came into the room and introduced herself, though they had briefly met once before at Manning Grocery. Or maybe it was at the flea market. Jo couldn't remember. Jane had a large Afro picked out to near perfection. And like Angela, Jane couldn't possibly weigh more than 100, 110 pounds, Jo mused. Perhaps she was one of those bakers who never ate the product.

"You can lay around another week or so," Jane said to Angela. "But then you need to get in your car and drive up Highway 64 and go put in some applications. West Mills Savings and Loan don't care nothin' about whose boss died and left them without a job. West Mills Gas and Electric don't care, neither."

Many of West Mills's residents worked in nearby Norfolk, Chesapeake, and Virginia Beach. Lymp had commuted to Newport News five days a week, when he worked as a foreman. That was before he was injured and went out on disability.

"Ma," Angela sighed.

"You won't find a job sitting here watching stories and sleeping all day," Jane lectured. "I know *that* much."

"Mama," Angela said. "You're really going to do this right now? In front of company?" She rolled her eyes. Then it was Jane's turn to sigh.

"Marian Harmon wouldn't shed a single teardrop for you, and—"

"Ma! Don't you have something in the oven?"

Jo looked down at the rose-colored shag rug then at the television. It was all the privacy she could offer the mother and daughter. She certainly wasn't going to suggest that she come back later. Too risky. Jo had questions for Angela, and she would be remiss if she didn't at least try to get them answered.

"Be glad you don't have any, Miss Wright," Jane said.

"Oh, please call me Jo."

"Okay, Miss Jo," Jane said. "I thank God I only had this one. Lord knows she's plenty." A timer dinged in the kitchen, and Jane dashed away.

It struck Jo that Jane knew she didn't have children. This was something Jo would have to get used to—people knowing things about others without ever having had a conversation with them. Small-town life, like Nate and Lymp had said.

"So, I guess you know all about what happened yesterday, don't you?" Angela asked.

"Some of it," Jo said. "First, let me say that I'm so sorry you had to be the one to find them. I imagine that was hard on you."

"Yeah, well. I guess nobody wants to find dead bodies. But to tell you the truth, I still don't know how to feel about it all. I worked for Dr. Harmon for two years, but I still can't say I was anywhere near to being friends with her or the others."

"No?" Jo asked.

Angela said that she was the fourth receptionist Dr. Harmon had hired since opening Friendly Pediatrics in '72. The word around town was that the doctor had initially wanted to open the clinic on the east side of the canal—the white side. Lymp had mentioned this once. He had been proud of his older sister for trying, but he also thought it was ridiculous.

En route to deliver fresh rolls to the customers waiting on her steps, Jane reappeared in the living room and said, "I don't like to speak ill of the dead, but I don't know who she thought she was. Them landlords laughed her right out their offices." Jane said she was working as a housekeeper when the Harmons returned to West Mills from New Jersey. Jane had heard one of the landlords telling his wife about it. "She was in the North too long," Jane added.

"Mama."

"No offense, Miss Jo," Jane said. "I know you're not like that. But if Dr. Harmon thought them white folk was gon' let her set up shop on *they* turf, maybe she *was* doing drugs. And she must've been planning for white patients."

"She might've gotten Black *and* white patients," Angela countered. "If they'd rented to her."

"I can't see it, baby," Jane said. "I'm sorry, but I just can't. I—"

"Anyway," Angela cut in, "I applied for the receptionist position and she hired me."

"Tell the whole story, Angie," Jane said.

"I will not. None of that matters," Angela shot back. "I hadn't worked as a receptionist before. I usually like to be up and moving around. Makes the workday go by faster."

"Miss Jo, Marian Harmon talked to Angie terrible," Jane said. "Looked her up and down and told her she'd have to get a perm if she wanted to work at her front desk."

Jo remained quiet, resisting the urge to pull her address book from her pocketbook and use it as a notepad.

"Oh, Lord," Angela bemoaned. "It wasn't that bad, Mama."

"Yes, it was. She came home cryin'. But she needed the work. So, I gave her the money to go to AnaFaye's and get her hair done. I ain't got nothing against perms, but hairstyles ought to be a person's choice. Am I right, Miss Jo?" And she headed toward her waiting customers.

"Yes. Of course," Jo said. But enough about Marian's beauty standards. "Angela, will you tell me about yesterday? If you don't mind, I mean."

"I don't mind at all. After they hadn't shown up at the clinic by eight o'clock, and I hadn't heard from them, I knew something must be wrong. She starts seeing patients at eight thirty, and the patients' mommas were getting fussy and asking me where Dr. Harmon was. So, I told them the Harmons must have been broke down on the side of the road or something. I thought they probably had a flat tire. I let another twenty, twenty-five minutes or so pass before I told everybody I had to close the clinic and go look for them. Told everybody I'd call them back to reschedule their appointments."

Jane came back through, said she needed to go and change for work, and disappeared down the hallway and into a room.

"Well, before I left the office," Angela continued, "I stopped for a minute and tried to think if it was one of those weekends they were going out of town."

Angela explained that every once in a while Dr. Harmon would clear all Friday appointments so that she, Marva, and Lazarus could take a weekend trip to New Jersey. Angela assumed the trips were to visit friends they had left behind when they moved back to West Mills after the Camden riots.

"To be honest with you, I had a hard time picturing them having friends, but I figured they were visiting somebody. Maybe Marva and Laz, but not Dr. Harmon. Actually, I take that back. Marva was the only one who was consistently social. Anyway, whenever they took those trips, they might come in dragging a lil bit. But they were never late for work. Dr. Harmon didn't like being late, and she didn't like *other* folk being late. It would tick her off *real* bad, Miss Jo."

Knowing all of this, Angela took the three-mile drive to the Harmons' property. With any luck she would help them change the likely flat tire—she hoped that was all it was—and they would all head to the clinic. Hopefully, Dr. Harmon would be able to shake off the morning's frustrations and see the afternoon patients, Angela said. But she didn't see the

Harmons on her way to their house. No sign of them or their car. So, she kept driving.

"Then I thought, if they *had* gone out of town, maybe they broke down on their way back here to North Carolina. Either way, I knew whatever had happened couldn't be good."

When Angela arrived at the property, she saw the Harmons' newer car, the sky-blue '75 Buick Riviera, and their older car, also a Buick Riviera—a white '72. Both vehicles were under the carport, off from the newly paved driveway. Angela remembered hearing Marva on the phone ordering the service a couple of months back. Marian had forced Marva to talk the price down.

"One of the doors was open. Just a little," Angela said. "And I—"

"One of the car doors?" Jo inquired.

"No, ma'am. Of the house. One of the double doors. And that was strange to me because Dr. Harmon couldn't stand for doors to be left open. At the clinic, she was always gettin' on us about letting in flies or letting out heat. So, I stepped up close to the door and saw them through its window. They were down by the foot of the staircase. All three of them."

Lazarus may have been the target. But with no known enemies? An aloof man like him?

"Let me tell you something, Miss Jo: I felt like my brain was spinning. You ever feel shocked, scared, and curious all at the same time? I know that sounds strange, to be curious when you see three people you know dead. But it just didn't feel real, like the first time you see a family member in a casket. You know they're dead, but because they're all dressed up, everything is still kinda normal."

Jo had never happened upon a murder victim, but she had some understanding of what Angela meant. Jo had felt that hint of normalcy when she and Herschel had seen their mother laid out at the funeral home in Brooklyn. Susan had looked so beautiful that Jo thought she might sit up and start giving orders. Jo remembered Herschel pulling up two chairs next to the casket. Just the two of them there in the viewing room. She stared at her mother's still face, wishing she'd had a better life; wishing her mother hadn't been widowed at such a young age; wishing her mother had found love again, just as Jo had with Lymp.

"Did it look like the place had been robbed?" Jo asked.

Angela hadn't taken the time to survey much. The Harmons' bodies had been what drew and held most of her attention. But she felt pretty certain that things didn't look tossed around.

Marian's body was on the stairs. She was wearing silver silk pajamas, her eyes staring toward the front door. Marva was at the foot of the stairs. Her eyes were closed. Her nightgown was green. Lazarus was wearing a white dress shirt and some slacks. He was on his side, his eyes also aimed toward the front door. "Anyway, I knew they were dead. Dead, for sure. Anybody with good sense in their head and a pair of working eyes could see that. They had a weird coloring about them, you know."

Angela said she ran back to her car, drove to the nearest pay phone, dialed the operator, and told them to connect her to the sheriff's department.

Jane reappeared. She smelled of what Jo believed to be Avon Sweet Honesty.

"I'm heading out, Angie. Miss Jo, please tell Lymp he has a friend in me. We've heard about all the talk and about the sheriff taking him in. Glad he's out and home. Anybody who thinks Lymp would do something like that is crazy. I blame Burrus for—"

"Don't be late, Ma," Angela interrupted.

"I'm goin'. I'm goin'," Jane said. "I can't lose that lil job. It's too easy."

"Where do you work, Jane?" Jo inquired.

"Just over at the nursin' home, doing this and that." She kissed Angela's forehead and told her to give Jo a few of the yeast rolls to take to Lymp. "He knows I usually charge twenty-five cents apiece. Tell him I'll stop by and see him once things cool down."

"Thank you so much. I'll be sure to tell him."

"Who's in charge of plannin' the funeral?" Jane asked. "Never mind. That ain't none of my business. Y'all let me know if you need me to bake something for the repass."

When Jane was out of the house, Jo could see the relief on Angela's face. She took off her robe.

"Now that she's gone, we can really talk. I don't tell her everything, Miss Jo."

Jo understood why. "You want something to wet your whistle? I've got Mountain Dew, Coke, Coors, orange juice, and water."

"Somewhere in this world, it's time for an after-work beer," Jo said. Angela smiled and went to get two beers. When they were poured and half drunk, Jo asked, "Do you know if any of the Harmons were dating?"

"No, ma'am. Marva told me she'd rather drive all the way back to New Jersey once a week for a date than see any man in West Mills. If that's how *she* felt, I know good and well the doctor wasn't dating anyone around here."

"That picky, huh?"

"Yes, ma'am." And when Jo asked if the same was true for Laz, Angela said, "Didn't seem to me that he was interested in women."

"Oh? You think he may have been interested in men?"

"No. Well, I don't think so. I heard a couple of people speculate that he was gay because he didn't have any kids or a lady friend and because he spoke kinda proper. But he didn't *act* gay." Jo cringed. "Women at the clinic flirted with him sometimes. He flirted back a lil bit. Mostly just by smiling and showing 'em those pretty teeth of his. He'd say, 'Thank you, ma'am.' When I first started working at Friendly's, I thought about setting him up with Mama. She likes tall, husky, quiet men like Laz. But once I saw how his sisters controlled him, especially Marian, I decided to leave it alone. Mama wouldn't go for that."

"I certainly wouldn't," Jo affirmed.

"Yeah," Angela said. "Laz was just—I don't know how to explain it. Just plain, like he didn't have much going on. For *himself*, I mean. Just did whatever his sisters said, mostly. Helped the doctor read up on new medicines and medical equipment and stuff sometimes and wrote up notes for her."

"Really?"

"Yep. I'd hear him in the office explaining the articles. He was smart as I don't know what, Miss Jo. When he wasn't doing that, driving them around, or cleaning the clinic, he'd find a corner and read romance novels and poetry books. Anyway, I guess you can say he was a sensitive guy. But no dating that I know of."

"Do you think he may have kept secrets from his sisters, like selling drugs? What do you think about this rumor that some of them might have been doing that?"

"Honestly, who knows? I don't know about Laz and Marva. But Dr. Harmon *loved* money. She was definitely doing things that weren't normal for a pediatrician."

"Like what?"

"Well, at least half of her patients were grown-ups. They'd call to make an appointment for a child and give me a child's age and all. But they'd show up with no kid. And Dr. Harmon would see them. I don't know what she was seeing them *for*, exactly, but they went back there and got examined and treated."

"Men *and* women?"

"Yes, ma'am. Dr. Harmon didn't turn money away, Miss Jo. At first, I thought it was real strange. But I called some friends of mine who went to nursing school and they told me it's perfectly legal. Unusual, but legal. I just figured, why call Friendly's a pediatric clinic if she was seeing some of everybody? Anyway, people wanted to support her. You know, her being the first Black doctor most of us ever met and all. People were all proud of her for that. Even though they complained about her."

"Complained about what?"

"Dr. Harmon was rude. Had no bedside manner whatsoever. And it's true what Mama said—she thought herself better than the rest of us on the west side. And Lord did she love money. More than loved it. She was greedy. Just as greedy as all get-out. She would charge those folks' insurance for every little thing you can think of."

Angela said that Marva handled most of the billing. But every once in a while, Angela looked at the books to see how much the clinic was making. She wanted a raise and thought knowing how much they generated each month might help her come up with a reasonable proposal.

"Miss Jo," Angela said, leaning forward on the couch. "She was hitting those folks' insurance and sometimes they hadn't even stepped foot *in* the clinic. For *months!*"

"No," Jo said.

"Yes," Angela said.

"And no one reported her?"

"Not that I know of. Unless she was charging them for something she was doing for them outside of the clinic."

"Such as?"

"Who knows?" Angela said, shaking her head, her eyebrows raised high.

"Any serious enemies that you know of, Angela? Besides the people who didn't care much for Marian's poor bedside manner, I mean."

"Not anyone who I think would *kill* them," Angela said.

Jo asked Angela what she thought about the recent disputes Marian and Marva had been involved in with Eunice Loving, Savannah Russet, and Ted Temple.

"I didn't catch it from the beginning because I'd walked over to Aiken's to get something for my gums." She had accidentally poked herself with a toothpick while trying to dislodge steak from between her teeth the previous night. The soreness had been driving her crazy, she said. Usually, she would've asked Laz to walk over and get something like that for her, but because she also needed sanitary napkins, she figured she'd go herself. "When I came back from Aiken's, Dr. Harmon had Eunice in the back and the door was closed. You know Eunice?"

"I don't," Jo said.

"She's a piece of work, too. She kinda acts like Dr. Harmon. I'm surprised they weren't best friends. Both being Black women with a lot of money and all. Anyway, I couldn't hear most of it, but I kept hearing Eunice say 'my son' this, and 'my child' that. And 'you are crazy!' Laz went in there and closed the door behind him. And when they got finished arguing in the back office, Eunice came out and said something like, 'You got the wrong one, Marian Harmon. You'll pay for this.'"

"Had they ever had any problems with each other before, that you know of?"

"Nope. They got along okay as far as I knew. Both in the choir and all. Anyway, it was a mess. And nosy me, I looked through the appointment books to see if Eunice had brought her son in. I thought maybe a medication had made him sick or something. But I didn't see his name on anything. No record of him being there. Ever. No file on him at all, Miss Jo. And I would have remembered if he'd been in there. He's not hard to miss."

"Oh? Why's that?"

"He's just—he's kinda different from most boys."

"I'm not following you, Angela," Jo said.

"He's not very boyish," Angela said, apologetically. "The way he talks and moves and all. You know what I mean. My cousins have kids who go to school with him at the junior high. They say he gets picked on a lot."

"That's terrible," Jo said. She thought about Herschel and all the name-calling he had suffered. There came a time when he seemed to no longer even notice. "Boys can be such rascals at that age."

"I think he catches it from boys *and* girls, to tell the truth. I told my cousins' kids they better not be picking on him, unless they want God to punish them with a child like that. I—"

"I don't think it works quite like that, Angela," Jo said, in lieu of *Please tell me you don't really believe that shit!* It was that kind of thinking that caused boys to run away from home and take their own lives.

Angela had put a bad taste in Jo's mouth, and it wasn't from the beer. In any other situation, Jo might get up and leave.

"I've heard that Savannah Russet's boys pick on Eunice's son a lot."

"Which reminds me, Angela. I know Savannah Russet and Marva were very close. Any idea why they'd recently fallen out? I hear they had a pretty serious argument."

Angela didn't know. She thought highly of the two women's friendship, she said, having never had one like that herself.

"When I was growing up, I mostly hung around with the fellas. So I thought their friendship was cool. And two people from opposite sides of the canal being close friends, to boot. They were so tight. It was cute. Sometimes they were like sneaky, giggling teenagers together."

"Sneaky?" Jo asked.

"Well, I probably shouldn't say. But hell, I might as well. The Harmons are gone. Marva took Valium. All throughout the day, sometimes. Laz did, too. Especially when Dr. Harmon was on a tear, which was every other day, seemed like. She liked things done a certain way. And that certain way was never the same. I just said, 'Yes, ma'am,' to everything she said and did the thing my way. She never knew the difference. But anyway, I used to wish *she* would take one of those chill-out pills. Shit. That's what I used to hear Marva call them. She didn't think I was listening, though."

"Did you ever see them sell—"

"Oh! I almost forgot why I brought up the pills," Angela said. "Savannah was taking them, too. Well, I should say I'm pretty sure she was."

"Was she one of Marian's patients?"

"Seemed to me like she was a patient of Marva's, really. I saw Marva giving her some kind of pills wrapped in tissue. So I assumed they were the chill-out pills. I don't know what Savannah needs them for. I mean, I know she's a single mom and all, but she never really looks stressed out to me."

Jo wanted to say that *stressed out* didn't always have a distinct look. But that was neither here nor there.

"Well, it seems that the pills are part of the reason that jive turkey of a sheriff has decided the three of them were dealers," Jo said.

"Sheriff Horton got people believing they were some big-time drug lords. Like it was tons of drugs in there or something. Marian Harmon would have never been that reckless. Easy for him to just call Black folk drug dealers and say, 'The end.' " Jo had seen that sort of thing happen all the time in New York. "I'm sorry Lymp's catching hell for this. But it'll pass. You know what they say: time fixes things."

"Yes, well, I'm told Sheriff Horton doesn't plan to do much. That he's likely to close the case pretty soon. But I say he owes it to the Harmons and the people of this community to do more than that. Wouldn't you agree? Three people have been murdered. *Three*."

"You plan on going over his head if he shuts it down too quickly?" Angela asked.

"It's a possibility," Jo said. "I've seen many cases reopened and police chiefs shamed. Many times. I've even helped. My neighbors and I have rallied behind more grieving wives and mothers than I can count, Angela. Where there's a will—"

"There's a way."

"That's right."

While Lymp's reputation and their happiness together was at the forefront of her mind, there was still the fact that three people had been murdered in their own home. And those who were tasked with finding their killer didn't seem to give a subway rat's ass.

She would go over someone's head when the time came. But she would only do so when she had evidence that would, without a shadow of a doubt, point to the Harmons' killer.

Jo didn't share that part with Angela. People talk.

"I have no interest in seeing Eunice, Savannah, or anyone harassed by the sheriff for something they might not have done. But it pisses me off that two other people who'd made direct threats to Marian and Marva have only been casually questioned. I wonder how things would have gone if they didn't have money or hadn't come from it. What if Lymp had been a white man who had run off at the mouth about the Harmons? Horton and his officers are either avoiding hard work or uncovering something they don't want to. Damn good-for-nothings."

"I hear ya, Miss Jo."

"Angela, thank you for speaking with me. You've been through a lot. Take care of yourself."

WHEN JO GOT back to her house, she went straight to her bedroom and lay across her bed. Her conversation with Angela certainly hadn't been a waste. But it might have provided her with more questions than answers. If Eunice Loving's son wasn't a patient at Friendly's, what could Marian have done to cause such offense? And what on earth had both of the Harmon sisters done to drive Savannah Russet to such rage? Savannah had threatened their very lives. Maybe they had refused her more drugs. Jo knew addiction could make people do and say the wildest of things. And with the two arguments happening on the same day, there was no doubt in Jo's mind that they were connected.

They had all them enemies, but everybody so quick to think I'd do *something horrible to 'em*, Lymp had said. To Jo, it sounded like Lymp would have had to get in line to kill the Harmons—the very end of the line, she hoped.

FIVE

EUNICE

Eunice Manning Loving loved her son, La'Roy, more than anyone or anything in the world. La'Roy was her heartbeat, and he had been that from the second the nurse placed him in her arms fourteen years ago, moments after she had delivered him.

Eunice could have had almost any type of life she wanted. She was a great singer, and she had been known around West Mills as one of the pretty girls. Once, during a visit to New York City for a choir competition a couple of years after La'Roy was born, a woman sitting in the back of a limousine rolled down her window and said to Eunice, "You are absolutely breathtaking, dear. Donyale Luna could be your twin sister."

"I don't know who that is, ma'am," Eunice had replied, smiling.

"One of the most beautiful models alive I've ever worked with," the woman said before rolling the window back up.

But Eunice didn't care. Being a great mother—someone La'Roy would always be proud of—was her top priority. He would want for nothing. Her adoptive parents, the Mannings, had done that for her. She would do the same for him.

Eunice and her husband, Breezy, had different expectations for their son's future. Breezy simply wanted the boy to someday finish high school and be employable. Eunice fantasized about him being the next Rod Carew or Walt Bellamy. If all went well, La'Roy would retire from the courts or fields young enough to help her run her businesses. By then, she would have several grocery stores all over the state, she imagined. Not just the one in West Mills and the second location in Currituck.

Then when it became clear after the fifth grade that he had no interest in sports but excelled in school, she envisioned him as a lawyer, a doctor, a professor, even.

If anyone asked, Eunice would tell them that everything she did was so that her son might have a head start in a world that could often be so cruel to Black men. Even her misguided attempts to shelter La'Roy were all made with the best of intentions. So, it caused her insufferable pain to know that he was hurting, and that it was all her fault.

Two weeks ago, Eunice had taken La'Roy to Dr. Marian Harmon to have the gay removed. Hypnosis would be the method, Eunice assumed. She hadn't bothered to ask. That was the second mistake. The first was thinking her son needed fixing.

And just a couple of hours after she had dropped him off at the Harmons' house for the treatment, on that Saturday morning at eleven thirty, Eunice would learn that violence was the intended method. But La'Roy had gotten away. (Thank you, Jesus.) Savannah Russet's sons had helped him.

With La'Roy knowing that Eunice had sought someone's help, and without Breezy's knowledge (he would have never agreed to it), the boy had every right to expose her for it. He was liable to tell Breezy. He might tell the Lovings. He might tell the Mannings. In a fit of sadness or anger, La'Roy might tell anyone who would listen. And Eunice could lose all respectability for taking such a matter to someone outside of her family. It was one thing for people to think something about your child. To confirm it was another thing entirely. If it meant regaining La'Roy's trust, a part of her wished he'd do it—place her before judge and jury. But she had begged him not to. It would ruin her, destroy the family, she had said to him. And he agreed to hold his peace.

"If there's nothing else, I'll head on out, Mrs. Loving," Stephanie, Eunice's one-day-a-week housekeeper, said.

"Are you in a hurry, Steph? Sit and talk with me for a while. How're your classes goin' over at the college? Come on. Sit down." Eunice pointed to the other end of the couch, hoping the younger woman would join her, take her mind off her worries. Just then, the telephone rang.

"Want me to get it?" Stephanie asked.

But Eunice, jumpy and nervous, was already halfway to it. "No, I've got it."

It was Mildred Pherebee, the assistant principal at the junior high school, calling for the second time in two weeks. La'Roy had been acting out. Eunice had to accept that Marian Harmon's death was taking a toll on him. He was liable to break, and this terrified her.

Eunice asked Mildred to hold, and she told Stephanie she'd see her in a week.

"Eunice, I meant to call you yesterday, but I got busy and forgot," Mildred said. "This just isn't the La'Roy I know." Mildred was also one of the singers in Eunice's choirs at Shiloh Missionary Baptist Church. She had known La'Roy from infancy. "He just stuck his foot out and tripped Darius Holley. For no reason at *all.* I could see if it was one of the Russet boys. At least then I'd know he was probably defending himself. But it looks like he's made peace with those two—which is beyond my understanding, though I'll take it."

Eunice knew why La'Roy and Savannah Russet's sons, Terrance and Troy, were no longer fighting. She wondered if La'Roy had convinced the boys to keep quiet about what had happened at the Harmons'.

"What did La'Roy say about it?" Eunice asked. "You sure the boy didn't do something to La'Roy first?"

But the boy La'Roy had tripped was so kind, Eunice often wondered if he were human. There was no way he had provoked La'Roy.

"Not this time, Eunice," Mildred said.

Mildred wouldn't suspend La'Roy. But she couldn't continue to let his behavior go unaddressed just because he'd previously been bullied. He would have to sit for after-school detention for three days—starting Monday. "I have to handle them all the same," Mildred explained. And Eunice said that she understood.

"I'll talk to him when he gets home. Mama wanted him to go up in her attic and get some ol' thing she doesn't need," Eunice said, her attempt to hide the fear. Thank God Mildred couldn't see her face. With all La'Roy had been through, she worried that every time he left the house, he might run away. "Did he say why he did it?"

"He didn't say much at all, really," Mildred said. "Didn't deny it, but wouldn't give a reason, either. He said he hadn't planned on doing it. Said it just happened." Mildred had asked La'Roy if he was angry about something. Asked him if he needed to get something off his chest.

"What did he say?" Eunice asked. Her heart felt as though it might come flying out of her chest and onto her pistachio-green kitchen counter. Another mess she'd have to clean up.

"He said he was sorry and asked if he could go apologize to Darius, which he did. But like I said, this is *not* the La'Roy I know. I called Cedar and Sequoia in and asked if they knew what was going on."

Eunice felt sick. She had to lean against the counter for support. Cedar and Sequoia were La'Roy's half sisters—children Breezy had with another woman. When Eunice scheduled La'Roy's treatment with Dr. Harmon, she forbade him from telling anyone about it. And she hadn't worried much about that. But she also guessed that if La'Roy was going to tell anyone that she was forcing him to go to Dr. Harmon's house on a Saturday for reasons that had not been explained to him, Cedar and Sequoia would probably be the first he would tell.

Mildred said the girls claimed to know nothing, though, and she believed them. La'Roy had honored his mother's request—as always. A consummate mama's boy.

Eager to end the call, Eunice assured Mildred that she would see to it that La'Roy got back on track. This, too, shall pass, she said to Mildred.

"I might speak with Terrance and Troy on Monday," Mildred said. "Since they seem to be friendly with La'Roy now, maybe they know what's bothering him. It's worth a—"

"Don't worry about it, Mildred," Eunice said.

"No?"

"Don't worry about it," Eunice repeated. She realized that the request had come out almost like a plea. "For now, at least. La'Roy's moody. Like you said last week, teenagers are something else."

"All right," Mildred said. Then: "You going to the Harmons' service on Sunday?" Eunice had wondered when it would come up. Her public row with Marian Harmon at Friendly Pediatrics was sure to follow. Mildred probably knew that she'd been questioned, too. Nothing stays secret for long in West Mills. "I always had a feeling Lazarus was up to something illegal. He was too quiet a person. What was he thinking, Eunice? Selling dope. At his age? Got his sisters killed behind that foolishness. Lord Jesus."

"I still can't believe it," Eunice said. "Never thought something like that would happen here."

"Shot him several times, I heard," Mildred said. She seemed more interested in the supposed reason they'd been killed than the fact that they'd been killed. "That's how I know it was his fault. The killer was after *him*. Had to be, Eunice."

Eunice didn't know what to make of this idea that Lazarus was selling drugs. About a year ago, on a Saturday, he had come into Manning's to shop and asked a cashier to get her.

"Mrs. Loving, I hope I'm not disturbing you," he said politely. And when Eunice invited him into her office: "I'll be straightforward. It saves time. I don't have much work experience. Working for anyone other than my sister, I mean. But I'm a quick study. I'll cut meat, stock your shelves, make deliveries, whatever you need. I'd love a job if you'd have me."

"What about the clinic?"

"I love my sisters very much, Mrs. Loving. They look after me. Too much, I think, though I've come to that conclusion a little late in life. Anyway, working with family is hard, Mrs. Loving. You know what I mean?"

Eunice knew exactly what he meant, having worked for her parents before the West Mills store became hers. She advised him to give Dr. Harmon two weeks' notice. She had plenty of work for Laz to do. But on the following Monday, Dr. Harmon called.

"Thank you so much for your willingness to hire my brother, Mrs. Loving. But he's decided to stay at Friendly's. I'll see you at choir rehearsal tomorrow."

Eunice couldn't imagine any of the Harmons being drug dealers, but anything was possible with those three. And Marian was a greedy one. Eunice was sorry the Harmons had lost their lives, whatever the reason. But she couldn't pretend she would miss Dr. Marian Harmon, the person who had tried to harm her child.

"Anyway," Mildred said. "It's all just awful. Terrible. God rest all of them."

"May He rest their souls."

"And how are *you* doing?" Mildred asked.

Here we go, Eunice thought.

Eunice said that she was doing well. The stores and the choirs were keeping her busy as ever. But she knew Mildred was likely asking something else entirely.

"Now, Eunice, as you might remember, I was a counselor for years before I got this position. I've never counseled adults, but I can."

"What you mean?" Eunice asked.

"Well, you've been through a lot lately. That business with you and Marian, and the police calling you, and La'Roy's acting out of sorts."

"Oh. I'm fine," Eunice said. "I'm embarrassed 'bout how I acted up there at the clinic, and I'm sorry 'bout what-all has happened. But I didn't have anything to do with any of that. I didn't mind the officer asking me anything."

No lies there. But if it were a crime to drive to Marian's home with plans to bang on the door, call her out onto the porch, and do unto Marian what Marian had instructed the Russet boys to do unto La'Roy, Eunice would be in jail. Thank God she had come to her senses that night and kept driving when she approached the Harmons' neighborless mansion.

"You already know what I'm about to ask next, don't you?" Mildred asked.

Eunice told Mildred the same lie she had told Breezy (and her parents, and her in-laws) about her argument with Dr. Marian Harmon: that the doctor had been speaking poorly about her, and she had gone to address it.

"Mildred, you know me. You know I don't usually let gossip get to me like that. But I guess it got me at the wrong time or something. I don't know. It wasn't one of my finest moments. I can admit to that."

"We all have our not-finer moments," Mildred offered. "And I don't know what Marian said about you, but anything coming from her probably would have set me off, too, to be honest with you."

Eunice heard a knock at the door. Maybe Stephanie had forgotten something. For this welcome excuse to end the call, Eunice was grateful.

"Someone's at my door, Mildred. But listen. We'll get La'Roy straight. Thanks for calling."

But wasn't that what had started this mess she was in—her wanting to get her son straight?

AT THE FRONT door, Eunice saw the woman who had bought Miss Gyther's house a few years back.

Eunice had seen her before at Manning Grocery, but they'd never spoken. Lymp's lady friend. That was how some of the cashiers referred to her when she'd leave the store. Eunice thought it nice that two middle-aged people still had hope enough for love that they'd rekindled an old flame. If the rumors were true, Lymp had proposed. Eunice had once fantasized about her and Breezy still being in love and romantic in their sixties. Now, it didn't seem likely.

With all that Lymp had been going through—the Harmons' deaths, and some people feeling so sure that he had killed them—surely his fiancée would've heard about Eunice's showdown at Friendly's.

"Hi, how you doing?" Eunice said through her screen door.

"Well, thank you," the lady said sternly. Not a lick of makeup on her face. Eunice would never do that. And why bother to put on all those bracelets but forgo a dab of lipstick? "I'm Josephine Wright."

"Eunice Loving," Eunice said. "But I imagine you know that already." Eunice offered the woman a hospitable smile and was about to invite her to come in.

"Mrs. Loving, I'll get right to why I'm here."

Miss Wright said that, for the life of her, she couldn't understand two things: why Eunice had been so upset with Miss Wright's sister-in-law-to-be that she had issued a threat and how Eunice had managed to escape the humiliating interrogation that Lymp had been put through.

"I don't mind telling you," Eunice said. And after telling the lie for the second time in less than twenty minutes, she continued, "I regret it. I really do. But that's all it was. An argument. A nasty, childish argument."

"That's all?" Miss Wright seemed skeptical. "Over gossip about you? Nothing else?"

"Nothing else," Eunice said.

"Nothing involving your son?"

Eunice thought her stomach would drop to her feet. Someone at Friendly's must have heard more than Eunice had imagined. Her face heated up.

"My son?" Eunice feigned surprise. "No, ma'am. Not at all."

"I've heard something quite different, I'm sorry to say. Did Marian give you some bad medical advice for your son or something?"

"I don't know who told you Dr. Harmon and I had words about my son, but they're wrong. We didn't. La'Roy's never been a patient of hers. Never. We go to Dr. Wassett for everything. My business with Dr. Harmon had nothing to do with my child." Eunice wanted to curse, cry, and vomit, all at once.

"I see," Miss Wright said. She wasn't convinced—Eunice could tell. "But don't you find it strange that people are saying you and Marian were arguing about him?"

"It's not strange for *people* to make shit up, Miss Wright. Pardon my language. But it happens all the damn time 'round here." *Get your act together, Eunice. Be respectful. Be respectable.* "Listen, Miss Wright. I didn't like Dr. Harmon. That's just the God's honest truth. But that's as far as it goes. Y'all want Sheriff Horton to lock me up for that?"

"I don't want anyone locked up for anything they didn't do."

"Good."

"But when I'm done turning over every stone, Sheriff Horton will have to do his job and lock someone up," Miss Wright said. "You can believe that. In what world do people threaten people's lives, and only have to answer a few questions over the telephone, or in their living room? I wish Lymp had been extended *half* the courtesy. *Half* the benefit of the doubt."

"Miss Wright," Eunice said. She was growing angry. "It sounds like you're accusing me of something, and I don't like it one bit. I won't have it. Not on my own porch. I hate havin' to say this, but Lymp didn't exactly love the Harmons. He hated them, from what I hear. You might wanna sweep around your own front door."

Eunice didn't mean it, but in the moment, it felt good to hurl something at Miss Wright, who looked as though she might take a swing with her pocketbook.

"My fiancé has cooperated with the police. *Fully.* And he's been cleared. Are you one of the people leaving notes? Calling and hanging up?"

"Was that another accusation? Goodbye, Miss Wright." Eunice turned to go back inside, hoping the woman would be on her way.

"Before I go I just want to say how sorry I was to hear that your son is being bullied at school. It must be awful for him. I hope someone, somewhere, is showing him kindness. I can't imagine he gets any from you."

"Get off my property. Now!" Eunice slammed the door shut and watched Miss Wright walk out of the yard.

In the living room, she sat on her brown leather sofa. If her large, oval glass coffee table weren't so heavy, she might have kicked it over. Eunice put her face in her hands. All she could see was La'Roy's face. *Do I embarrass you, Mama?* he had asked recently. *You ashamed of me?*

"Lord, they say you don't give us more than we can bear," Eunice muttered. "Right now I'm feeling pretty weighed down."

SIX

EUNICE

On the last Sunday in February, three weeks before the Harmons were found dead, Eunice sat in the first pew in the choir box, surrounded by singers wearing mauve robes with tan collars, listening to the pastor's sermon. The scents of at least twenty different perfumes and colognes mixed with the odor from the cigars three of the deacons had puffed on before entering the church.

"The Word says all you got to do is ask!" Reverend Stephens shouted from the pulpit. He turned to face the choir then back around to the congregation. Usually, Eunice hated when he did that. Did he believe the choir members were more in need of his sermons than anyone else? But on that Sunday, Reverend Stephens said what Eunice needed to hear. At one point, she even felt as if the sermon had been written just for her.

"The Lord God already knows what we need, people!" the reverend said. "Sometimes he'll put what or *who* you need right in your very path! Won't he, y'all?"

"Yes!" the congregation cheered.

"God's just waiting on *us*," he said, pointing at himself. "Waiting on you and me to *ask* Him for what we need. Y'all hear me talkin' to ya today?"

"Yes!" the congregation shouted again. He looked toward the deacons, Lazarus Harmon sitting among them. "Am I telling the truth, deacons?" With a handkerchief, he wiped sweat from his forehead.

"Yes!" the deacons shouted back.

Eunice lowered her head and closed her eyes. She asked God to send her help for La'Roy. It wasn't the first time she had prayed that prayer. And she'd whisper it every Sunday if she had to. Breezy might have given up, but she couldn't. She was terrified of what La'Roy's life might otherwise become. It would be miserable, she imagined. A life of ridicule and isolation. Certain things just are what they are, Breezy had said to her on the subject. "It ain't my fault," he'd said. Did he believe it was hers?

When Eunice opened her eyes and lifted her head, her gaze landed on the Harmon sisters. They wore solid-colored dresses—much like ones in Eunice's repertoire. Marva's was gray; Marian's was black. They sat in the third pew, right of the aisle.

Funny, they usually sat on the left.

The reverend was revving up to conclude his sermon. The organist and lead guitarist egged him on, both smiling and craning their necks to watch him. Marva Harmon stood and waved a hand, slowly, from side to side—her eyes shut tight.

"Glory!" Marva shouted. She was never shy about praise and worship. Eunice could not remember a service in which Marva did not participate verbally or with a stomp of her heel against the hardwood floor. When Marva attended a service, everyone knew it.

As for Dr. Marian Harmon, she sat still, mostly, responding with only a faint smile. Every once in a while, Eunice might see her sway, ever so slightly, from side to side—careful that her shoulders wouldn't touch the person sitting next to her. It had been a topic of discussion at the beauty parlor, how different the sisters were, though they looked so much alike. To Eunice, the Harmon sisters looked like the actress Rosalind Cash.

"Maybe she oughta go to the white folks' church," one of the salon's patrons, Wanda, said as her hair was being lathered. "She acts like our services scare her."

"Well, shit. She'd call the police on the folks over at the House of Prayer," the salon's owner, AnaFaye, said. Every woman in the shop bent over with laughter, nearly toppling onto the mustard linoleum. The House of Prayer was West Mills's only Pentecostal Holiness church. Some people called it a dance club because there was more music and dancing than there was preaching and praying.

"Marva seems nice," AnaFaye's sister, Nova, said, her chainlink earrings hovering just over her collarbones. "I see her smoking sometimes at the shopping center with that white girl."

"Yeah, they tight," AnaFaye said. "Marva brought her in here one time. On a Monday."

"Say what?" Wanda's mother, Miss Charlotte, said. She clutched her blouse, having left her pearls at home. "And on a Monday?"

AnaFaye only opened her shop Tuesdays through Saturdays. Appointment only. She said her doorbell rang on a Monday evening, around six thirty. AnaFaye's daughter had come into her bedroom and said, "It's Dr. Harmon's sister and that white lady." And when she asked which white lady, her daughter had said, "You know which one, Ma."

All the women had turned and looked at AnaFaye, eager to hear more.

"Asked me if I'd cut her hair," AnaFaye said. "Savannah Temple's hair."

"You mean Savannah *Russet*, honey," Miss Charlotte said. There were giggles.

"Tell them what happened next, Ana," Nova nudged.

"I did it," AnaFaye said. "It's just hair, y'all."

"That's not what we're asking, Faye," Wanda said, exasperated. They wanted to know if the white girl talked about them—since she lived near many of them. Had the Temple girl mentioned her late husband, FitzAllen Russet? (Wanda and Nova had both dated him at different points in high school.) Was she seeing anyone new? If so, was he Black or white? AnaFaye explained to the group that the three of them made small talk about the weather, the rising cost of this thing and that.

AnaFaye shared that Marva had noticed the stack of records in the living room, and she asked for AnaFaye's permission to flip through them. And once the permission was granted, Marva had talked on and on about how her older sister turned her nose up at soul, blues, and disco music.

Hearing this didn't surprise Eunice as much as it had the other women at the salon. Eunice had, without fully realizing it, been observing Dr. Harmon for some time. The doctor was always draped in rigid stoicism. Eunice imagined her listening to string symphonies or opera. Something Marian might consider respectable. But in truth, Eunice thought that rigidity might be helpful to her own cause.

★ ★ ★

WHEN THE WORSHIP service was over and the congregants were hugging one another and bidding each other a blessed week, Eunice saw that La'Roy was occupied with the girls he so often sat with at church—the same girls with whom he spent much of his free time: Cedar, Sequoia, and others. And when Eunice saw that he was at the back of the sanctuary, deep in conversation, she looked for Dr. Harmon. She found her standing alone, waiting for Marva to finish a conversation with one of their patients.

"Dr. Harmon," Eunice said.

"Good afternoon, Eunice." Her gloved hands were clasped together. "Good to see you, dear."

Somehow, even then, Eunice didn't believe this was how the doctor spoke behind closed doors. But who would know?

"And you," Eunice replied, awkwardly. She felt like a little girl in Dr. Harmon's presence. All three of the Harmons had that effect to varying degrees. Eunice had felt this way since the day she'd met them in '71, when they had just moved back to West Mills from Camden, New Jersey. The rioting was the straw that broke the camel's back, Dr. Harmon had told them. Eunice's adoptive father, Brock Manning, knew the Harmons from long before Eunice was born.

"The choir was wonderful, as always," Dr. Harmon said. "I may have to join *that* one, too." She smiled. Eunice smiled back, and she remembered the evening the doctor had popped up at the church on the night of choir rehearsal for the Senior Inspirational Choir. Eunice was getting out of her car when Dr. Harmon walked up and asked if she could join. She couldn't carry a tune from one side of the street to the other, she admitted. But she claimed to want to feel involved, a part of the community, part of the church family. Dr. Harmon said that she, her sister, and her brother had been away from West

Mills for so long, it was like they'd never been born and raised there.

Community, my ass, Eunice had thought to herself that evening. Almost every woman in the choir had at least one child, or a grandchild, or was raising someone else's. Choir members weren't short on elderly parents or grandparents, either. Eunice believed Dr. Harmon was joining the choir to get new patients, since more than half of the people on the west side of the canal went to white doctors on the east side. If Dr. Harmon's sudden desire to be active in the church wasn't sign enough, the advertisements all around town were. There were flyers on bright, colorful paper, one on every other telephone pole. FRIENDLY'S PEDIATRICS, they read, with the address and phone number included at the bottom. And when those signs got weathered, Eunice saw Lazarus going around pulling them down and replacing them with fresh ones.

"That song you all sang just before today's word," Dr. Harmon said. "What's it called again?"

" 'Rise Up and Walk.' "

"That's it. 'Heartache and pain will soon be over.' It's a beautiful song. A perfect song."

"Yes, ma'am," Eunice agreed. She wanted to get to the point. "Dr. Harmon, I was wondering if there's a day this week I can come by your office and have a word with you." She glanced around to make sure no one was eavesdropping. "About my son?"

Dr. Harmon tilted her head and frowned slightly.

"Of course," she said. She would alert her receptionist that Eunice would be calling to book an appointment, adding that thirty minutes was all she could spare. Eunice had hoped Dr. Harmon would ask for at least a hint of what they might discuss. But the doctor likely had her suspicions. Eunice saw how people looked at La'Roy. It was an open secret.

"Be sure to bring your health insurance card along," the doctor said.

"Yes, ma'am," Eunice replied. Was Dr. Harmon really going to bill her insurance for a short talk?

"I'll see you later this week, then," the doctor said, and she wished Eunice a great rest of her day.

And on that Wednesday, Eunice met with Dr. Harmon, who handed her a box of Kleenex to wipe her tears. La'Roy's problem, Eunice explained, was concerning her more and more with each passing day. There was no sign that his femininity was a passing phase. All he wanted to do was hang around with his sisters and the girls in the neighborhood, comb their hair and the like. Eunice couldn't bring herself to tell Dr. Harmon that she had even noticed that his eyes lingered on handsome men when he saw one. Nor could she mention that she'd found department store catalogs in his dresser drawer. The corner of a page always turned down on an ad for men's underwear. The lean model standing there, hands on hips. Something had to be done, she told the doctor. Something had to be done quickly before he had a chance to act on it, Eunice pleaded.

"Say no more, Eunice," Dr. Harmon said. "I know just what to do."

"Oh, thank God," Eunice sighed out, dabbing her cheeks with a tissue.

"I need one session with him."

"Only one?"

"Just one. The key is to make the treatment memorable. Lasting. I've seen it done before. Years ago. At the very least, the effects should last well until he's old enough to be out of your care." Eunice thought that was a strange thing to say. A child is always in their mother's care, one way or another. "Bring him to my house on Saturday."

"Not here in the clinic?"

"No. My house. Saturday," the doctor said. "Does your husband know you're here?"

"No, ma'am," Eunice said sheepishly. "He'd have a fit if he knew I was talkin' to anybody about this. I'm leaving him out of it for now."

"I think that's best at this stage. In my experience, most fathers usually only care about the results, anyway."

They discussed a time. Light refreshments would be served about an hour before the short spurt of treatment. "It helps to relax the patient," Dr. Harmon explained. Eunice was to drop La'Roy off at eleven o'clock and leave. She would be called when he was ready to be picked up.

But as Eunice expected, getting La'Roy to go to a doctor's house on a Saturday resulted in a lot of questions and protest.

"You're going, and I don't want to hear another word from you about it," Eunice said to La'Roy that morning around nine o'clock when she went into his bedroom to make sure he was awake. Breezy had already left for work at the auto repair shop.

"What she want to talk to me about?" La'Roy asked.

"Your future," Eunice said. It wasn't a lie. La'Roy sucked his teeth. "Too early for attitude, Robert La'Roy Loving. I want you up, clean, and ready to go by ten thirty." He flipped over in the bed.

As scheduled, Eunice took La'Roy to Dr. Harmon's home. La'Roy sulked the whole ride there.

Eunice couldn't remember the last time she had been to that corner of West Mills where the Harmons lived. The tree-lined property was gorgeous. The paved, U-shaped driveway was lined with shrubs. Did they hire groundskeepers, or had Laz done it all himself? And the white-painted steel yard furniture sat perfectly centered in the front yard. The mansion itself was the cleanest white. It all looked like something from some Hollywood film. It also reminded her of estates on the east side of the canal.

"Dr. Harmon will call when she's done talking to you," Eunice said. "Behave and do what she says."

"Why you not coming in?" La'Roy asked. He gave a look of confusion and dread that nearly shattered her into a million pieces. But this treatment was necessary, Eunice reminded herself. She had read that hypnosis could solve many problems in people's lives. "Other people gon' be here?"

"La'Roy Loving," Eunice said. "Don't ask me any more questions."

"Ma, why do I have—"

"Go! Now!" And in an instant, looking into her son's face, she saw her own, and Breezy's, looking back at her. *He will thank me for this one day*, she thought to herself. When he's married to a beautiful woman and has children of his own. Boys, she hoped. To keep the Loving name going.

About an hour and a half later, while Eunice was measuring the living room windows—she was thinking of buying new curtains—she looked up to see La'Roy getting out of a car she didn't recognize. When she went to the door, she realized it was Murphy Daniels, one of the art teachers at the junior high school. She had once worked as a cashier at Manning Grocery. All the students loved Murphy, a young, pretty lady who was barely ten years older than them. Perplexed, Eunice went to the door and opened it. La'Roy rushed up the porch stairs. He looked as though he wanted to huff, puff, and blow her house down, and nearly knocked her over.

"How you doin', Murphy?" Eunice called. She did all she could to conceal her surprise that La'Roy was home, her fear that something had gone wrong, that he had not been changed.

"Pretty good," Murphy returned. "Saw these three walkin' toward town and told them to get in." Eunice stepped down from her porch and walked toward Murphy's new Chevy Caprice. That's when she noticed Terrance and Troy Russet in the back seat. "Edge of town's a long way to walk, even if you do have all afternoon."

"It sure is," Eunice said. She glanced at Terrance and Troy. They both looked away. "Boys will be boys. Thanks for bringing them back. You want me to take them home? I have to go that way."

"No," Murphy said. She got out of the car and led Eunice a few paces away from it. "Something's got La'Roy upset. He's been crying. I asked him if Terrance and Troy had done anything. He swore the three of them are friends now. Said it wasn't them at all. I—"

"It's nothing, Murphy," Eunice cut in. "I've just been getting a little tougher on him lately. The only-child syndrome was gettin' out of hand. I'm having to say no more often these days. That's all."

"Oh," Murphy said. She raised her eyebrows.

"You sure you don't want me to take these two home?" Eunice asked once more.

"I've got it," Murphy said. "I'm going that way, too. To tell the truth, I'm glad to see the three of 'em gettin' along." Murphy had witnessed Terrance and Troy bullying La'Roy before. Eunice remembered her being there in the principal's office to report what she'd seen.

"Me, too," Eunice said, forcing a smile.

She watched Murphy back out of her driveway and head toward Walker Avenue, where Savannah and her boys lived. She thanked God Breezy wasn't home.

Inside the house, Eunice could hear La'Roy in his room, crying into a pillow. She opened his bedroom door.

"Get out!" he yelled. He ran toward the door, trying to block her entry. She grabbed him by his shoulders and held him steady.

"What happened?"

"Get outta my room!" he shouted again. On any other Saturday, she might slap him and remind him that his room was inside her house. But it was not any other Saturday. Tears ran from his eyes at a speed she'd never seen.

"La'Roy!" she said. "Talk to me. Tell me what happened."

"She tried to get Terrance and Troy to beat me up!"

"She, who?"

"The doctor! And she punched me in the chest and told me to be a man. That's what you took me there for, Ma? To get beat up?" La'Roy tore himself from Eunice's grip. He stood there staring at her, his arms hanging limp at his sides. "She called me a fag and told them to knock it outta me!"

Though Eunice couldn't remember when, she had, at some point walked to the chair in the corner of La'Roy's room and sat down. It was covered with clothing, but she didn't care. He was still standing, and he was staring at her. Tears still dangled from his chin.

"Did Terrance and Troy hit you?" Eunice asked. La'Roy, after an extended silence, shook his head. They wouldn't do it, he said. Terrance, the older of the two, told Dr. Harmon that they didn't want to get into trouble.

"Then what happened?" Eunice asked.

"Did Daddy tell you to take me to her?"

"La'Roy, please." Eunice felt she had no right to plead for anything. She was lucky he'd allowed Murphy Daniels to even bring him home. Lucky he and the other boys hadn't told Murphy what a doctor, a respectable member of the community, had put them through. "Tell me everything."

"I don't wanna talk about this," La'Roy said. "Ma, can you just leave me alone, please?"

"What did she say when they said no? Tell me and I'll leave you alone, baby. Please."

"She started yellin' 'faggot' at all three of us and we just ran. Why'd you take me there?"

"Did the doctor come after y'all?" *The way I'm going to go after her*, Eunice thought.

La'Roy looked at Eunice and asked again, "Did Daddy tell you to take me to her?"

Eunice almost said, *Yes, your father wanted this, La'Roy. You know I'd never put you in harm's way like that.* It would have been so easy to tell that lie. And La'Roy would have believed her. Of that, Eunice was certain.

"We won't tell him," Eunice said. "He might lose his mind and I—"

La'Roy didn't say a word, but his eyes judged her and sentenced her to a life of guilt.

"Baby." She stood and grabbed both of his hands. "That's not what was supposed to happen. Dr. Harmon was only supposed to *talk* to you. I didn't know anything about—"

"I embarrass you, Mama?" he interrupted.

"No," she lied. "You're the best thing I got in this world."

"Then why you'd want her to fix me? She said I was there to be fixed because I'm a—"

"Come here, baby," Eunice said, throwing her arms around him and pulling him to her. She hoped he would hug her back, but he didn't.

"Please forgive me," Eunice said. She released a wail she didn't know her body was capable of producing. "Please forgive me." And after what felt like several minutes, though it couldn't have been more than one, La'Roy raised his arms and embraced her. He laid his head on her shoulder.

"It's okay, Mama," he said. "I didn't get hurt. And I'm sorry, too. I'll try harder."

Eunice gently pulled away, just far enough to look him into his eyes. "You don't have nothin' to be sorry about, baby. Nothing."

They went to the kitchen and both had a glass of water. She begged him to keep all that happened a secret, and he agreed. They wouldn't tell Breezy or anyone else. La'Roy swore that he wouldn't tell a soul.

"But what about Terrance and Troy?" he asked. He was such a smart young man, her son. She had forgotten about those two. And she was grateful to them for resisting Marian Harmon's demands. She would have to go and speak to them, which meant she would have to speak to their mother. There would be more begging to do.

DRIVING WELL OVER the speed limit, Eunice went to Savannah Russet's house—stray dogs and cats darting from the path of her butterscotch-colored Dodge Monaco. A visit to Dr. Harmon would have to wait. If Eunice went there now, she would surely find herself in jail for disorderly conduct—or in prison for doing far worse. But any other

mother—one who hadn't put her own child in danger—
might feel differently.

"What have you gone and gotten yourself into, Eunice?"
she said aloud to herself. "Shit, fuck, damn, fuck, damn!"

Eunice arrived at the narrow dirt road called Walker
Avenue and approached Savannah Russet's house—the small
house was where her childhood schoolmate, Savannah's late
husband, Fitz, had been raised by his grandparents. She saw
Mrs. Russet marching to her car, angry-looking, her boys
walking behind her with trepidation, like kittens leaving
their birthplace for the first time. The breeze tossed
Mrs. Russet's blonde hair around her head. Eunice turned
into the driveway and blocked her in.

"Please move your car," Mrs. Russet said, forcefully. "My
boys just told me what happened and damnit, I'm heading up
there to—"

"I understand, but I need you to wait," Eunice said. She
got out of her car and approached the woman hastily and put
her hand on her arm. "Please, Mrs. Russet. Can we talk for a
few minutes? Just the two of us, mother to mother?"

Mrs. Russet looked bewildered. And after a few moments
of staring, she ordered Terrance and Troy to go back inside.
She would honk when she was ready, she told them. She went
into her pocketbook, got a cigarette, and said, "My boys said
Marian told them to knock La'Roy around. Called him *and*
them awful things. What the *hell's* going on?" She went on
to say that Dr. Harmon had invited her sons there for some
sort of early career-counseling session for teenagers. "The
boys told me she started picking on La'Roy and that she tried
to get them to join in. Told them to beat him up because
he—well, I'm sure La'Roy's told you the rest."

"Yeah," Eunice said. "Mrs. Russet, I—"

"Excuse me, but can we cut the missus crap, please? I'm Savannah. Just plain Savannah, as you well know."

"Okay," Eunice replied.

"Anyway, my youngest is rattled half to death," Savannah said. She blew smoke away from Eunice. "You and I both know mine aren't angels. But darn it! I would've headed to Marian's sooner, but it took me twenty minutes just to get the boys to tell me what in hell happened. Then it took me another few minutes to calm down." Another drag from her cigarette.

"I need a favor from ya," Eunice said. Savannah frowned. "Don't say anything to the Harmons."

"Excuse me?" Savannah said, taking a step back. "My best friend's sister just tried to get my sons to assault yours, and you're asking me not to do anything about it?"

"Just for now," Eunice said. "I—"

"No. There's no way I'm saying nothing. I—"

"Please, Savannah. Let me deal with Dr. Harmon first."

"Doctor," Savannah scoffed. "What kind of doctor picks on kids?"

"I just need you to trust me on this. It would be a big favor to me if you and your boys kept this to yourselves."

"You *do* know that I talk to Marva all the time, don't you?"

"I assumed so. But please, Savannah."

"I just tried to call her, but no one's answering."

Savannah took the last pull from her cigarette and flicked the butt into the ditch. "I don't know what you're planning to say to Marian, but my boys have given La'Roy some bad days in the past. To make it up to you I'll back off, but you've got to keep me in the loop on this thing, Eunice. Marian tried to use my boys like they're animals or something."

Later that night, Eunice lay in bed, waiting for Breezy to fall into a deep sleep. And when he did, she threw on some clothes, snuck out, and headed for the Harmons'. She would raise all kinds of hell to wake them from their beds. Eunice would allow herself all the cursing and name-calling the moment warranted.

Then, as she approached the Harmons' house, she realized she couldn't go through with it. After all, it was she who had gone to the woman and asked her to fix La'Roy—to get the gay out of him. The last thing Eunice needed was for that to get out. What did Marian Harmon have to lose? Not a thing. If what Dr. Harmon had tried to do ever got out, it wouldn't stop people from going to her clinic. Eunice knew the people of West Mills well enough to know that.

"I can't do shit," Eunice whispered to herself. "Not a fucking thing." She turned the car around and drove back home. When she turned the key and stepped into the foyer, Breezy was standing there.

"What's wrong?" he asked, standing there in boxers and a T-shirt. "Where you been?"

"Went to the store to grab Midol from my office," she said. "Cramps starting."

"Wake me up and let me know next time. You ain't got none of that here in the house? You scared me."

"I'm sorry. Just wanted to catch the pain before it got rough," she said, heading toward the kitchen. "G'on back to bed. I'm all right."

But on the following Monday morning, when Eunice dropped La'Roy off at the junior high, he broke down before getting out of her car. She didn't need to ask why he was crying. What other reason could there be?

Eunice held La'Roy. She didn't mind if he was five, ten minutes late for his first class. He needed her, and she had failed him. The very least she could do was let him cry in her arms. When he was done, he told her he loved her and that he would see her later. There was a tug in Eunice's heart that nearly made her say, *Skip school. Hang out with me today, baby.* But if that was what he wanted, he would have asked.

Eunice watched La'Roy walk into the building. He wasn't the only one running late. There was a group of boys walking in front of him. They were horseplaying—pretending to beat up on one another. And at the sight of it, Eunice knew where she would go next. Errands be damned.

"Where is Marian?" Eunice shouted when she walked into Friendly Pediatrics, startling mothers and children—what few children were there. The waiting area smelled of baby formula, Cheez Doodles, and grape-flavored candy.

"You lower your voice," Marva said, stepping out from behind the reception counter. "Dr. Harmon is—"

"Doctor, my ass." Eunice wouldn't dignify the woman with the title ever again.

"Please lower your voice, Eunice," Marva repeated.

"You ain't heard noise yet, honey," Eunice said. "Get your sister out here *right* now or I'll do some serious talking. And I mean it!"

"Mrs. Loving," Dr. Harmon said. It seemed that she had appeared out of thin air, standing just behind her sister. "You seem quite upset. Let's speak in my office. I'm sure we can—"

"Don't you '*quite*' me!" Eunice yelled. Mothers pulled their children closer to them, but Eunice knew they were all enjoying the show.

"In my office, please," Dr. Harmon said calmly. "I won't ask again. You're frightening the babies."

Once they were in the office, Dr. Harmon closed the door. "You've obviously lost your mind," Dr. Harmon said. "How dare you barge into my place of business and behave this way?" She looked as though she'd smelled something rancid. "Come on, Eunice. I thought you had more class than this."

"And I thought you were a—"

"Keep. Your. Voice. Down," she said through clenched teeth.

"I thought you were a decent doctor. A decent *person*," Eunice said. She was beginning to cry. "You tried to get Terrance and Troy to hurt my child! They both bigger and stronger than La'Roy is. You told them to stomp him, Marian. What's *wrong* with you? You sick in the head or something?"

"They didn't lay a finger on La'Roy. They're buddies now, apparently."

"Thank God!" Eunice shouted. "Thank God they have more decency than you!"

"You have a lot of nerve, talking to me about decency." She folded her arms. Her lab coat was so heavily starched, it made sounds with her every move. "*You* came to *me*. Remember?" She stepped closer. There was a hint of victory in her smirk.

"I thought you were going to hypnotize him," Eunice said. "Not—"

"Don't tell me what you *thought*. You didn't even bother *asking* what I had in mind. You want to know *why*? You didn't ask because you didn't *give* a damn. All you cared about were the results. If that husband of yours was any kind of man, he would have done it himself. I bet any other father around here would have. *Mine* did. But that's neither here nor there."

"You're supposed to be a fuckin' doctor!"

"Such awful language."

"How could I know you'd try some ol' backwoods shit like that?"

"As I've said, you came to me. Drove right up in my driveway and forced him out of the car."

"I didn't force him!"

"Oh, yes, you did," Marian said. "I sat in my parlor window and watched La'Roy pleading, begging you. And you put your red little fingernail in his face, poked him in the chest, and pointed to the passenger door. I saw you."

"You were going to watch those boys beat my son to a pulp. And then what, Marian? Bandage him up and call me to come and get him, like he'd just had a tooth pulled or something? Are you crazy? You think I'd want my child to be assaulted?"

"I know what you *didn't* want," Marian said. "You no longer wanted your son talked about around here. You no longer wanted people calling him the sissy that he is."

"You go to hell."

"This is all your doing," Marian said. She didn't have a worry in the world, it seemed.

"You didn't turn me away."

"Of course not. I wanted to help. I've seen far too many of our fellows lost. Their mothers and fathers unable to hold their heads high in their communities." She wore an expression of utter disgust as she spoke. Eunice felt she had never seen so much hatred in her life. "I want to see it *all* rooted out. My parents taught us at a young age that a man is to walk and talk as a man, and a woman as a woman should. You're a God-fearing woman *just* like I am."

"Jesus," Eunice said. "You think you're God-fearing?"

"Absolutely. It is an abomination and it must be rooted out. But I don't have to tell *you* any of this. You know it already. So, yes, I wanted to help."

"You don't have the good sense God gave you, Marian Harmon. You're crazy."

"Oh, dear, I've been called worse."

"I'll make sure everyone knows what—"

"No, you won't, Mrs. Loving," Marian said, chuckling. "Not unless you're willing to tell everyone you were going to have La'Roy fixed. To get the *fag* out of him. I know your type. Mrs. PTA Mom. Mrs. Choir Director. Mrs. Member of This Board and Member of That City Council."

Eunice found it nearly impossible to swallow.

"I'll bring you down," Eunice said. "No one messes with my son!"

"Figure out how to tell your husband what you, without his knowledge or permission, wanted me to do," Marian said. "I imagine he still doesn't know anything. Otherwise, he'd be standing in here next to you."

"What my husband knows and doesn't know is none of your fuckin' business."

"Whatever you say, Mrs. Loving."

Just then, Lazarus came into the office. "Everything all right in here, Marian?"

"I've got this under control, Laz. Thank you," Marian said without releasing Eunice from her gaze. "Mrs. Loving and I were just finishing up. Please see her out. And she will keep her mouth shut as she leaves, if she knows what's good for her."

"If you think you can threaten me and I'll just roll over, you're dead wrong," Eunice said.

"No," Marian said. "I don't think I am. Now get out." She looked past Eunice and gave Lazarus a nod.

"I think it's best you follow me now, Mrs. Loving. Please," Lazarus said to Eunice, standing tall and broad just a couple of feet away from her. She couldn't imagine that he'd forcibly remove her from the clinic. But she glanced up and saw pure ambivalence in his eyes. He might pick her up and throw her if Marian commanded it.

In the hallway, he gently tapped Eunice's shoulder, and when she turned to face him, he said, "Let it go, Mrs. Loving. Whatever she's done that's got you angry, it's best you let it go and move on."

"Oh, now *you're* threatening me, Laz?"

"No, ma'am," he said. "Not threatening. Just advising."

Eunice turned and headed toward the waiting area. When she arrived at the double glass doors, Eunice spun around and found Marva and Laz standing side by side.

"People always said y'all was strange. But *strange* ain't got nothing on her! She's pure evil!" The people waiting to be seen might as well have been pieces of furniture. Their presence mattered nothing at all to her. "This ain't finished, Marian Harmon!" she shouted as loud as her voice would allow. "Just as sure as I draw breath, you'll pay for this!"

The moment it was over, Eunice knew she had made an awful mistake. How would she explain it to Breezy? Surely, he would hear about it before the day was over. With all the people in Friendly's waiting area, someone would run home and call a sister, who would tell their husband, who would go to the auto repair shop for an oil change and ask Breezy, *What's goin' on with your wife and the doctor?* How would Eunice explain this to her parents? Her mother-in-law, Pep Loving, would relish Eunice's bad behavior. La'Roy would be shamed and ashamed.

Eunice saw no sure way out. Lying would have to suffice.

★   ★   ★

ON THE DAY Angela Glasper found the Harmons' bodies—
it was one week after Eunice had barged into Friendly
Pediatrics—a customer came into Manning Grocery and
reported the news to anyone within earshot. Lymp had been
picked up on suspicion of their murders. Apparently, he'd
spouted off at the mouth recently as well. Said horrible things
about the Harmons in public. Eunice knew Lymp wasn't on
the best of terms with them; everyone on the west side of the
canal knew that. But had he disliked the Harmons enough to
kill them? Eunice couldn't imagine it.

And when Breezy called her at the store to ask if she'd
heard, he said, "I hope you didn't run out of Midol again,
without me knowing."

"Don't talk crazy, Breeze," she replied, offended.

"Well, you might as well be ready to tell Sheriff Horton
'bout your boxin' match with the doctor. Anybody who
watches TV knows you sure as hell gon' be questioned."

"There was no boxing match, Breezy, and you know it."

"Y'all might as well have boxed," Breezy said. "That's how
folks was making it out to sound."

And a couple of hours later, Deputy Brent Wolfe called.
He needed to speak to her. Ask a few questions.

"Sheriff Horton says it's fine to talk to you at your home
or at your store, since he's known your father for so long and
whatnot."

*Oh, you mean my father's keepin' his head down? Stayin' in his
place?*

"My home, please. Thanks. Me and Breezy'll be there."

"Be there in half an hour," he'd said.

It was true that Eunice's father had had a longtime cordial
relationship with Sheriff Horton. But she also knew that all

the donations she'd made, year after year, to Wolfe's wife's food drives and charity events were paying off.

"How can we help you, Officer Wolfe?" Eunice said after offering him refreshment, which he declined.

"Anyone see you two here at home late Saturday night?" Wolfe asked.

"How we s'pose to know, man?" Breezy asked. "We didn't have any visitors or nothing. Just in here watching TV and all. Living. Like any other Saturday night. Like any other family."

By the look on Wolfe's face, there was no question in Eunice's mind that he disliked Breezy's irritable attitude—the kind of orneriness one felt when a white man came into his house, half accusing his wife of something he hoped to hell she hadn't done. But Eunice hadn't killed anyone, and she trusted Breezy to know.

"I don't know," Eunice said. "Maybe the neighbors can vouch for seeing my car here. And Breezy's truck was here all night, too. We were in by seven something and didn't leave."

"And your son?" Wolfe asked. "He was here all night with y'all?"

"Yes," Eunice said. "Playing his records, or on the phone. Probably both." That was half true. La'Roy was home in his room, but he was in bed with the covers pulled over him. And that had been the case almost all that day.

"You sure 'bout that? Absolutely?" Wolfe asked.

"Yes," Eunice replied.

"So what was the problem exactly?" Wolfe said. "Between you and the doctor."

"It was silly," Eunice said. She told him the lie about gossip, and that she regretted going to the clinic to address it. "Not the right place or time. But—"

"Mind tellin' me what Dr. Harmon said about you?"

"Just church-related stuff. That I'm bossy, don't know how to run a choir, things about my husband's past. That sort of thing." Breezy took a deep breath and leaned against the wall.

"Yeah, that does sound pretty foolish," Wolfe said. Eunice heard Breezy take another deep breath. "Do you know Savannah Temple?" The question was like a mosquito bite. Not painful, exactly. But she would feel it later. "Russet, I mean."

"Yeah," Eunice said. "Because of our children. We don't know each other very well."

"But y'all's boys are friends, right?" he asked. "Murphy said she gave the three of them a ride home a week or so ago."

"Yes, I remember that," Eunice said. She'd forgotten that Murphy Daniels and Wolfe were first cousins and neighbors.

"Gave the three of them a ride from where?" Breezy broke in, confused.

"I guess what I'm askin' is, did your dispute with the doctor and Savannah's argument with Marva Harmon have anything to do with each other?" Wolfe inquired. "Happenin' on the same day and all."

Eunice wanted to strangle Savannah. She had asked her—begged her—to leave it alone. And Savannah had agreed.

"I don't know anything about that," Eunice replied.

"You got all you need?" Breezy asked Wolfe. "My wife ain't done nothin' wrong. Unless fussin's a crime now."

Wolfe sighed and said, "Pretty sure I'm done here. Probably their dope customers who done—"

"Dope customers? They were dealing dope?" Breezy asked.

Wolfe looked as though he'd ruined a surprise birthday party. "I've said too much. Don't y'all repeat that."

"Why y'all got Lymp in custody if you think some junkies did it?" Breezy pressed.

"Breezy," Eunice said, shaking her head no.

When Wolfe was gone, Breezy stood there, hands on hips, looking at Eunice. She thought he was about to launch into another lecture about how ridiculous it was to fuss over gossip, and to do it at someone's place of business, no less. Or maybe he would ask why La'Roy had been driven home by the art teacher and why he had been with Terrance and Troy Russet—given the trouble they'd caused him.

"Damn," he said. "I knew they were weird. But dealin' dope? Old as they are? Were, rather." He walked to the couch and sat on the arm, both hands on his knees. He breathed in and exhaled loudly. "Weird people. All three of them. Especially Laz." Eunice knew what was coming next. "I tell you 'bout that time he came to the shop for an oil change? How I saw him lookin' at me? Like he wanted to—"

"Yes, Breezy," Eunice sighed out. "You told me." If she had to hear, one more time, about Lazarus's lustful gaze at Breezy, she would scream. The thought of it infuriated her.

"You don't think Lymp did it, do ya?"

"No. Not for a second."

"Me, neither. Lymp's a decent guy."

"Sure is," Eunice said. "But you never know."

After a couple of minutes of silence, Breezy said, "You got lucky, Eunice. You know that, don't ya?"

"What you mean?"

"You cussed the doctor out. To her face. In public. And told her you'd make her pay for talkin' shit about you. Look where you at right now and where Lymp is."

"And?"

"I'd call that pretty damn lucky."

"What? You want them to haul *me* into the station, too?"

Stay calm. It's better that he talk about this than ask why La'Roy was with the Russet boys.

"Of course not," Breezy said. "That's not what I'm sayin'."

"What *are* you saying, Breeze?"

He shook his head. Another deep breath. "That Manning money buys—"

"Don't start with that mess, Breezy. You know how many times white boys tried to tear our store down when it was just a little thing up by the bridge?"

"Yeah, I know," Breezy replied. "Poor Black folk like Lymp can't catch a break. That's all I'm sayin'."

"That's not *my* fault."

"Yeah, I know." Breezy walked down the hallway toward their bedroom, shaking his head.

TODAY, IT WAS Eunice who couldn't seem to catch a break. Between Mildred calling about La'Roy and Ms. Sherlock Holmes Josephine Wright coming around asking questions—the kind of questions that might have Wolfe knocking on her door again or expose the harm she had put La'Roy in—Eunice didn't know whether she was coming or going.

She had not spoken to Savannah since the Harmons had been found dead. It was clear that they both felt there was no reason to reach out. But also, for Eunice, it was too risky. Her being seen speaking to Savannah now would be just what Miss Wright needed. All it would take was for Miss Wright to ask one person if they'd seen Savannah and Eunice together lately and that person would tell it all—right down to the time and what they were wearing.

Even now, as much trouble as Josephine Wright could cause, Eunice had to admit that she felt some admiration for the lovestruck lady. All Miss Wright wanted was to protect Lymp and their relationship. Eunice understood that impulse. She would do the same for Breezy.

Did Eunice and Breezy have a perfect marriage? It was probably one of the least perfect marriages in the county. Yet Eunice stayed with him.

"Where's Calvin Lockhart today?" some of the women who came in to the grocery stores often said to Eunice. They swore Breezy and Lockhart could be twins. Eunice felt certain that every woman in town wanted Breezy. How could she blame them? But Eunice had long since determined he was to be hers and how far she would go to have him.

SEVEN

EUNICE

In June of 1960, when Eunice was seventeen years old, she learned that everything she had thought about herself was a lie. She and Fran Waters, the girl who had the other half of Breezy's heart, got into a fight. Breezy's father, Otis Lee Loving, was a farmhand for the Penningtons. Breezy's mother, Pep, was a midwife. When there were no babies to be delivered, Pep cleaned houses on the east side of the canal.

Assuming that Breezy would be home alone for several hours, Eunice made the quarter-mile trek from her parents' store—it was just a small general store then—to Antioch Lane to surprise her man. When she arrived, she found Breezy and Fran on the porch, grinning from ear to ear, tight in each other's arms.

"If you don't get your arms from around her, I'll break 'em!" Eunice threatened. "I might break her arms, too."

Thinking back, Eunice could not remember what Breezy had said in response. Nor could she remember Fran leaving Breezy's embrace. All she could remember was her and Fran going at each other. They fought as though their lives depended on winning, as if Breezy were the only man in the world.

Breezy managed to pull them apart twice, briefly. But each time, Eunice and Fran found their way back to each other. No words exchanged. There had been an unspoken agreement that their hands would do all the talking.

Then, Eunice felt a stinging smack on her back, then her arms, then her shoulders. And instead of her yelling ouch, Fran was the one to say it. Pep appeared and served Eunice and Fran more licks with her shoe. Had the older woman come a few minutes earlier, when Eunice was still in the trance, she might have taken one of Eunice's blows.

"Stop this foolishness right now!" Pep yelled. "What in the devil's wrong with y'all?"

She turned to Breezy and struck him several times with her shoe as well.

"Mama, I—"

"Shut up!" she said. "I don't wanna hear nothin' from you. This is all yo' fault in the first place! Sit down!" She pointed at the porch. "All three of ya."

"You ain't my momma," Fran proclaimed, and she stepped toward Eunice as though to finish what she'd started.

Pep grabbed Fran by her arms and flung her to the porch, next to Breezy.

"Listen to me now and listen to me good." Pep wiped her brow with the back of her arm. "I ain't never, never in my whole life, thought I'd come home from work and find two girls that I helped bring into this awful world fightin' in my yard. Never!"

"I was already here and she came startin' shit," Fran said. "She asked for it, so I—"

"Shut up, Fran!" Then, just like spitting out a hangnail, Pep said, "Y'all sisters. Knot's y'all's mama. I pulled the both of ya from the same woman's womb. There it is. The truth's out. And I won't have you fightin' each other. Not over my son, or over anything else. I just won't." Then Pep walked over and hit Breezy on his thighs with her shoe.

Pep explained to the girls that Knot had become pregnant with them but was unprepared for motherhood. In '42, Phillip and Lady Waters adopted Fran just hours after she was born. And in '43, Ayra and Brock Manning adopted Eunice. There was no mention of fathers. And Eunice did not care. In fact, she wanted to unknow all of it.

Eunice couldn't take her eyes off Pep, nor could she bring herself to look at Fran, the girl who might be her sister. No, the girl who *was* her sister. Pep had no reason to make up such a story. And in truth, Eunice had always felt a pull to and from Fran Waters. When they were little girls at the schoolhouse, something about Fran always interested Eunice. And when Fran began playing the piano for the church, and Eunice started singing in the choirs, there was something unexplainable there. A knowing of some sort.

So, when Pep spit it out, all Eunice could do was stare at her. Fran stood and walked away. And after about a minute, though it felt like an hour, Eunice rose and went back to her parents' store on Busy Street.

When Eunice arrived at the store, she entered and found that her parents, Ayra and Brock, were both standing at the counter with colas. There were no customers in the store.

"When was y'all gon' tell me?" she asked calmly.

They looked at each other, bewildered. Had they forgotten that they'd adopted her from West Mills's most notorious alcoholic? Had it slipped their minds that the disgraced schoolteacher, Azalea "Knot" Centre, had birthed a baby girl and kept her for only a couple of hours before summoning them, the people Eunice knew as Mama and Papa, to come and get that baby girl?

"Tell you *what*, baby?" her mother asked.

"About Knot."

A few days later, Eunice happened to see Knot at the general store. Though Eunice had accepted that Knot had given her life, she would not allow the woman to be a part of it. So, she treated the woman as she always did. With indifference. The same way Eunice regarded all her parents' customers. When the woman dropped her groceries, Eunice couldn't summon the urge nor the interest to help Knot pick them up. Eunice just stood there, watched her, and said, "I hope you found everything you needed in the store, Knot. Come again."

Within a week's time, Eunice was on a train headed to New York City. Giving her some money and setting her free, if only for a while, was the least her parents could do, she told them.

"I'm not mad at y'all," she promised the Mannings. "Y'all the only mother and father I know. I love y'all and always will. Just need some time away from here."

They understood. They hated to see her go, but they understood perfectly well, they said. Eunice would try her luck with singing, she told them.

"Maybe I'll cut a record, make it big, and y'all won't have to run this ol' store anymore," Eunice said just before boarding the train in Norfolk.

"Be careful, my child," her mother said. She cupped Eunice's face and kissed both her cheeks. But that was just it: Eunice was not her child. She was the child of the town drunk and some traveling musician, apparently. Eunice would do everything in her power to avoid becoming like the woman who had birthed her. She would be a big success. She would always be honorable, respectable, wherever she was.

FIVE MONTHS INTO Eunice's stay in New York City—she was living in a boardinghouse on 140th Street in Harlem—she learned that Fran Waters was expecting. Breezy was the father. But the couple had broken up. Fran wouldn't allow him anywhere near her, it was said. Breezy had been sneaking around with someone else.

"He don't love her, Eunice," Nita, another girl from West Mills, said. They were sitting on the stoop of the 132nd Street boardinghouse where Nita lived. "I believe he misses you, girl. You goin' home for Christmas, right? You oughta see him."

"Easter," Eunice said. And on her first night back in her parents' house, Breezy did as he had done so many nights before she moved away. He tossed handfuls of dried beans at her window until she opened it.

"G'on away from here, Breezy Loving," Eunice teased. "You oughta be somewhere plannin' a weddin'."

"With who?" Breezy retorted.

"Don't play stupid with me. I know you got a baby on the way."

"Yeah. So?" Breezy said. "Me and Fran ain't together. We decided."

On the porch of Manning General Store, Breezy explained that he and Fran had come to an agreement. They were too young to get married just because Fran was in the family way. "Lots of folk got children without getting married nowadays. It's the sixties."

"So, you figure you just gon' have girlfriends all over town?"

"What you talkin' 'bout?" Breezy asked.

"Gayle Richards," Eunice shot back, naming the girl Nita had told her about.

Breezy played the fool. "I miss you, Eunice. If I didn't have a child coming, I'd move to New York with you." In spite of herself, she appreciated that he wanted to be in his child's life. *Breezy ain't all bad*, she thought to herself. "How many records you cut?"

"Not a one," Eunice said. She had found that there were hundreds of girls from the South who had gone to New York with the same idea. She went to audition after audition. And each time, she heard voices that made her want to crawl under a table and never open her mouth again.

"Good as you can sing, Eunice?"

Eunice was proud of her vocal abilities. "But some of them gals *sang*," she explained to Breezy. "Some of 'em sang and turn flips and play instruments and all. Anyway, things ain't easy as I thought they'd be. Colored girls with voices come a penny a dozen in New York."

"Well, I still say you better'n all of 'em." Breezy told her she might need to give it more time. Stick it out.

Eunice went inside and got the keys to her father's car, and the two of them drove out by the Harmons' place. In the front seat of Brock Manning's black Plymouth Savoy, they made love.

In '62, not long before Breezy and Fran's daughter, Cedar, took her first steps, Eunice had moved back to West Mills and given birth to a colicky baby of her own. She named him Robert La'Roy Loving—the middle name taken from an actress with whom she'd been briefly obsessed.

"The two of y'all need to go on to the courthouse," Brock Manning said to her and Breezy a couple of days after La'Roy was born.

"For what?" Breezy asked.

"What you mean 'for what'?" Brock said. "No disrespect to the Waterses. But Eunice ain't Fran. Whatever kind of arrangement you got with Fran about y'all's baby, that don't work for me and *my* daughter and *my* grandchild. You gon' keep *my* daughter decent."

"I don't know," Breezy said. He laid La'Roy down in the bassinet. "I—"

"I hear tell you want to open up your own business," Brock Manning said. "Work on cars and so forth. Well, I done already talked to Mr. Bridges. The one's got that lil fillin' station over on Blood Field Road. You know it's for sale, don't you?"

"Yes, sir," Breezy said. Eunice could see a glimmer of joy in his eyes. But would he think ill of her? Think she had put this all together—an attempt at trapping him? It was not her plan at all. It was all her parents' doing. But she hadn't asked them to abandon the idea.

"Offered me a good deal if I made a down payment on it within the next week," Brock said.

Eunice had a child, and she wanted a husband. She wanted to be nothing like Knot, who drank away nearly every dime that came into her hand. The woman who'd given birth to two children, two years in a row, and gave them away like extra carrots harvested from a garden. Eunice would never be like that, she swore to herself. She wasn't the first or even the hundredth girl to have a baby before marrying, and she wouldn't be the last. But she wanted to be able to hold her head up high in the community. And she wanted the same for her son.

One day, Knot came to Eunice and Breezy's home unannounced. At the time, they were living in the apartment over Manning General Store. It was the morning after Fran Waters buried her own adoptive father, Phillip Waters. Lady Waters had died the previous week. (It was a sad time in West Mills. Phillip had dropped and taken his last breath at Lady's funeral.) Eunice had just lain down, hoping for a nap. La'Roy was with Pep and Otis Lee. Eunice heard Breezy dash out their front door and down the stairs that led to it.

"Hey, Knot," he said. "What you need?"

"You ought to have somethin' on yo' chest, boy," she scolded.

He asked again, "What ya need?"

"I come to talk to yo' wife." At this, Eunice rose from the bed and went to the window. Hearing wasn't enough. She needed to see Knot. She wanted to see what it looked like for a woman to come and have a conversation with her child—not the grocers' daughter—for the first time. Knot wore a black dress that looked as though it had been thoroughly inspected for lint or wrinkles. She looked like she were about to attend yet another funeral. Breezy told Knot that she didn't need to worry about apologizing to Eunice about the past.

"She got a good life," he said. "Trust me on this, Knot. Best not to bother with it."

"I know she's got a good life," Knot said. "But I figure she might want to say somethin' or ask me somethin'. No better time than the pres—"

"She don't, Knot," Breezy cut in. Eunice was both impressed and warmed by his determination to protect her. Hearing Breezy's words felt like a tight, reaffirming hug.

"Eunice made peace with you bein' her real momma years ago. She fine. *We* fine. But if you go up them steps, it might bring on trouble ain't nobody lookin' for." He glanced toward the door nervously. Eunice backed away from the window, lest she be seen. "Eunice said she grateful it had all happened the way it did. Good for everybody." Knot asked if he was certain there might not be something Eunice wanted to get off her chest, to which Breezy said he felt more than certain. "Everything's all right, Knot." And he was right. Eunice did not want to talk to Knot. In fact, she was grateful to Knot for placing her in the care of the Mannings. Eunice only wished it had remained a secret. A secret to her and everyone else.

Eunice's marriage to Breezy didn't stop him from loving Fran Waters. And eventually, Fran would give him another daughter, Sequoia. It pained Eunice deeply. But she decided that Fran and Breezy would have to suffer any ridicule that might come their way, from God and from others. Eunice was the injured party. The dutiful wife who stayed by her man's side, just as her vows required of her. An honorable, God-fearing woman who would raise her baby boy to someday be a respectable, God-fearing young man. And she had made the decision that nothing would get in the way of that.

EIGHT

EUNICE

Eunice decided it was best that she not attend today's memorial service for the Harmons, and she didn't think anyone would question that choice.

"You askin' *me* to go?" Breezy shouted. "Now I *know* somethin' crazy's in the water 'round here!" He was standing in their bedroom doorway when she asked him to attend and represent their household. She had already sewn a button back onto his one dress shirt and hung it back in his closet. "La'Roy's 'round here mad for God knows what and slammin' doors like the world owes him something. And you worryin' about me goin' to the funeral of some people you didn't even like? Folk I don't even half know?"

"It's not a funeral," Eunice said. Rumor had it that the Harmons had a living will that dictated that they be cremated within forty-eight hours of their deaths. When Reverend Stephens heard, he insisted that there be a memorial service at the very least. They were members of the community, members of the church, he had been heard saying.

"You know what I mean," Breezy retorted. "I can't believe you even askin' me to do this. Ain't a person in this town who don't know you and the doctor was on the outs. Shit, half the town knew about it before *I* did."

"That's exactly why you should go," Eunice said. She was tired of explaining it.

"If it's that damn important to you, just go. Shit."

Eunice looked at her watch. It was one o'clock. The service was scheduled to begin at two thirty. Eunice knew Reverend Stephens would make sure the Sunday worship service ended with enough time to allow him a break. She just needed Breezy to agree to attend the service, get dressed, and get off her last nerve. Of course, she felt bad for asking, given how supportive he'd been of her in the past week. Some men in West Mills would have given their wives the silent treatment, used the public argument their wife had been in as an excuse to go spend a few nights (or weeks) with their girlfriend. Eunice was no fool. She knew Breezy had likely been to Fran's to confide and do whatever else they did. But he'd come home every night since her blowup with Marian Harmon. To Eunice, that was worth something.

"Please do me this favor, Breeze," she said.

"Nope," he said definitively.

"Okay," Eunice said. "Forget it. I'll go and give everybody even *more* to talk about."

He stood there, looking at her like she had four heads. The telephone rang.

"Well, answer the phone, at least," she said. And she ran into their master bathroom, eager to avoid whoever was calling to ask if she was going to the Harmons' memorial service.

"Eunice in here trying to get me to go. By myself," Eunice heard Breezy say. She figured it was his mother. "For what?"

Silence. "Ma, why in the world should—" Silence, then a grumble. "See, that's y'all problem. Y'all worry too much about what folk think." More silence. "All right." Silence. "All right, all right. But I'm sittin' somewhere in the back." She heard him put the receiver back in its cradle.

"How long you gon' be in there, Eunice?" Breezy asked from the other side of the bathroom door. "I need to get in the shower."

When Eunice came out, she asked Breezy who had called. He rolled his eyes and went into the bathroom. She waited to hear the water running before going to La'Roy's bedroom door and tapping. He opened the door just enough for her to see his puffy eye.

"You all right in there?"

"Yeah," he said.

"Want to go to the mall?"

"No," he replied.

She asked if she could come in for a couple minutes. This wasn't something she normally did. After all, it was her house. Still, La'Roy stepped aside. And when she entered his room, all she wanted to do was dust, vacuum, and spray air freshener. At least a week's worth of his clothes were on the floor. And now she knew where her bowls and spoons were disappearing to. At least he was eating, though it hadn't been much more than Frosted Flakes, potato chips, and the occasional ham-and-cheese sandwich.

"Your daddy's still asking 'bout your mood," Eunice said, softly. "You think you can come out and chitchat with him a little this week?" La'Roy was wearing a football jersey her parents had bought him a couple of Christmases ago. He hated sports. "I need you to cheer up for me, baby. We gotta hold it together. Okay?" He lay on his bed and stared out the window. "La'Roy, look at me, please. I'm talking to you."

"Yes, ma'am," he said.

"Thanks."

She told him to take a shower. They would ride to Norfolk, have a late lunch, and go to a mall. She asked him to be ready in thirty minutes.

Shortly after, Breezy emerged from the bedroom dressed and looking like the handsome husband she'd won from Fran Waters. And, grumpily, he headed for the door. He would pick up his mother, and together they would go to the service, he said. Pep had agreed that his presence was important. Going was the right thing to do. Breezy was always a mama's boy. He'd do whatever Pep asked or demanded of him. La'Roy was the same way. Ever obedient. Ever loyal.

So, when forty minutes passed and La'Roy hadn't come out of his bedroom, Eunice walked down the hall to check on him. His door was ajar. He was fully dressed, sitting on his bed with a small, floral-covered notebook and a pen. The tablet looked like the ones the teenage girls brought with them to choir rehearsals. Eunice had never seen him with it before. Her impulse was to remind him that boys didn't write in those. But it was that kind of thinking that had gotten her into this mess. At the mall, she would find him something more masculine. A brown leather journal, perhaps.

"You ready?" Eunice asked. "Let's hit the road."

"I ain't goin'," he said. He didn't look at her.

"Listen, La'Roy, you need to get out. You gotta move past this. We—"

"You're ashamed of me, Mama. I know you say you aren't. But you are."

"La'Roy, we already talked about that. I—"

"I'm not goin'," he said.

"Yes, you are," Eunice shot back.

La'Roy turned to her, his nostrils flaring. His lips pursed as though he might spit all his anger, all his pain, onto her purple angora sweater. "Can you get outta my room?"

Before Eunice realized it, she had leapt toward him. "Don't press your luck too hard, boy. I'm still your mother and I'll knock you into—"

"Touch me and I'll tell Daddy what you did. I'll tell everybody."

NINE

Jo

In Lymp's living room, Jo and Nate sat waiting for the right time to leave the house for the church. Lymp alternated between sitting and pacing. The instability of it all nearly drove her crazy.

Lymp didn't want to arrive at the church too early. For the past two days he had told Jo over and over again how foolish he thought it was that Reverend Stephens had insisted on holding a service for people who had gone out of their way not to have one.

"Stephens just likes the attention," Lymp said. It was at least the fifth time he'd said it to Jo and Nate. He resumed pacing. He had been at it, off and on, for the past fifteen minutes. "Wouldn't surprise me if the bastard's got himself on the program to sing two solos." He kicked his TV stand.

"Lymp," Jo said, startled. She didn't like this display of anger. "I know today is a tough day and that you're nervous about who'll be at the service and if anyone will be rude. And I understand that. But try to calm down."

"I don't even know why I'm goin'," Lymp said. "Marian and them didn't give a *shit* 'bout me. To hell with 'em."

"Lymp!" Nate shouted. "See, that's the kind of talk that got you hauled into the sheriff's department." *Sweep around your own front door,* Jo remembered Eunice Loving saying. "Stop sayin' shit you don't mean."

"I *do* mean it! Every word!"

Goose bumps prickled on both her arms. In bed later that night, she would ask God to forgive her for the image her mind conjured of Lymp holding a gun, aiming it at the Harmons.

"Sit down and breathe, honey. Please."

"Get yo'self together, man," Nate said. "Imagine if your father heard what you just said. Think about that for a minute."

Lymp stopped pacing. He sat down in his favorite chair and pulled a handkerchief from his shirt pocket, wiping his entire face.

"I apologize. I shouldn't talk like that. Jessie Earl'd be hurt. The only reason I'm goin' today is because he would've expected me to."

When Lymp wasn't looking, Jo offered Nate an appreciative smile. She admired his ability to calm his father down. Though Nate was only twenty-nine, he seemed to have more wisdom than most of the middle-aged people Jo knew.

"And I don't want to give these no-good backstabbers 'round here anything else to talk about." *Then insist on a fucking polygraph!* Jo wanted to yell. "Now you watch," Lymp continued. "That church gon' be jam-packed. And nary a one of the motherfuckers liked Marian or Marva or Laz. You mark my words. I probably won't be able to get a seat at my own sisters' and brother's service. Watch what I tell y'all."

Nate sighed. "It's five after two, y'all. Let's head on out."

"Naw," Lymp said. "It don't take but seven, maybe six minutes to get to that church. We can wait, Nathaniel."

"Lymp, honey, we should get going. Come on, now."

"Listen to me. I'm not doing a bunch of standing 'round talkin' with folk when it's over," Lymp declared. "And I mean it."

Jo agreed with Lymp that at least half of the west side would attend the service. But she couldn't bear to tell him that she doubted many people would stick around to speak with him once it was over. Since she'd found the note placed under her windshield wiper, another five had been placed in her mailbox. She had only told him about a couple of them.

TEN

SAVANNAH

Savannah Temple Russet's two sons were all she had, and she would do anything to protect them. But she had let down her guard, entrusted someone else, briefly, with their care. She could only hope Terrance and Troy would someday forget how poorly Marian Harmon had treated them, how she sought to use them to inflict harm. And Savannah would never tell the boys that Marva Harmon, the person she believed to be her very best friend in the world and Terrance and Troy thought of as their aunt, had been unwilling to stand up for them.

Savannah didn't blame Eunice Loving one bit for confronting Marian—whether privately or at a place of business—for bullying La'Roy. Savannah, too, had cause for anger toward the Harmon sisters. *But my God, woman. Did you kill them?*

Savannah looked at the clock on her nightstand. The Harmons' memorial service was set to begin in an hour, and she was still sitting on her bed, back against the headboard, crying and trying to smoke a cigarette without dropping it and burning her sheets. If Terrance and Troy had not brought in a toasted waffle and a half glass of orange juice, she might not have had the strength to sit upright.

Next to the clock sat the old, empty Tylenol bottle where Savannah used to hide the Valium. She felt as though the mildest of withdrawal symptoms would kill her. But this wasn't new to her. She had gone through it years ago, just before moving back to West Mills from New York.

Savannah hadn't had a pill in almost a week, having run out of them the day after the Harmons were found dead. A damn crime, she had thought when she realized she'd taken the last one. She knew she would need at least one to get through the memorial service. And one would certainly come in handy in a couple of days, when she would go to the county clerk's office to ask for another extension on the property tax bill. The house where she, Terrance, and Troy lived—the same house they had moved into after returning to West Mills—was a godsend. Mortgage-free. But, oh, the taxes. Sometimes Savannah wondered if she was better off paying rent.

Savannah couldn't bring herself to look at the notice again. It, too, occupied space on her nightstand. It was printed on yellow paper, as if it brought joyful news of some sort. If the payment wasn't made within ten days, the marshal would be there to install padlocks. Then where would they go? Not across the canal to the east side, where her father and grandmother would say, *We told you not to marry him.*

But none of that mattered today. She had a service to attend. With what feelings exactly, Savannah couldn't say. It was a strange notion, paying respect to someone who had been your best friend and then your enemy. Even so, one thing remained undeniable: Savannah missed her badly.

"Come on, Savannah," she whispered to herself, looking across the room and into the mirror. She had to sweep her long blonde hair to the back of her head to see her own face. "Get up. Get moving." The boys didn't want to go with her to the memorial service. She didn't blame them. But she was still shaken by the murders, and there was no way she was leaving them home alone. Not with a killer on the loose. Whether it was Lymp Seymore, Eunice, or someone else, Savannah couldn't be sure. Regardless, the boys would just have to be mad at her. She would make them join her at the church.

In the shower, Savannah lathered her hair with the last few remaining drops of Body on Tap and thought about her friendship with Marva. They had been so close, like the pair on that new television show, *Laverne & Shirley*. Despite the yelling match she'd had with Marva at the shopping center, people would expect Savannah at the service. Some might even expect her and her boys to sit in the front row with what little kin might be in attendance.

Savannah was in no way oblivious to the fact that she and Marva had been an odd pair. Savannah had grown up in West Mills, where close friendships between Blacks and whites were exceedingly rare. There was also their age difference. Savannah was in her thirties, Marva had been in her late fifties. But their closeness made perfect sense to Savannah. Among other things, they both enjoyed a bit of bad behavior: gossip about the shopkeepers in the shopping center, chain-smoking, and the little pills—reintroduced by Marva; Savannah had had her first Valium the day after she became a widow—that helped them get through the day without cursing people out.

Living on the west side of the canal, Savannah thought she would become friends with many of her neighbors, people who had grown up with her husband. But it wasn't so. Marva was her only friend in West Mills. In truth, Marva was Savannah's only friend in the world, which was why Savannah would have never thought Marian would mistreat her children, or that Marva would defend it.

A COUPLE OF days after Savannah took her sons to the Harmons' for what she had been told would be an early step in getting them to think about career paths in the medical field, a customer came in to Aiken's Rx and More and asked if anyone knew what had happened with Eunice Loving at the doctor's office.

"She just came out of there cussing and fussing," the customer reported.

Savannah figured Eunice had given Marian a piece of her mind about what happened on Saturday. *Good*, Savannah thought. Now she, too, would be able to address it with Marian. But she would speak to Marva about it first, during their usual smoke break in the narrow alley between Aiken's and Friendly's. How the two of them had never fainted from the unusually strong smell of perc coming from Gresham's Dry Cleaning and Alterations would forever be a mystery.

"I don't know anything about it," Marva said. But Savannah could tell she was lying. "I wasn't there. But I don't believe Marian would do anything that mean. Bullying children? No. She has her limits."

"I know you weren't there, Marva. But come on. You don't know anything about it?"

"I just said I didn't."

"Where were you?"

"In Norfolk, browsing the malls. What was I going to sit around the house and listen to Marian talk to kids about medical school for? I can't even imagine how things would get to what you say the boys told you."

"It has to be true, Marva."

"Oh, girl, just let it go. No one got hurt."

Savannah could not believe what she had just heard her best friend say.

"No one got hurt? Marva Harmon, are you hearing yourself? Marian told Terrance and Troy to—"

"But they didn't, Savannah." Marva sounded exhausted by the conversation—as though they'd had it many times before. "I think you might be overthinking it all."

"Well, *I* think maybe you don't have the right to tell me what I'm overthinking when it comes to my kids. You don't have any. You're not a mother, you don't understand what it's like to—"

"I don't *have* to be a mother to understand, Savannah! Look. What Marian did was wrong. It was wrong as hell."

"So, you *do* believe it."

"But it's done and over with, dear. Move on. Just forget it."

"Are you shittin' me? What kind of doctor, what kind of grown woman, tells two kids to call another kid bad names and to beat him up?"

"Get off your high horse, Savannah. That's nothing. You're not on the east side anymore. And don't get righteous. As many times as Terrance and Troy have picked on that boy? Hell, they probably didn't do what Marian said because they're *bored* picking on him. Been there, done that."

Where was this venom coming from? Who was this woman? She wasn't the Marva Harmon Savannah adored.

"No wonder Marian thinks my two are a couple of brutes," Savannah said. She hadn't wanted to cry, but it was happening. "You must think they are, too. How *fucking* dare you!"

A man walked by them slowly, staring. "Good afternoon," he said. Savannah and Marva ignored him.

Marva would not make eye contact with Savannah. She took a final pull from her cigarette and said, "I think you'd better calm down, young lady. I have to get back to work. Your children are fine. La'Roy Loving is fine. Learn to pick your battles."

"Pick my battles? We're talking about my kids, goddamnit!"

"Savannah."

"Save it, Marva. I'm going to the police," Savannah declared, surprising herself. It wasn't something she'd considered before. "I know she's your sister, but what she did was *fucked* up. She shouldn't be around *anyone's* children."

"You need to take a pill and put your thinking cap on, Savannah Temple," Marva said.

"Russet!" Savannah shouted. "And don't talk to me like I'm a child! I cannot and I will not just turn a blind eye to this, Marva."

"But you will," Marva said. This was a threat. Unmistakably.

"What did you just say to me?"

"I wonder how long it'll take Social Services to be at your door if they find out you're taking pills you've never had a prescription for."

At the very thought of it, Savannah felt that she could lift a car.

"Don't *fuck* with me and my children! I'll send you *and* Marian to early graves!"

Just then, Savannah looked to her left and saw that they were no longer alone.

"Y'all all right?" It was a woman known by many as Knot. Savannah had seen her around town, in Manning Grocery, in Aiken's, and at other places. From what Savannah had gleaned, the woman was a big drinker. Knot was with her friend, a man known to be gay. Savannah did not know his name, but she often saw them together. To Savannah, Knot seemed to be perfectly sober, but her friend was three sheets to the wind. "I said, you all right? I don't like seeing grown womenfolk fussin' and fightin' and carryin' on."

"We're fine," Marva snapped at the duo. "Move along."

"You sure?" the man asked. "'Cause this white girl sound like she ready to go upside yo' neck."

Marva unfolded her arms and sighed. "Keep moving and mind your own *fucking* business!"

The man scowled and called both Savannah and Marva stuck-up. Knot told him to shut up.

"Let 'em shame themselves in the streets, if that's what they want to do, Val," Knot said before pulling her friend along.

With the audience gone, Savannah turned her attention back to Marva and asked, "Who *are* you?" The silence between them was louder than the motorcycle that had just passed the shopping center.

"I'm done talking about it," Marva said. "You keep quiet, we'll keep quiet." Then Marva walked away just as she would after any other smoke break on any other day.

A week later, when an officer came into Aiken's to buy a package of salted peanuts and said, "The colored doctor and her family's been killed," Savannah sat on the floor. Right there near the checkout counter, in front of her co-workers and the officer who had brought the news, Savannah went down Indian-style. It reminded her of the day she'd been told Fitz was dead. She had felt as though someone had ripped a vital organ from her chest.

The day after the Harmons' bodies were found, Savannah received a phone call at work from an old childhood friend, Brent Wolfe. Deputy Brent Wolfe. He needed to ask her some questions about Marva Harmon, he said.

"I'll come down to the station if you need me to, Brent," Savannah offered. "I don't mind." She could use an extended lunch break from the drugstore. But no such luck.

"No need for that. You're a Temple. People'll just talk if anyone sees you coming in here and whatnot. I'll save you the trouble. Just a few quick questions for ya." Only because someone had reported her argument with Marva, he explained. Savannah had to admit that she appreciated Brent's discretion, but she knew he was bending the rules.

"It wasn't anything too serious," Savannah said.

"Well, *I* believe you," Brent assured her. "But there's some who might think different, with you sayin' you'd kill 'em and whatnot." She and Brent had only been on the phone two minutes, and he'd said *and whatnot* at least four times. Was everything going to be *and whatnot*?

"Yes, but I didn't mean it. Things just got heated. I would never—"

"We know, Savannah. Relax yourself. You don't exactly fit the profile, if you know what I mean."

From what Savannah had heard from Miss Lynn, a co-worker at Aiken's, not long before Brent called, Lymp Seymore had been taken to the station the day before. Apparently, he had been kept for hours.

"He'd been talking ugly about his sisters and brother, I'm told," Miss Lynn had said. But to Savannah it didn't sound as if he had quarreled with them directly—not recently, at least. Savannah didn't know Lymp well. She didn't know him at all, really. But she'd never heard anyone speak ill of him—except Marian and Marva.

"Y'all think you know who might've done it? I heard y'all have their half brother."

"We had him for a while, but it wasn't him. He was home with his son Saturday night," Brent said.

Savannah thought it a weak alibi. But she had to admit that hers—being home with her own sons—wasn't exactly iron-clad, either. Not that Brent had even asked her for an alibi.

"Oh," Savannah said. She remembered some of the things her late husband had said about America and Black men. He was so worried about their boys' futures. "Then why was he taken in at all?"

"Protocol." Savannah knew it was bullshit. "We don't have an exact person in mind. But like I said, you shouldn't worry. I'm just callin' you out of due diligence."

Savannah would hardly describe what Brent was doing as due diligence. But he was right about one thing: Savannah was as innocent of murder as one could possibly be. And with all Eunice had to lose—the stores, her highfalutin positions around town, and the like—she probably was, too. But a mother might do anything to right a wrong done to her child.

"Sorry for your loss, by the way," Brent said. "Should've said that from the start."

"Thank you, Brent. Marva was my best friend. I haven't slept a wink since—"

"Care to share what you and Marva Harmon fussed about?" Brent asked. He kept saying her first and last name as though Savannah might know multiple Marvas. Savannah knew that question was coming, but she hadn't much time to come up with something anyone would believe.

"She and her sister criticized my parenting."

"Your *parenting*? Well, I guess that's what pediatricians do, isn't it?"

"Sometimes," Savannah confirmed. She told Brent that Marva, in particular, too often gave unsolicited opinions about how Savannah disciplined—or didn't discipline—Terrance and Troy. "She'd started up with that again, and I just wasn't in the mood for it that day, I guess."

This was not a total lie. Marva often told Savannah that she thought Terrance and Troy could both use a swift kick. Savannah didn't believe in hitting children. She and Fitz had debated that topic over and over before their oldest was even born. Savannah won.

"I see," Brent said. "You know anything about all that fussin' and doin' at Friendly's between Eunice Loving and the doctor? From what we're hearin', it was just a couple of hours before you and Marva Harmon had it out."

"I don't. Did y'all speak with Eunice? Mrs. Loving, I mean." They had, he said. If Savannah had money to spare, she might have paid Brent to know what Eunice had told them.

"She don't fit the profile, either," Brent said. "Ladies raised in Christian homes, like the two of you, rarely commit crimes like this, unless it's in self-defense."

"Oh." Savannah was fairly certain that wasn't true. Did he ever read or watch the world news? Hell, did he ever read news from other cities in North Carolina?

"Seems like the doctor had it out with some of everybody lately."

"What do you mean?" Brent shared with Savannah that her father had also had a somewhat public dispute with Marian.

Savannah hadn't heard about that, surprisingly. It was probably just something to do with his being the clinic's landlord, she imagined.

"When's the last time y'all spoke?" Brent asked. "You and your dad."

"Are you asking that as part of the investigation, or for some other reason?"

"Never mind," he said. "I just think it's a shame y'all don't—"

"Brent."

"Sorry. You know anybody who might have a problem with Lazarus Harmon? He was shot differently than his sisters."

"Yeah, I heard," Savannah said. Poor Laz. He was so kind. The boys thought highly of him. Two Christmases ago, he had bought them a brand-new football.

"I figured I'd get y'all something you can share," he had said to Terrance and Troy in Savannah's living room on Christmas afternoon. The football was half-exposed in its box. Savannah could smell the leather. "Teach Troy how to throw, Terrance." They both nodded. "My father once bought me one. Brought Lymp over to show me how to throw it. My hand was too small at the time, so I kept dropping it. But I didn't care nothin' about football. I just enjoyed hanging with my big brother."

Savannah had been moved to tears—by the gift and his anecdote.

So, to Brent she said, "No. I can't think of anyone who'd have an issue with Laz. I can't imagine him giving anyone a reason not to like him." Brent said that was the consensus.

"You ever see any funny business with them?" Brent asked. "Illegal stuff. Like using or selling drugs."

You mean other than the pills Marva and I used, without having a prescription? No. Not at all, Brent. She knew Marva and Laz smoked reefer. But if they were indeed selling it or anything else, she truly didn't know. And she wished she could say she didn't believe it. But Marian and Marva had proven themselves to be mysterious. Who knew what they sold and didn't sell?

"Marva and Laz smoked. Yes. But selling? At their ages? No." Savannah feigned shock. "I don't believe that."

Without much reservation, Brent told Savannah that, based on what had been found in the Harmons' house, the sheriff was more than certain it was drug-related. Likely people from somewhere else, since illegal drugs weren't a big problem in West Mills, and since the Harmons were said to have returned to West Mills from the North.

Returned to West Mills from the North, Savannah thought to herself. *I guess that makes me and my boys liable to do anything, too, doesn't it, Brent?*

Savannah wondered if Sheriff Horton could get any dumber. What addicts or drug lords would leave drugs behind?

"I think I got all I need, Savannah. Case'll probably be closed soon, I expect. How old are your boys now?" When she told Brent that Troy was thirteen and that Terrance was fourteen, he said that he also had two boys. Seven and eight years old. Savannah knew this already. Brent's wife's grandmother was in Aiken's at least twice a month, chatting away with Miss Lynn.

"Stairsteps," Savannah said, using a term she'd often heard from her own grandmother, Hera Temple. At least once a week, Savannah saw the petite, energetic eighty-three-year-old driving around town. Still wearing those cat-eye-shaped glasses, her hair dyed to an auburn perfection.

"Yeah," Brent said, smiling. "Both of 'em mama's boys. And we're done. Two's enough. I'm hoping they'll rack up football scholarships."

Though Brent couldn't be more than thirty-five—Savannah knew this because she was thirty-four—he sounded like the old men on the east side of the canal, those who sat at the gas stations eating honey buns and talking about farming and the old days of war. In fact, Brent sounded like his father, Toliver Wolfe, who had also worked for the sheriff's department. It had been Toliver who had come to escort her and Fitz off her father's property on the day they proclaimed their intention to marry.

Before Brent said goodbye, he told her to take care of herself. She should watch who she got herself mixed up with over on that side of the canal, he said.

"What do you mean by that, Brent?"

"You know what I mean," he said.

"No. I don't." But she did, and she despised him for it.

"Well," he sighed as though he were speaking to a lovestruck teenager who was resisting his big-brotherly advice. "I'll let you go. Thanks for your time, Savannah."

Fuck off, Brent, she thought to herself.

ELEVEN

SAVANNAH

Nervous and alone, Savannah drove to Shiloh Missionary Baptist Church. It was a short, wide redbrick structure that sat in the center of a large yard with pine trees evenly spaced in front. The boys had convinced her to let them go to a friend's house.

Savannah's husband's funeral had been held at Shiloh Baptist. She had been the only white person in the building that day. She wondered if the same would be true today. In any case, Savannah hoped the Harmons' service would be short. And she was glad there would be no bodies present. As angry as she had been with Marva and Marian, she didn't want to see them lifeless in caskets.

Would Lymp be there? Would Eunice? It was unlikely that Eunice had shot three people. Savannah couldn't even imagine her holding a gun with those dainty, well-manicured hands she had. Brent Wolfe had evidently made the same assessment. But Eunice had been so insistent on handling Marian Harmon herself for what she'd attempted with the boys. *Let me deal with Dr. Harmon*, Eunice had begged of her. What had that meant?

THE MEMORIAL SERVICE was beautiful and modest. There were three gorgeous sprays at the front of the church. Red roses—all three. Hymns were sung, prayers were offered. And some people—there were very few—stood and spoke of how nice Marva or Lazarus had been to them at one time or another. Those testimonies, along with Savannah's own memories, brought her to tears. A lady sitting next to her who smelled a bit like kerosene and green rubbing alcohol— Savannah didn't know her name, but she knew she lived down the road from her on Walker Avenue—patted her knee. "You don't have to worry 'bout them, child. They're just fine. It's us, here on earth, we should cry for."

Of the six people who stood to give testimonies, only one mentioned Marian. And Savannah got the distinct feeling that Angela had only done so because no one else had. Always a nice person, that Angela.

There was no sign of Eunice Loving.

Savannah had thought her father might have the decency to show his face. Marian rented the second-largest unit in his shopping center, and there was no doubt that he profited from Friendly Pediatrics being on his property. Surely, Marian had paid well to have a space to practice.

But Savannah also knew how her father felt about Black people. Not quite a Klansman, but he wasn't inviting Black people over for dinner, either.

With the service concluded, Savannah wanted to get out of there, have a cigarette, and get home to her bed. But since so few people lined up to express their condolences to Lymp,

Savannah thought perhaps she should. Not doing so would hardly go unnoticed. While she waited, she scanned the sanctuary for familiar faces. She saw many. Neighbors, customers at Aiken's, and the like.

Savannah imagined that if the Harmons had had a regular funeral—one with bodies and caskets—they might be stretched out where the sprays stood, where Lymp and his son and Lymp's fiancée were standing. The woman—what was her name again? Something with a G or J—was dressed quite fashionably. She wore a black skirt suit with a milk-white blouse. Her salt-and-pepper hair hung just above her shoulders. And her black hat (veil down) reminded Savannah of Saturn.

The woman gave Savannah the most curious look. A mix of acknowledgment and skepticism. It was similar to ones Savannah had received shortly after moving back to West Mills and onto the west side. But this gaze, Savannah felt, said, *I've got my eyes on you.*

In the line, two people ahead of Savannah, stood Breezy Loving. Surely, Eunice would have been at her husband's side if she had come along. Eunice Loving was that type of wife.

"Mr. Seymore," Savannah said to Lymp when she reached the front of the line. "So sorry for your loss. As you know, Marva meant the world to me, and—"

"Thank you for comin', Miss Temple," Lymp said, and he looked to the person in line behind her. If he had made eye contact with her for even a second, she had missed it. What had she done to deserve such an insult? And to be called *Temple*. Savannah believed that even West Mills's unborn knew she was no longer a Temple. Marva had once told Savannah that Lymp was grumpy. In fact, she had said he was mean. But whenever Savannah saw him around town, he seemed kind. Maybe Marva had been telling the truth about him all along. Or maybe all the nastiness the Harmons had told her about Lymp had been their way of covering their own dishonesties. Either way, with all that had happened to Lymp in the past week, Savannah supposed he was justified in having an attitude.

"Thank you for coming, Mrs. Russet," his fiancée said, extending her hand. Savannah accepted it. "I know this hasn't been easy on you, either." This took Savannah by surprise. So few of the people Savannah had spoken to in the past week had offered her condolences. Not a soul had seemed to remember that she, too, had suffered a loss.

"Well, thank you for saying that, Miss——"

"Wright. Josephine Wright."

"I still can't believe it, Miss Wright. Just doesn't seem real. Like some awful nightmare."

Savannah left the church and headed straight for her car. After the awkwardness she'd just experienced with Lymp, her next cigarette was liable to smoke itself. What a cruel March it had been. Cruel to her sons. Cruel to La'Roy Loving. Cruel to the Harmons. And outright vicious to her.

"Mrs. Russet," a voice called out. Savannah turned; it was Miss Wright.

Jesus Christ. Just let me go home.

"May I speak with you for just a moment? I won't keep you long," she said. "I just wanted to say, again, how sorry I am that you've lost such a close friend. I think people sometimes forget how hard it is to find true friendship, Mrs. Russet."

"Yes, that's true. And please, call me Savannah." She waited for Miss Wright to reciprocate the permission to be less formal. But she didn't. "Anyway, my boys and I are still pretty shaken up. And something like this happening *here*?" Savannah almost brought up the fact that the killer—assuming it was only one person—was still walking free, possibly in West Mills. But now wasn't the right time to mention things of that nature. She didn't want Miss Wright to think she was some insensitive hick.

"Mrs. Russet—Savannah—I have a question for you."

Right here? Right now? Minutes after the memorial service? "Well, I should probably get back to my boys. They're probably—"

"Was Marva seeing anyone?" Miss Wright asked. "Romantically, I mean."

"No," Savannah replied, a little hastily.

"You seem pretty sure about it."

"Well, to be frank, Marva didn't like the men around here. She always said they were too country for her. I know of at least five gentlemen who would've gladly—"

"What about Marian?"

Savannah remembered Marva joking that Marian had a *gentleman caller*, as she liked to say. But Marva never said who he was—only that he was a man their father had introduced them to not long before he died. Since Marva had been so vague about it, Savannah assumed he was married. Reluctantly, Savannah shared all of this with Miss Wright. What harm could it do now? Even Savannah had nearly forgotten about the doctor's mysterious man. Whoever he was, Savannah imagined he must be suffering. To lose a companion that way. Unthinkable.

"Marva never mentioned his name?" Miss Wright pressed. She would put Brent Wolfe to shame.

"No, ma'am."

"Marian had a fight with your father, I'm told. Do you know what that was about?"

"I don't. Business, probably," Savannah said. "But that's just a guess. I really don't—"

"When was the last time you spoke to Marva? Did the two of you get a chance to reconcile?"

"Sadly, I'm afraid we didn't get to repair things." Savannah resumed walking toward her car. But not too fast. She didn't want to appear to be running away. "I'm sure we would have, though. I feel terrible about it. It just wasn't like us to go at each other like that. Wasn't pretty at all. I imagine you've heard about it."

"Yes," Miss Wright said. "I heard it got pretty heated."

Then, just like those news anchors on TV, Miss Wright switched gears. What was Savannah's opinion of Sheriff Horton's conclusion? she wanted to know. Savannah paused and thought for a moment.

"Well, at first, I thought it was pretty ridiculous," Savannah said. "I mean, imagine them selling drugs."

"And now?"

"Now I just don't know, Miss Wright. And I guess it doesn't really matter."

"It *does* matter. It matters quite a bit that a sheriff and a district attorney would claim to believe that a triple murder was drug-related, yet they found drugs *undisturbed* in the house. I'd say it matters quite a bit."

"Yes, ma'am. I just meant that knowing whether they were drug dealers or not won't change how everything ended."

"Hmmm," Miss Wright hummed. "You know, some think Marian may have been writing people prescriptions to satisfy their habits. Addictions, to be frank."

Savannah felt her blouse dampening.

"I don't think she'd do anything like that," Savannah said.

"I certainly hope she wouldn't. She was West Mills's first Black doctor. I'd hate for her legacy to be dragged through the mud. She and I weren't close, and maybe she wasn't the nicest, but the town owes her some respect for what she accomplished. Wouldn't you agree?"

"Yes, ma'am," Savannah said. "Of course."

"Just as Lymp's name and good reputation shouldn't be tarnished. People want him to leave town. For *us* to leave town. All because of some grumbling he did about Marian. He didn't *threaten* anyone. I don't mean to pry, but Lymp and I just can't understand what Marian and Marva could have said or done to make you so angry that you'd—"

"Miss Wright." Savannah's stomach churned and her mouth went dry. She would have to end this conversation quickly. "I don't really want to get into it. We had a falling-out. It wasn't our first. I loved her like a big sister. We—"

"But you threatened to kill her," Miss Wright said. The wind blew her hat off and she caught it in midair. Her hair was pushed from her face to show her smooth, blemish-free skin. "You threatened to kill her *and* Marian. And your father had words with Marian days before that, and you say you know nothing of it. I suppose you know nothing of Eunice Loving's argument with Marian just before yours with Marva, either."

"I don't."

"What on earth did they do to you all? Why won't you tell me what Marian and Marva *really* did that upset you so?"

What did she mean by *really*? Her testimony to Brent must have gotten around, which was good, but only if people believed it.

"Excuse me, Miss Wright, but this isn't the time. We're all going through a lot right now. And I can't even imagine how Mr. Seymore must be feeling. But I won't do this with you. I *can't* do this. I just can't."

"Did it have something to do with your medication?"

"What?" Savannah asked. *How in hell?*

"I won't stand here and lie to you, Savannah. There's a rumor that you and Marva misused sedatives. I'm not judging you. But was that what you two fought about? Did she or Marian cut you off?"

"I'm done here. Goin' now," Savannah said. She was almost to her car. A few yards, maybe. Miss Wright followed.

"Between you and Eunice Loving, I don't know which of you is hiding the most," she said. "Something isn't right."

Despite her better judgment, Savannah swung around and said, "Are you accusing me of murder, Miss Wright?"

"I'm accusing you of withholding information. We'll start there."

"I gave a statement to the authorities. And you, ma'am, are *not* the authorities."

"Yes, I know. That so-called investigation is a joke."

"Listen. I don't know what Marian and Eunice had goin' on. I barely know Eunice Loving at all. Now please, leave me alone. *Please.*"

"I am not finished with this, Savannah. Sheriff Horton and Attorney Boothe have a lot more work to do. And I'll see that they do it."

"Well, you know what, Miss Wright? From what I hear, your fiancé had it out for Marian, Marva, and Laz for decades. Maybe the sheriff should revisit *that*! Maybe *you* should think more about it."

Miss Wright looked as though she'd just seen the Harmons' ghosts. Without another word, she turned around and headed back toward the church.

The last thing Savannah wanted to do was cast more doubt on someone who might be innocent. But Miss Wright had backed her into a corner. Savannah had no choice but to come out swinging.

Yet when Savannah got to her car, she felt too shaky to drive off right away. She sat there, gripping the cold steering wheel, fighting the urge to tear the car apart in search of a pill.

TWELVE

SAVANNAH

Savannah went back to work at Aiken's Rx and More the day after the memorial service. She had taken Friday off. Feeling out of sorts, she had told her boss, Stewart Aiken. And he understood perfectly. But because she and Marva were not family, he would have to deduct the time from her allotted sick days. Josephine Wright's questions had nearly made her ill. Savannah thought she deserved at least two days for that alone.

In a wobbly chair, at the long, wobbly table in the cramped break room at the back of the drugstore, Savannah ate a tuna sandwich (relish only). The room was used for more than eating midshift meals. It was also a stockroom and a closet for their coats. Some of the women Savannah worked with even left their purses there, unattended. But not Savannah. Having lived outside of West Mills, she found herself unwilling. Not that there was much in there to steal besides cigarettes and money for the soda machine. Keeping her belongings in eyeshot had simply become habit after living in New York. She had never been mugged, but Fitz had.

Sandwich nearly eaten and Pepsi all gone, Savannah began to crave the requisite postlunch cigarette. It was another harsh reminder that she would no longer enjoy the weekday smoke breaks with Marva. Savannah found herself just staring into the Tupperware bowl that held the last bite of her tuna on wheat. Two co-workers entering the room broke Savannah's trance. They were going on about the Patricia Hearst case. It had been the topic of the day on every other radio station, it seemed.

"I think she's innocent," said Miss Lynn, the drugstore's oldest employee. Savannah thought Miss Lynn might be the oldest employee in the world. She was eighty-eight years old and wore a long, brunette wig like Cher. She and River, the youngest cashier—River was also girlfriend to one of Miss Lynn's great-grandsons—had been listening to talk radio all morning, adding their own commentary. Savannah didn't want to get into a debate with Miss Lynn or with any of the others. But she was dying to know how Miss Lynn had come to that ridiculous conclusion. It wasn't so much that she cared what the old lady thought. It was more that Savannah knew that she would have to return to being at least halfway social at some point. Why not start with Miss Lynn? What Savannah wanted most was a Valium. If she had any, Miss Lynn could turn cartwheels around the room and Savannah wouldn't care.

In lieu of *How in holy fuck did you come to that dumb conclusion, Miss Lynn?* Savannah politely asked, "May I ask why you believe she's innocent, Miss Lynn?"

"Well, haven't you *seen* her?" Miss Lynn sat in one of the other wobbly chairs at the wobbly table. Then she turned to River and said, "Where's that newspaper we were looking at this morning, honey? We haven't thrown it out, have we? Jesus, I hope not." She opened her own Tupperware bowl.

Meat loaf and string beans. "Nice girl like her wouldn't rob banks unless she was *forced* to. Why *would* she? She's from a *good* family. From respectable people. Lots of education and that sort. Young lady like her—"

"Is just as liable to rob a bank as any of us in this room, Miss Lynn," Savannah put forward. She imagined few people thought Eunice Loving, with all her businesses and elbow-rubbing, might have killed the Harmons. But that didn't mean she hadn't.

Miss Lynn looked at River, shrugged, and stuck her fork in the meat loaf, which gave Savannah ideas for dinner. Then Miss Lynn went off on a tangent, causing Savannah to regret her decision to engage.

If Marva had been alive and the two of them hadn't fought, Savannah would tell her all about Miss Lynn's verdict, and the two of them would laugh. She would also update Marva on what was happening with the property tax bill that was coming due. Savannah only had savings enough to cover half the balance. She had asked for extension after extension, payment plan after payment plan. Late fees were piling up. Savannah would have to get a second job. But that would mean leaving the boys alone. Was it safe to do that now? That was something she should have done before the Harmons were killed. In any case, her forty hours at Aiken's wasn't making ends meet. But she'd rather work eighty hours before asking her father, or her grandmother, for help.

SAVANNAH GOT THE job at Aiken's Rx and More in '73, when she had moved back to West Mills. The drugstore wasn't the worst job in the world, but Savannah wanted more for herself. For a while, it paid the household bills and the loans she'd taken out to go to college and her car note and insurance. And it kept her, Terrance, and Troy fed and clothed. When property taxes increased in '74, things got a little harder, but she was still able to manage on her own.

Having earned a bachelor's degree in chemistry in New York—she had attended Manhattan College—and with her experience working in a pharmacy in Riverdale, just a few blocks from the campus, Savannah thought applying to West Mills's newer drugstore would be the right move. The owners of the other drugstores wouldn't have given her a job if she'd applied. Savannah was certain they would sympathize with her father and her grandmother—to whom her father deferred. Savannah had never known her mother, who passed away fewer than twelve hours after Savannah was born.

Savannah had been pleased and surprised to receive a call from Stewart Aiken so soon after dropping off her application. She had no doubt that the moment she left the drugstore that day his employees jumped at the chance to fill him in on who her father was and who she had married.

"There's something I should probably tell you, if you don't already know it," she had said at the interview, after she'd been welcomed to start the very next day.

"I know your children are Black and I think it's beautiful," he said. Savannah looked down at her lap. As she saw it, she had two options: telling him how she felt about his comment, or ignoring it because she needed the job.

"My father is the landlord here."

"Oh, yes!" He didn't seem the least bit embarrassed about having mentioned her children's race. "I knew that, too. And I know you two are having difficulties. But Mrs. Russet, that's none of my business." *That* was none of his business? He explained that he was a city guy—originally from Chicago.

"I don't judge people based on who they're related to, married to, friend to, or foe to. None of my concern. Any of it. You need a job and we need the help."

On the one hand, Savannah felt so appreciative she wanted to hug him. On the other, she wanted to tell him he'd been in West Mills too long to say he didn't care about others' personal affairs. But she neither hugged nor scolded. Instead, she thanked him and asked how he came to live in West Mills of all places. He explained that his wife had, some years ago, visited to do research on the history of the canal.

"She fell in love with this place. So, here we are," he said. "And I got tired of the cold weather. Arthritis." It was the oddest *Why we moved to West Mills* story she had ever heard. But Stewart was kind.

Before she left his office that day, Stewart told her that he looked forward to having her on his staff and that he thought she was quite brave.

"Brave?"

"Doing things on your own," he clarified. "Quite modern."

A few weeks went by and Savannah got into the groove of her new life back in her hometown. Academically, the boys were doing well. Getting them to behave in school had been a different story. They were always pushing another kid to the ground, taking someone's chocolate milk at lunchtime, telling a teacher about their bad breath. Name it, they did it.

A little over a month into working at Aiken's, Savannah met Marva Harmon, who worked in the shopping center at her sister's pediatric clinic. She and Marva became smoke-break friends. One day during one of their workday interludes, Marva looked at Savannah and asked, "What's it like being the only white person on Walker Avenue?"

"It's fine. The boys love the big yard." Savannah told Marva about the house, its coziness, its draftiness, the fixtures she had been impressed by when she visited it for the first time, and the two big trees out front. "Perfect for a hammock. I'll get one when I can."

"Well, that's all very nice," Marva said, blowing smoke toward the sky. "But that's not what I asked. My question was, what's it like being the only white person?"

"It's not my first time, Marva."

Having married FitzAllen, Savannah had become quite accustomed to being the only white person in spaces. When they eloped and moved to New York, she was the only white person in their Harlem building, to the super's dismay.

Savannah told Marva so much in those first couple weeks of their friendship: about the beauty of falling in love with Fitz, her family casting her out, her time in New York City with Fitz before the boys came along, the boys' births, Fitz's sudden and fatal aneurism in '67—he died while mopping the floor at an all-white high school in the Bronx; thank God he'd had a bit of life insurance—and her reluctant but necessary return to West Mills. Savannah had come back to her hometown with more uncertainty and fear than money, she told Marva. But in West Mills, she and the boys had a home waiting for them, thanks to the Russets.

"You know something, Savannah?" Marva said to her after handing her a tissue to dry her eyes. "You've been through a lot, and you've held strong for your sons. I respect that. I respect it a lot."

"Thank you, Marva," Savannah said. Marva took hold of Savannah's hand and gave it a quick squeeze. "You're all right for a white girl." The two of them nearly toppled over from laughing. "In all seriousness, you're savvy. You're the type who'll always find a way to take care of herself. Get what you need."

Just a couple of months ago, in January, when Savannah first mentioned the tax bill, Marva said, "You probably don't want to hear this, with things being so strained between you and your family. But maybe this is a chance for you to reach out to your father. Or maybe your grandmother. I'm aware she doesn't think highly of Black people, but I don't believe she'd want to see you and the boys homeless."

"You know I can't do that," Savannah replied.

"I know that's what you keep saying," Marva said.

Years before, Savannah had told Marva everything that had happened in the past with Fitz, her father, and her grandmother, as unnecessary as it was. Anyone who took one look at Savannah and her sons could imagine what her relationship with her family might be like. Marva had told Savannah, time and time again, that she would pay the whole tax debt off for her if she could. But Marva only made a very modest salary working for her sister at Friendly's. If most physicians' assistants made twelve thousand a year, Marva made six thousand working for Marian.

"And that doesn't bother you?" Savannah had asked Marva some time ago.

"When I was younger, it did. But I'm okay with it now. Marian knows best, most of the time, at least. She looks out for me and Laz. Always has."

SAVANNAH PUT ON her coat and hat, and she went outside for a cigarette. She should quit smoking, she mused. Not now. Maybe later. But when she found herself unable to stop glancing across the parking lot at the closed clinic and felt the trouble brewing in her stomach, she ran back inside. The pack of Marlboros never made it out of her purse.

In the bathroom, Savannah sat on the toilet and held a wastepaper bin in front of her face, waiting for the wave of panic, nausea, and sweats to pass. Residual withdrawal symptoms. She didn't need a professional to diagnose it. Fortunately, the vomiting had stopped days ago. The bin was a precaution. Breathe, she whispered to herself. Just breathe, Savannah. She prayed no one would come in until she was done.

Without trying, Savannah thought about the doom and gloom that had become her recent life: the loss and betrayal; the threat of losing her sons; their being used as pawns in some vicious game; the argument she'd had with Josephine Wright; the possibility that there was a secret band of killers on the loose in West Mills. It was all too much for one person.

Savannah had taken two Bayers with her sandwich to ease the headache. When would it end? It took everything in her not to go to Stewart and flat out beg, no prescription in sight and no doctor consulted, for something to help her relax. But she couldn't. She would surely lose her job, as well as any respect Stewart might have for her.

Having survived her body's attack—the withdrawal episodes were lightening up—Savannah headed back to the break room to hang her coat. It was time for her to get back to restocking shelves with those products she was always surprised to see people buy. Face creams and hand moisturizers. Weren't they all the same, just in different packaging?

Savannah felt chilly. She would keep on her long sweater. The day was cool, and she felt it each time customers came in or out. As she approached the break room door to return her coat, she heard Miss Lynn and River whispering.

"I'm talkin' about Savannah," Miss Lynn said. "I, for one, think Stewart needs to let her go. She was friends with *drug lords*. No tellin' what they had her hooked on."

"I don't know, Miss Lynn," River countered. "I've got good friends who smoke a little and drink a case of beer every single weekend. That doesn't mean *I* do it. I don't touch the stuff. Not a day in my *life*. We oughtn't judge her by what her *friends* done."

"It ain't the same, child," Miss Lynn retorted. "She's done *other* things that got to be taken into account. I'm not talkin' just about the drugs. And I sure do hope Davey ain't one of your *friends* who smokes that stuff."

"He's not, Miss Lynn. I swear. And what other things are you talkin' about?"

"Oh, you don't have to play coy with me, River Monroe. You know exactly what I'm talking about. There ain't a person in this whole town who hasn't talked about it. Even y'all who're too young to remember her leavin' know what I'm talkin' about."

"Because she married a Black man? Miss Lynn, times have—"

"Times have *not* changed. Not *that* much. Don't give me that. She should've stayed right where she went. She knows how things are here in West Mills. That's why her folks won't have a *thing* to do with her. Ted's such a nice man. And Hera. Poor Hera. After all that woman's been through. A mean husband, a dead son, the other one widowed young. Then Savannah grows up just to bring the poor woman *more* pain."

STANDING OUTSIDE THE break room, listening to Miss Lynn, Savannah wanted to throw the door open, walk up to the old woman, and say everything she had been holding in for the past three years. Savannah wanted to remind Miss Lynn of her own lot—the two sons in prison, the granddaughter who would steal your fingers right off your hand if you didn't watch her. The same one who had dropped all her children on Miss Lynn's front porch in the middle of the night, knocked hard and left. Every fiery word that Savannah wanted to serve to Miss Lynn would have felt wonderful, would have given her unspeakable joy, even if that joy lasted only a minute.

But what about after the joyful minute? Savannah would still be left with everything she was going through: no friends, a bill she couldn't afford, unpredictable children who, she believed, needed a positive male figure around, and her own lonely heart. All of it would still be there, staring her down.

Let God deal with Miss Lynn Pettigrew. If there is a God. Lately, Savannah was less sure.

She took a few steps away from the break room's door, turned her head away from it and coughed loudly. If she let on that she'd heard them discussing her, Savannah might be expected to acknowledge it. She had not the strength, the interest, nor, at the moment, a single diplomatic word with which to do so. So, Savannah would do what any proper white lady of West Mills would do. She would pretend not to know her name was being dragged through the rows of overpriced junk at Aiken's.

SAVANNAH HAD MET Fitz in 1961. She was eighteen, Fitz nineteen. She had grown tired of sitting around doing nothing to help the Black people who were being mistreated in North Carolina and around the country. In whatever small way, she wanted to take part—lend a hand. First, it was sending donations to various organizations. But when she'd heard about marches in the state's capital, she went to the west side of the canal, and to West Side High School, where people her age congregated and strategized about protests.

Savannah first saw Fitz on the steps of West Side High. It was a Friday evening, just after sundown. He was standing with a group of his friends discussing who would make what signs, how they would respond to opposers, and who they would call if they were arrested by Raleigh police. The following morning, Savannah went to see if she could offer a ride to and from Raleigh. She would take her father's car while he was still sleeping, leave a note telling some lie. Fitz and two others accepted Savannah's offer.

Savannah and Fitz became lovers after that Saturday. Using a pseudonym, he sent her letters, and she replied only in person. The forbidden couple took risky Saturday excursions to the Outer Banks, where they sat on deserted corners of the beach at night.

"Let's run away together," Fitz said, as the waves crashed out in the distance. "Someplace where it'll be legal for us to be together."

"New York, probably." Savannah leaned in closer to him. Even through the blanket, she could feel the coolness of the sand seeping through her plaid wool skirt. There was no need to feign surprise about Fitz's idea. She'd believed he would soon propose something like this. And if he hadn't, she would have done so herself. "I've been there a few times. Everything's fast there. People don't have time to care what others are doing."

"Oh, I'm sure there'll be people who'll care and won't like us," Fitz said. "But it'll be better than here."

"Yeah," Savannah said.

"You love me, Savannah Temple?"

"Of course, I love you, FitzAllen Russet. And don't you ever doubt it."

They had the old conversation about how their lives would be forever changed—likely to be shunned by all her people, likely to be shunned by at least half of his. He needed to know that he could trust her.

"There's gon' be times when you just want to be a white lady. Have white lady freedoms and privileges," Fitz said.

"We've talked about this. And what have I said to you each time?"

"As long as you still mean it, Savannah."

"I do," Savannah assured him. "Do you promise to love me?"

"I do. Love is the biggest part of what we need to make it." They would combine their savings and get jobs. They would be all right. "We can go to college up there."

"You won't jilt me when you see all those pretty girls up there, will you?" Though she'd said it with a smile, it was a real concern. Fitz was smart and stunning. He could have anyone he wanted.

"You know I don't play around with stuff like that, Savannah. I'm a man of my word. You know that."

It was all so simple. Almost too simple, really. Fitz would tell his grandmother—he couldn't run off like a thief in the night. Savannah loved her father and wanted to offer him and her grandmother a similar courtesy. But she hardly expected them to welcome Fitz with open arms. Hera didn't like Black people approaching their front door, much less entering it. Few on the east side of the canal did—regardless of the fact that West Mills had been built, nearly every brick, by Black hands.

"Jesus Christ, Savannah. Have you lost your mind?" her father asked when she told him she was in love with a Black man from the west side of the canal. They were outside in the gazebo. It was a Wednesday evening after dinner. He sat his whiskey glass on the nearest ledge. "You'll ruin your life, and this family. And the only reason I'm not screamin' at the top of my goddamn lungs right now is 'cause I don't want anyone in the house to hear."

"I love him, Daddy. No one has to be ruined because two people love each other. Fitz is a wonderful man. He—"

"You don't know a *thing* about this Fitz, about this world, about life," he said. "End it. Now."

"Daddy, will you just listen to me?"

"Savannah, I don't wanna hear another word about it. I love ya. But right now, I want you to leave me alone. Please." He grabbed his glass from the ledge and finished it in one swallow. Savannah sat still, hoping to restart the conversation. "I said leave me alone. I can't *look* at you right now."

Savannah avoided her father for three days. They avoided each other. If she heard him upstairs, she went downstairs. And when she stood before him on the evening of the fourth day, Fitz was by her side.

"Daddy. Nana," Savannah had said while standing in the foyer, hand in hand with the man with whom she planned to spend the rest of her life. "This is FitzAllen. We've been seeing each other for just over a year now. We're going to be married."

Her grandmother sat down in the middle of the floor and yelled toward the ceiling, "Lord God, help me!" Her father called out for the maid to come and help her into another room—anyplace but where she was.

Savannah's father put his cigarette out in the nearest ashtray, moved closer to them, and said, "Young man, by coming here today, you've shown yourself to have been raised with dignity and respect. Others might have run off with my daughter without a word. But—"

"I love Savannah, Mr. Temple. And I—"

"I'm sure you *think* you love her, and I'm sure she *thinks* she loves you. But you won't be marrying her. I won't have it. Now, turn around and g'on out that door. Please."

Savannah had always admired her father's ability to remain calm, even when she knew he likely wanted to pull his hair out. He had always been a gentle-natured man. Always caring of others' feelings—hers and her grandmother's, at least.

"Daddy, I—"

"Savannah, go to your grandmother and apologize for upsettin' her," her father said. "And fella, you need to leave my property quickly, before I have to arm myself."

"No," Savannah shot back. She told him that she, too, would be leaving and that they would be leaving West Mills. Leaving North Carolina. Savannah heard her grandmother wailing from the study. One would think the woman had seen the ghost of her late husband or her late son sitting at the desk.

"If you leave this house with that boy," Savannah's father said, "you go with nothin' but the clothes you're wearing and the money in your pocket. You are to never step foot on this property again. Either of ya."

Savannah had been prepared for that. She had already packed and withdrawn all the money from her savings account. As they left the foyer where four generations of Temples had greeted guests, Savannah looked back at her father and saw tears running down his face. She wanted to hug him, but what message, in that moment, would it send? Savannah took hold of Fitz's hand.

"Take care of yourself, Daddy. I hope you'll find some happiness again someday."

When Savannah and Fitz got out to the porch, Toliver Wolfe was walking up. Someone must have called the station and begged him to come before something awful happened.

"Glad to see you leaving quietly, boy," Toliver said to Fitz, smiling, his face flush with eagerness to do harm. He smelled of sweat and cigar smoke. "You savin' me and you both a lot of trouble. More you than me, of course."

"My name is Mr. Troy FitzAllen Russet," Fitz said to Toliver. "My mother and father have both been dead for many years. I'm no longer anyone's boy."

"Well, listen to you," Toliver taunted. He turned his head slowly and spit in the bushes, never taking his eyes off Fitz. "A fancy-talkin' nigga. Boy, I'll—"

"I just want 'em off my land, Toliver," Ted Temple cut in, appearing at the door.

Toliver Wolfe stared at Fitz for what felt like an hour. Then Toliver turned to Savannah.

"You lucky she's like family to me, and I don't want her hurtin', boy," Toliver said. "You *real* lucky."

The couple walked to the west side of the canal, headed for a friend of Fitz's. Toliver Wolfe, from a distance, followed them. Whether her father had asked Toliver to see her safely across the bridge, or to make it clear she was no longer welcome on the east side, Savannah couldn't be sure. The next morning, she and Fitz rode in separate train cars from Newport News to New York City. Of her father, Savannah would later say to Fitz, "You know, he didn't really look mad."

"Who are you talking about?" Fitz had asked.

"My daddy," Savannah clarified. "He was crying, but he didn't really look mad."

THIRTEEN

SAVANNAH

The next day, while at work in an aisle, counting quart-sized tubs of body lotions, Savannah thought about Terrance and Troy. She wished Fitz was alive to talk to them, love them, teach them, watch them grow into stunning, kind, intelligent replicas of himself. Savannah had once spoken to Marian and Marva about the boys' behavior. The three of them were having lunch together at the Harmons', in Marian's home office. A rare occurrence.

Marian, like a teacher in New York City, had suggested taking them to an analyst.

"They're grieving the absence of their father," Marian had said. "Acting out is common."

"But they were so little when Fitz died. They can't possibly remember what it was like to have a father around."

"You'd be surprised," Marian had replied. "I wouldn't worry too much about it, Savannah."

Savannah remembered thinking how unusual and maternal it was of her. Marva had always been the soother. Later, during that same lunch, Savannah noticed a large snow globe on one of Marian's bookshelves. Inside was a little human figure holding a rectangular sign that read MY SWEETHEART TOOK ME TO THE POCONOS.

"That's one big, pretty snow globe. Who's the sweetheart?" Savannah had asked.

"Cute, isn't it? I bought that for myself," Marian had said. "I saw it and liked it. Well, I broke the first one and ordered another. The people at the resort tried to charge me an arm and a leg. More than it cost in their shop. The nerve. Nickel-and-diming me."

"And the sweetheart?" Savannah had asked again.

"There wasn't one. Just a gift to myself. Now, you two hurry and finish your salads and move along. I need to read up on these new antibiotics. There's always something to do. Eat up."

Now Savannah could see that Marian might have been right about the boys' behavior and the absence of a father figure. But it was too bad Marian had used their acting out for her own entertainment—or whatever her reasons were.

While Marian's treatment of Terrance and Troy was abhorrent, Savannah still believed she could have prevented it. Had she not been so foggy from excessive use of the Valium on the evening Marian had called her to invite—it was more like a summons—Terrance and Troy to the so-called career talk, she might have thought it strange that Marian was inviting them only fourteen hours before it was to happen. In fact, Savannah would have taken the last-minute invitation for such an event as a slight. She wouldn't have taken them at all. Had Savannah been clearheaded at the time, she might have asked, "How many teens are you having over?" She almost certainly would have said, "I'll help you and Marva set up," at which point she would have learned that Marva wasn't even going to be there. And on the morning of that awful so-called career talk, had Savannah not started her day with two chill-out pills to get the tax bill off her mind, she might have had an opportunity to think of all the questions she hadn't asked Marian the evening before. And she would have called Marian and said, "They'll have to catch your next career talk. I forgot we'd made plans to spend the day in Norfolk." If Terrance and Troy hadn't been there, Marian wouldn't have tried to get them to assault La'Roy Loving—that poor troubled boy. The whole day might have gone differently for her sons. She shuddered to think what might have happened to La'Roy, though. Would Marian have tried to knock the boy around herself?

Savannah dropped a tub of lotion onto her foot. It was just the wake-up she needed.

"How you ladies doin' today?" Savannah heard a familiar voice say. It was her father. Miss Lynn and River stood at the counter sharing jelly beans from a sandwich bag. Miss Lynn ate at least twenty after lunch each day, followed by salted peanuts to cut the sweet taste in her mouth, she'd explained.

The chorus sang, *Good afternoon, Mr. Temple.*

"Need help finding anything, Ted?" asked Cynthia, the cashier who received twelve or more phone calls per day from her daughter and another six from her husband.

"I'm just here to grab some usuals," Savannah heard her father say. How would anyone at Aiken's know what his usuals were? Neither he nor her grandmother shopped there regularly, even though it was on his own property. He came into Aiken's once every couple of months, at most. "I'll find them. Thank y'all."

Savannah kept at her work. She would not go to him. He would have to seek her out, if that was why he was there. And she had the distinct feeling it was. Likely there to ask her questions about the Harmons.

"Hello, Savannah," he said.

"How's it going?" she replied without looking at him. *I need you to loan me some money,* she had an urge to blurt out. *No. I need for you to just give me some money, but I'd sooner pull every strand of hair out of my head than ask you for it.*

"Doing fine. Can't complain."

"Am I blocking something you need to get to?"

"Oh, no," he said. "I came for Band-Aids." Band-Aids were four aisles away. "Thought I'd say hello. Been a while. You and the boys doing all right?"

"We're getting by. Thanks."

"Saw them a couple of weeks ago. They'll be askin' for your car keys before you know it." Savannah decided not to acknowledge his comment. If he bothered to contact them, he'd know that neither of them—for reasons Savannah hadn't quite figured out—was particularly eager to learn how to drive. "Well, as you know, Dr. Harmon was one of the tenants here. And I know you and her sister got on well. I imagine it's hard to lose a close friend, and 'specially in that manner."

"Thank you for saying that," Savannah said, now shelving tubs of Happy Face washing cream. If she looked him in the eye, she might see the old him—the one who had comforted her when she was a child. The one who chased away the monsters in her closet. If she got a glimpse of that version of him, she might collapse into his arms. She might tell him all she'd been through in the past couple of weeks, the past few months. She might even tell him how rough things had been in the years since Fitz's passing. But he might mistake it for an admission of regret—remorse for not listening to him that night she left home hand in hand with Fitz. She regretted nothing where Fitz was concerned.

"Must have been shocked to hear about the other part," her father said.

"What other part?" She imagined he was referring to the drugs. And she found herself curious to know what he'd heard.

He referred to the Harmons' possible drug selling as their *other enterprise.* He moved slightly closer to her. No doubt he was hoping to learn whether she had known and whether she, too, partook. It was then that she took the risk. She looked at her father.

"I'm not sure that's true," she said. She nearly mentioned that she had also expressed that opinion to Brent Wolfe. But she thought better of it. The less she said, the better.

"I hope you're right, but who knows? We can't always know the people we—"

"We can't always know the people we call our friends—or family, for that matter. Can we? Yeah, I know that all too well." Savannah saw him swallow hard.

"Now, Savannah, I didn't come here to upset ya."

"Good."

"I've just come to pick up a few items for Mama and to offer you my condolences. The Harmons were decent people, far as I knew."

Savannah felt a bit guilty for having snapped at him. "How is Nana doing?"

"Oh, you know how she is. Still thinks she's forty. Givin' me hell." He chuckled. "I'm happy for it, though." Savannah tried to fight back a smile, but she lost that battle. Her grandmother was a hell-raiser indeed, a force to reckon with. Secretly,

Savannah hoped to be as strong and spunky as her when she reached that age. "Anyway, I'll leave you to your work. Good seein' ya." He turned to leave, but paused. "Oh, quick question for ya." *Finally,* she thought to herself. Had he heard about her tax bill and decided to offer assistance? "Had Marva mentioned anything to you about their plannin' to move the clinic to some other location?"

Savannah sneered.

"What?"

"Maybe try 'Do you and the boys need anything, Savannah?' Or 'Mind if I visit the boys once in a while?' Just you and your business. But it's okay because we're fine. My children are fine. You know why?"

"Savannah."

"Because the three of us have one another. And my sons are strong, like their father. A man you *hated* without even knowing." It took everything in her not to curse her father high and low. "Now, unless you need help finding something, I've got work to do."

"I'm sorry, Savannah," he said. "I'm truly sorry."

The odd thing was, she believed him. Maybe it was the way he looked down at the floor. Maybe it was the whisper with which he delivered the apology. She couldn't be sure. But she knew he meant it.

As he turned to leave the store—he didn't buy anything— Savannah thought how peculiar it was for him to ask if Marian had planned to move the clinic. Why would such a thing matter now? Was that what he and Marian had been seen arguing about—her breaking a lease?

★ ★ ★

AT HOME, BEFORE dinner, Savannah took a moment to watch Troy and Terrance as they read in the living room, a science fiction novel and a comic book, respectively. They were beginning to mature. Her boys were learning to think for themselves, seemingly more aware of their impulses to snap at each other, talk back to her, be nuisances to teachers, be unkind to their peers. Savannah was certain that if Marian had asked them to call La'Roy awful names and to hit him five or six months ago, they might not have passed on the opportunity. But they had come a long way. Savannah was thankful for mercies—big and small.

"Homework done?" she asked, having given them both a kiss on their foreheads. Neither of them replied. "Hello? Are all four of those ears clogged again?"

"Yeah," Terrance said. His voice seemed to be getting deeper by the day.

"Then go clean them," she joked, but the boys didn't laugh.

"Yeah, we did our homework," Terrance clarified. Troy lifted his comic back up to shield his face.

"What's going on, big guy?" she said to him. "How's everything at school? Still no visits to Mrs. Pherebee's, right?"

"Nope."

Savannah had not had much of a conversation with them about the Harmons' murders. Maybe it was time. After dinner, perhaps. She felt certain the kids were whispering about it at the junior high school.

"I'm going to start dinner," she said. Hamburgers and fries. In the meantime, there was clean laundry that needed to be folded and put away. She would leave that to them, she told them.

On her way out, she heard Troy say, "I'm gonna ask."

"Don't, dumbass," Terrance whispered.

"Why not?" Troy asked.

"Because. Just don't. I told you. You can't believe everything you hear."

Savannah turned back.

"Is there something you two wanna talk about? Maybe about the Harmons?"

The boys glanced at each other.

"Nope," Troy said. "I'll start foldin'." He tossed the comic book onto the coffee table and started for the kitchen, where the baskets of clothesline-dried laundry sat on top of the washing machine.

"Boys," Savannah said.

"Is it true their brother killed them?" Troy asked, and Terrance rolled his eyes.

Savannah invited Troy to sit next to his brother on the couch. She got a chair from the kitchen table and sat before them.

She explained that Lymp Seymore had been questioned and released, and that the police had no idea who had taken the Harmons' lives. There wasn't any evidence left behind to point them in any particular direction. "But they do think it was someone the Harmons knew," she added. "They don't think it was just some random thing, from what I've heard. So, there's no reason for you two to be afraid."

"So, the person was mad at them for something?" Troy asked.

"Of course, dummy," Terrance teased.

"Cut it out," Savannah reprimanded. And to Troy she said, "Seems that's the case."

"You were mad at them," Troy said. "Did you kill them?"

"Gosh, you so stupid," Terrance said. "I told you not to ask that dumb shit."

"Language, Terrance!" Savannah knew both of the boys swore; she'd overheard them more times than she could count. But swearing to her face? Had she lost Terrance's respect? "Honey," she said softly. She reached out and touched his hand. It was cold. "Of course I didn't. Why would you even—"

"People at school said you told Aunt Marva that you'd kill her," Troy reported.

"Her *and* Dr. Harmon," Terrance added. "Did you say that?"

"I did, guys, but it was the same way you two say it to each other every day. I didn't *mean* it."

"But why'd you even say it at *all*?" Terrance inquired. "What were y'all fussin' about in the first place?"

"Was it about what happened with La'Roy?" Troy chimed in.

"No," she lied, not wanting them to feel in any way responsible for, or more connected to, any of that drama. "Nothing to do with that. Just other grown-up crap."

"Was it over pills?" Terrance inquired. He had slid to the edge of the couch cushion, as though preparing himself to leave the room.

"What, sweetie?" Savannah was dumbfounded by how much they'd heard at school. "What pills?"

"People are sayin' Aunt Marva was a pill popper and that you are, too," Terrance said.

Had Marva told someone about this? Or was it that damn receptionist, Angela? Always eavesdropping on her and Marva whenever Savannah dropped by the clinic for a quick hello.

Well, Savannah imagined saying to her sons, *I misused Valium, but I wouldn't call myself a pill popper. And I don't want you calling people "pill poppers." It doesn't sound nice. Not at all.*

Then she thought of Marva's threat to call Social Services. There was no way she could tell such a truth to her sons now. They weren't the most talkative two on Walker Avenue, but they had begun opening up to people, making new friends. It would be Savannah's luck that they'd share her confession with some kid who would, without a doubt, tell his own mother. Terrance and Troy could be snatched from her with only a moment's notice. Social Services would make an example out of her—Ted Temple's daughter. Why risk it?

"The pills I take are for women's pains," Savannah assured them. "Normal things most women take at certain times." Maybe they would carry that back to whatever gossiping kid had called her a drug addict. "I don't know what Marva was taking, but I doubt it was anything bad. She was older than I am. Sometimes people have ongoing pain when they reach a certain age. We all will someday, probably." The boys were skeptical. Both scowling—Terrance more so than Troy. "I'm sorry you had to hear that nastiness about her and me, but it's not true." The boys exchanged glances. Terrance scratched the cornrows he had had done by a girl down the road. Troy's hair was cut too short for the girl's fingers to catch. They would most certainly discuss it among themselves later. "Is there anything else you want to ask?"

"What did you and La'Roy's mom talk about that day she came here, the day all that stuff happened?" Troy probed. It was the third time he'd asked that question. The first time had been the evening of Marian's so-called career talk. The second time had been a couple of days later. *I'm too tired for this, big guy,* she'd said, and, *None of that's important.* But it was important to Troy. And though he was the one asking all the questions, Savannah could see that Terrance was just as eager to know. Though he was sitting back on the sofa, his neck was craned forward. It was something Fitz used to do when he was listening closely. "Why'd you change your mind about going to talk to Dr. Harmon that day?"

Was there a right answer to any of it? To tell them that Eunice had wanted to handle it on her own would lead to more questions. *Handle it how? Kill her?*

"Mrs. Loving and I wanted to schedule meetings with Dr. Harmon to discuss what had happened," Savannah told the boys. She hated lying to them, but it was a necessary evil.

"Well, did y'all get to talk to her?" Terrance asked. "Dr. Harmon."

"I decided to speak to Marva first. And—"

"And that's when y'all fussed," he said.

"That's right. But it didn't have to do with that. I'm sorry all the talk at school is bringing this stuff up. It would be nice if we could all just move on. Let's try."

"Well, something's up with La'Roy," Terrance said. He had picked up the habit of starting his sentences with *well*. She would be glad when that was over. He was beginning to sound like the old men her father spoke with while she was growing up. "He's been actin' weird. Like, gettin'-in-trouble kind of weird." The boys explained that he'd been fussing with teachers, shoving his shoulder into people in the hallways, not eating his food at lunch, putting his head down in class and crying, then sleeping. "Ms. Hathaway told him she was gonna speak to his mom and he said, 'Tell her. I don't care. She won't care, either. She don't even like me.'"

"And he called me a faggot today," Troy added. The boys giggled.

"Guys."

"It's funny because he—"

"I don't think it's funny! Not one bit. And I don't want to hear that word again."

She, too, would have to banish the epithet from her vocabulary. She used the term at least once a month, in the boys' presence, when a male driver pulled out in front of her, or when a male employee at McDonald's wouldn't let them in five minutes before closing time. But Savannah knew it was wrong. And she was glad the word, on any regular basis, had never been used to describe her sons.

Savannah hadn't seen Eunice around in a while. Not even at Manning Grocery, where Savannah had gone twice, hoping to catch a glimpse of her, hoping to observe something in Eunice that would show anything but guilt—the guilt someone might carry for having done the unspeakable. The guilt of taking three lives. *Oh, get off it, Savannah. Eunice didn't shoot three people.*

"Have you seen Mrs. Loving at the school?" she asked her sons. They had.

"She came to pick him up after Ms. Hathaway sent him to Assistant Principal Pherebee's office," Terrance said. He had seen it. Eunice had tried to hug La'Roy in the hallway. But La'Roy had pulled away from her, told her that she didn't care about him. "La'Roy said he was gonna tell everybody what she did."

"Wait. What? What did she do?"

"I don't know."

"What do you mean, you don't know, Terrance? Weren't you standing there listening?"

"Mrs. Loving just kept saying 'La'Roy, please don't talk like that. Please calm down.' Somethin' like that."

After dinner and dishes, Savannah went to her room and collapsed on the bed. She needed time to herself. She was glad her sons felt comfortable telling her what they'd heard about her and asking her hard questions. But it was an interrogation nonetheless, and she was exhausted. She imagined they were, too.

Was it possible that Eunice killed the Harmons, and somehow La'Roy found out? *Hell, it's not out of the question.* From all she'd heard, it was the work of someone who knew how to handle a gun. An experienced shooter, she would wager. And with Laz having been shot more than his sisters, Savannah once again had to wonder if he had been the target.

But with Marian's reputation, it was more likely that Laz had taken a couple of bullets trying to protect her. Savannah sighed. No one will ever know the truth, she decided. But Eunice had obviously done something unsavory—something La'Roy was holding over her head.

Savannah needed a cigarette, and when she reached to get one off of her nightstand, she saw the tax bill. It was almost as if it were taunting her, always there, no matter how many times she thought she'd thrown it in a drawer. She would need to think of something soon.

La'Roy said he was gonna tell everybody what she did, Terrance had said.

Having finished her Marlboro, Savannah went out into the living room and got the telephone book. First, she looked up the phone number to Manning Grocery. She used a piece of junk mail to hold the page. Then she flipped to the *L* section, found the *Lo* names, and ran her finger down until she located LOVING ROBERT AND EUNICE.

FOURTEEN

SAVANNAH

Savannah's calls to the Lovings' residence went unanswered, so she dialed Manning Grocery. A staff member picked up on the first ring. Her voice was upbeat and inviting. It was clear that Eunice had urged them to always make customers feel welcomed, whether in person or on the phone. Mrs. Loving was still in the building, the lady said. She would go and find her.

"This is Eunice. How may I help you?"

"This is Savannah."

"Hey, Savannah," Eunice said cheerfully after a pause. "Hold on a minute, please." Savannah heard her telling the staff member to transfer the call to the office. Savannah nervously fingered a loose string at the tail of her mustard-colored wool sweater. "Hey, I hate to rush you, but we're really busy in here tonight for some reason. You'd think it was Thanksgiving Wednesday or something. How can I help you?" How Eunice so effortlessly pretended everything was normal was baffling to Savannah. It was impressive.

"I've heard that La'Roy's having a tough time and I think we—"

"La'Roy's fine. He's still a little upset about what Marian tried and all, but he'll—"

"Cut the shit, Eunice. I know what you did. And it's time you dealt with it. Head on."

What Savannah knew and what she suspected were two very different things.

"I don't understand," Eunice said. "What did I do?"

With feigned confidence, Savannah said, "I know you're the reason Marian tried to get my boys to hurt La'Roy and the reason he's mad as hell with you right now." Savannah could hear Eunice close the door to her office. There was a slow creak before the sound of it catching.

"I don't know what it is you think you know, Savannah Temple. But I—"

"You know that's not my name, Eunice. And what you've done is—"

"You have *two* teens. You ought to know, better than *I* do, how easy it is for them to wake up one day and be mad at you. If me or Breezy sneeze the wrong way, La'Roy's rolling his eyes and wishing he had different parents. You *know* how they are. But go ahead. I'm listening, since you know so much."

Before placing the call, Savannah had sat in her bedroom thinking about the things Terrance and Troy had told her after the art teacher dropped them off on that awful Saturday. Marian had instructed them to call La'Roy vicious names. She had told them that he needed it knocked out of him. *This will help him, gentlemen,* Marian had insisted. *This is what La'Roy needs.* And when the boys had refused, Marian had said, *Well, I guess you're a couple of fags, too, aren't you?* Terrance and Troy had reported these things to Savannah and she believed them. Every word.

"You are wasting my time, Savannah. I have businesses to run."

For Savannah, it was like playing roulette. She placed all her chips on red.

"Eunice, you hired Marian to fix him. You wanted her to change him, and she told you she could. I know it all." Silence, save for the humming of some machine in Eunice's office. "Are you still there?"

"I don't know where you got that crazy shit, but you're wrong," Eunice said, unconvincingly.

"You wish I was wrong."

"Did Marva tell you that bullshit?" There were another handful of silent seconds. "Oh! I see what's goin' on here." Eunice laughed. "You're tryin' to blackmail me. I can't believe this shit. You pill popper. If you were a Black woman, your kids would've been taken away the day word got around about you and Marva and those pills. You do know that, don't you?"

Blackmailing Eunice might not be as easy as Savannah imagined. People like Eunice Loving—people with so much to lose—were supposed to be easy targets.

"I have never, never had a pill problem! That's all lies."

"Oh, of *course* they are," Eunice scoffed. "I guess it's all lies that you're behind on your property taxes, too, isn't it? 'Cause if it is, you oughta go talk to Annie Ballance up there at the county clerk's office. She's telling *everybody* about your tax bill. And here you come, thinking you gon' blackmail *me*? To get *your* bills paid? Oh, no ma'am, Miss Temple. Fuck. That. You scheming junkie. No wonder your boys are two wild animals. If Fitz wasn't already dead, the three of you would probably kill him."

Savannah heard very little after Eunice said *Your boys are two wild animals.*

"What did you just say to me?"

"You heard what I said," Eunice shot back. "Get your life together, Miss Temple. And do *not* call me again." She hung up.

It was a good thing Savannah had called Eunice instead of going to the store. Savannah would be on her way to jail for assault, at the very least.

Savannah, having seethed for several seconds, ripped the phone from the wall and threw it across the room. It landed in front of her closet door. Soon after, Terrance and Troy burst into her room without knocking. She hadn't even heard them coming down the hall, she was so engulfed with anger. Eunice Loving had crossed a thin line, and Savannah would not be able to let it go unanswered.

"What's the matter, Mom?" Troy asked.

"Damn!" Terrance exclaimed, looking at the destroyed telephone. Thank God there was another one in the kitchen.

Savannah rose from her bed, walked over to them, and pulled them close. There, near the entrance of her bedroom, she stood hugging them.

"You are good boys. Don't ever let anyone tell you different. Do you hear me?" Savannah took a couple of deep breaths. "Go on back to your room. I'm sorry about the noise. I love you both very, very much."

She kissed their foreheads and ushered them out.

Now you've fucking pissed me off, Eunice Loving. Forgive me, Fitz.

FIFTEEN

Jo

Jo was five minutes into a phone call with Herschel. She wished she could have shown more enthusiasm about his news. He and Dean had been on several brisk, ten-block walks since they'd last spoken. He had found them quite energizing, he reported.

"That's good," Jo said solemnly. "Happy to hear it. Your doctor will be, too."

"Uh-oh. What's wrong? Still getting those wonderful little take-your-man-and-leave notes in the mailbox, breadbox, icebox, and wherever else the lovely people of West Mills are putting them?"

"Not a good time for jokes, Hersch. I have a lot on my mind."

As if Savannah's biting remark in the churchyard hadn't been enough, a couple of days ago, Jo was at the grocery store—she drove all the way to Price Chop in Pasquotank County because she didn't want to give Eunice Loving a dime of her money—and an old woman she didn't know walked right up to her and said, "You Susan and Shem Wright's girl?" She looked to be at least ninety-five years old. Maybe a hundred. She was wearing a black-and-white houndstooth coat that looked as though it had only been worn once or twice. Not a dingy spot in sight. Jo heard bangles collapsing onto one another every time the woman raised her right arm to push her large, dark sunglasses up the bridge of her nose. Coarse, snow-white hair peeped out from under her black toboggan.

Jo had said, "Yes, ma'am. Have we met?"

And the woman replied, "Naw, but I knew your people. Now, you listen to me, child. If you know what's good for you, drop that no-good Lymp. Anything that came from Jessie Earl Harmon is mean. Them three that got killed ain't no exception. And just 'cause they couldn't prove Lymp ain't kill 'em, don't mean he *didn't*."

"Forgive me, ma'am. But this is both unfair and inappropriate. It's this exact kind of talk that ruins a person. And with all due respect, you should be ashamed of yourself. Now, if you'll excuse me."

The old woman stepped in Jo's path and said, "Save all that fancy talk for the white folks, child. Lymp told the boys, right up there at Sutton's, that he couldn't stand Jessie Earl's other children. He—"

"Ma'am, I know all about what Lymp said at Sutton's."

"I know you do," the old woman said. "That's what's troublin' me. After the way he cut up at Sutton's, I'd drop him like a hot comb. My son was there, and Burrus Mitchell was there, and at least five, six other ones was up there. The Stokes fella, probably. I can't think of his first name. But I bet you this bag of oranges he was there, too. I know you ain't a young girl, but you that scared of bein' without a man that you'll be with a killer?"

"Then she walked off with her bag of oranges," Jo told Herschel.

"Did you get her name?"

"I didn't get a chance. And I certainly wasn't going to follow her."

"That's bold."

"I know. The audacity to just approach someone and—"

"Oh, I'm not talking about her," Herschel said. "I'm talking about Lymp. Don't you think that's bold of him to speak that way about the Harmons? So publicly like that? And you said he wasn't even drunk. Right?"

"You've said this before, Herschel. And again, I don't think it's all that unusual. He'd asked for help and Marian not only refused him, she talked down to him. Humiliated him. Besides, siblings don't always get along well. Think of all the people we both know who aren't speaking to a sister, a brother, a father."

"But come on, JoJo. People in the South are different. They don't go around wishing their siblings ill will. Southerners are too conservative for that sort of thing. I know you love your man, and you want this one to last . . ."

"But?"

"What's the latest on the polygraph?"

"There's a lot of bureaucracy involved, apparently."

She had called Percival to inquire. In addition to not having the authority to submit the request, Percival had said scheduling and paying an expert to administer the test couldn't be done without Horton's knowledge. And Horton had reiterated, multiple times, that he had no intention of using his resources on three dead drug pushers.

"Well, I hope they test him soon," Herschel mused. "Because that alibi . . . whew!"

"That's not helping, Herschel."

"I'm not saying I think Lymp's a murderer, Jo. But—"

"I know what you mean. I hear you."

"So, what's next?"

Jo told her brother that she had considered speaking to some of the men the old woman at Price Chop mentioned. What if one of the men had added things to the rant that were never said at all?

"You need to be prepared to learn things you don't want to know, JoJo. Again, not necessarily that he's guilty of murder, but other things."

Jo appreciated her brother's candor. But sometimes she resented him for it.

"Either way, I don't know how much longer I can keep going behind Lymp's back, asking questions."

"You don't have to go behind his back. What would Susan Wright do?"

Their mother would call witnesses to the apartment and hold court in her living room if Jo had been accused of doing something wrong on the block. She'd call in as many children as she could reach in earshot of the window. And she would say, "Reba says my Jo used a swear word whilst y'all was playin'? I wanna know what swear word it was, and how many times. And if I even feel like you're lyin', I'll paddle you, too."

"I don't know about that, Herschel," Jo said. "Lymp is fragile right now."

"Eventually, he'll find out you've asked around about him, you know."

And she did know. But Lymp would have to understand. Or she hoped he would.

★　★　★

WHILE LIVING IN New York, Jo had never allowed her phone number to be published in the telephone book. Why would she? If she wanted someone to have her phone number, she would just give it to them. Why did all of New York City need to be able, on a whim, to call her home or know her address? But now Jo found herself grateful to whoever had the bright idea of inventing the telephone book. West Mills's was coming in handy.

Moments after Jo turned onto Mill Sound Lane and into Burrus Mitchell's driveway—he was said to be the man who reported Lymp's rant about the Harmons to the sheriff's department—her unannounced visit was welcomed with more warmth than she'd expected. It was almost as if they'd been waiting for her. This was an especially nice surprise because she would use it to soften the blow when telling Lymp that she'd gone there, without his knowledge, to speak to Mr. Mitchell.

The Mitchells served Jo water with lemon.

"A week ago you would've gotten a Coke," Mrs. Mitchell announced. "But we on diets. Cuttin' back on sugar." One of their granddaughters was getting married in two months. "My dress's being made. I got to be able to slide into that size fourteen, Miss Wright." She laughed. Jo smiled politely. "How's your brother? I went to school with him."

"He's doing well, thank you."

"She had a big ol' crush on him," Mr. Mitchell teased. "He wasn't thinkin' 'bout her, though. Or any other girl."

"Burrus!" Mrs. Mitchell said, slapping his thigh. "He didn't mean nothin' by that, Miss Wright."

"It's all right," Jo said. "Herschel found freedom when we moved north." The Mitchells smiled awkwardly.

"Oh. Well, we'll keep him in our prayers," Mrs. Mitchell said. "God fixes things when He gets ready."

"Leaving small-town life *was* the fix for him."

Then, as her segue into why she'd come, she told them about the lady in the Price Chop. "Was she a short lil light-skinned woman with big, big, dark sunglasses on her face? Sunglasses so dark you couldn't see her eyes? And with 'bout twenty or thirty jinglin' bracelets on her wrists?" Mrs. Mitchell asked, and Jo confirmed.

"That was Miss Cret," Mr. Mitchell said. "Miss Lucrezia Hathaway. Her grandson, Horace Hathaway, is a coach up there at the high school. And his wife teaches up at the junior high."

"Ah," Jo said, wondering why any of that information might be important. "Mr. Mitchell, I hate to put you on the spot, and I don't want to drag you into anything. But as you might imagine, Lymp and I have heard that you called to the sheriff's department and told what you heard him saying about his sisters and brother. Now, he doesn't deny saying unkind things about them, but—"

"You want to know exactly what he said. I don't blame you," Mrs. Mitchell said. She had invited Jo to call her TeeTee, but Jo could tell the Mitchells were at least twelve to fifteen years older than her. She wouldn't dare. "He know you're here?"

"Yes," Jo lied. "He's not happy about it, but he says he has nothing to hide."

"Well, first off, I didn't go and report *shit*," Mr. Mitchell said.

"Don't cuss at the lady."

"It's fine," Jo assured them. "Please, tell me everything. From the beginning."

Mr. Mitchell confirmed that he and a group of other men were sitting around at Sutton's Petro smoking their pipes and cigars, and talking about this, that, and the other. Lymp was on duty that day.

"I can't remember how, but somebody said somethin' 'bout ol' Jessie Earl Harmon." Mr. Mitchell scratched his nose for a few seconds. "Oh! Yes, I do. It was somethin' 'bout how Jessie Earl used to help us get summer work on the east side when we were boys. Raking the white folks' yards and that sorta thing. Well, Lymp got to talkin' 'bout how much he missed Jessie Earl. Said somethin' 'bout how he wished he was still around to teach the other three how to be kind to folk, especially family."

"Tell her 'bout the loan, Burrus," Mrs. Mitchell chimed in.

"I'm gettin' to it, Tee."

Lymp had shared with the men that, just the day before, he had called Marian at Friendly's, told her about his plumbing issues, and asked if she'd be kind enough to loan him the money to have the work done. Marian refused and said, "I don't even loan money to Marva and Laz. I'm certainly not loaning you any."

"So, Lymp said the doctor and the other two forgot where they come from. Said he was the one looked in on Jessie Earl after Miss Louise died—and the other three went back up north. Said he hated all of 'em. Called 'em some names I won't repeat, Miss Wright. But you can imagine." Mrs. Mitchell slid back on the couch and crossed her arms over her chest.

"Yes," Jo said, hoping he'd soon share things she didn't already know.

"So, I told him to hush up before he go too far. But he was on fire, Miss Wright. Said the doctor treat people any ol' kinda way. Lymp said if she or the other two was drownin', he wouldn't throw 'em a rope. Said somebody was gon' get Marian one of these days for her ways.

"See, Miss Wright, that's the kind of *too far* I was talkin' about. Anyway, he broke down and cried. Right there in front of us. Cried like a lil child. Then he started kickin' and hittin' things. I felt bad for him. About all of it. We all did. We told him don't worry. We told him we'd all pitch in and lend him some money. He wouldn't hear it, though. I'll tell you the truth, Miss Wright, Lymp kinda scared me, the way he was talkin' and doin'."

"Was there a particular reason you called the sheriff's department, Mr. Mitchell?"

"Like I said, I didn't call and report Lymp. Quinten Stokes did, and it was Quint who told Sheriff Horton who all was there and heard Lymp. Then Horton sent his boys out to talk to each of us. I told the officers that Lymp ain't said nothing everybody on earth hasn't said 'bout a family member at some point in their life. Only difference is, Lymp said it out in the open, 'round lots of people. That's the only difference. No law against talkin' shit, though."

"I don't believe I've met this Quinten," Jo said.

"That's a *good* thing," Mr. Mitchell said. "Just an ol' troublemaker. Still mad at Lymp 'bout some ol', ol' stuff."

"What old stuff?"

"Quinten loves him some Willoughby," Mr. Mitchell said. "Always has."

"Oh," Jo said. Willoughby was Nate's mother.

"But I been tellin' Quinten for years, if Willoughby wanted him, she would've gone back to him after she broke up with Lymp damn near thirty years ago." There it was: this Quinten and his old grudge was the reason half the town knew about

Lymp's harsh words. "I don't think Lymp killed them people, Miss Wright. Not for one minute. He's good to the core."

At that, Mrs. Mitchell glowered. She seemed to be waiting for an invitation to elaborate on the gesture.

"Mrs. Mitchell?" Jo said.

"Well, since you asked, I—"

"Tee, his boy ain't got nothin' to do with it."

"Shut up, Burrus."

Mrs. Mitchell explained that while she didn't exactly think Lymp was a murderer, she wouldn't swear on a Bible that Lymp, or Nate, were the most honest people in town.

Seven or eight years ago—Mrs. Mitchell couldn't be exact—Nate had been half the reason for the hairdresser AnaFaye's divorce. AnaFaye's then husband, Bernard, had been told that his wife was seeing Nate and that the lovebirds were getting together at the salon on Mondays—the one weekday AnaFaye didn't see clients.

"Bernard confronted Nate one night up there at the lodge. It got ugly. Our grandsons were there. Heard every last word of it. Didn't they, Burrus?" Mr. Mitchell sighed and sat back. Jo had slid to the edge of her seat. The thick, clear plastic that covered the cushion made sliding effortless. "Bernard said he'd buy a gun and shoot Nate in his privates if he even *looked* at AnaFaye again. Said he'd shoot AnaFaye too! Folk lose their minds over some lovin', don't they?" Mrs. Mitchell said, causing Jo to square her shoulders. "Anyway, the next day, I was up at the savings and loan making payments. That's where Bernard works, you know. And Lymp came in there, walked right to Bernard's desk, and said, 'Bernard, I'mma say this to you one time. Somebody's got it all wrong. Me and Nate been to Nags Head every single Monday for the past two, three months. Gatherin' oysters and mussels to sell in Pasquotank."

Jo, knowing neither Lymp nor Nate knew the first thing about gathering and selling oysters or mussels, could tell where this was going, and she didn't need to hear the rest. But there was no stopping Mrs. Mitchell.

"Lymp said, 'My boy ain't thinkin' 'bout yo' old lady. You accuse him again and we gon' have a problem. And if you shoot him, you best shoot me, too. And shoot me dead, damn it, 'less you want to be always lookin' over your shoulder for the rest of your days.' But Lymp's lie was a waste, Miss Wright. When Bernard filed them divorce papers, AnaFaye told every woman who came to her salon how good Nate was in bed."

"Tee!"

"Well, that's what happened," Mrs. Mitchell returned. "Anyhow, you hear what I'm tellin' you, Miss Wright?"

"Yes, ma'am. You don't believe Lymp's alibi?"

Mrs. Mitchell raised her chin and said, "Want some more water before you go?"

Obviously, this didn't ease Jo's concerns. What other secrets, big or small, might Lymp have? She might never know. But this didn't mean he was a killer. Did it? After all, Lymp, on the day the Harmons' bodies had been found, had been willing to take a polygraph. It wasn't his fault that one wasn't available and that the lazy sheriff wasn't doing his job.

Jo almost said all of this to Mrs. Mitchell. But what difference would it make? Until the test was taken or the killer found, people would have their eyes narrowed on Lymp. Jo knew Mrs. Mitchell thought her a fool in love. *And maybe I am. But I won't give up on him just because he displayed some anger, a human emotion, in public. I just won't.*

Mr. Mitchell walked Jo out to her car.

"She don't think Lymp's a killer, Miss Wright," he said, stuffing his pipe with Dunhill tobacco from a red tin. "Really, she don't. She just don't like home-wreckers, and she feel like Lymp helped his son wreck a home."

Jo didn't know what to say in response. A shrug was all she had to offer.

Mr. Mitchell remarked again on how sad the triple murder was. He said he wouldn't stand there and pretend he liked the Harmons. But he always felt bad for them. "I always feel sad for folk that seem like they never satisfied. That can wear you out, you know. Always wanting a lil more of this and a lot more of that. That's how the doctor was, you know."

"Did you go to her sometimes? As a patient, I mean."

"Yeah, me and Tee both went to her a couple times. Wanted to show some support to our own. You know?"

"I understand. We should all do that," Jo said.

"Well, we stopped goin' to her. She talk to me kinda rough and I told Tee I might as well go to the white folk if I want to be talked to like I was simpleminded. Miss Wright, I don't talk like the people on the news. And I don't know a bunch of fancy words like she did. But I'm not dumb. And she told us we were fat. We know we ain't the thinnest two in West Mills, but I'll be damned if I'm gon' sit and listen to a doctor call me fat. And seem like she kept saying it over and over. Like she was tryin' to make sure I remember it. Her sister was in there, grinnin'. But anyway, it's terrible what happened to 'em. Nobody deserves that."

"They weren't always like that," Jo said. "I don't know what changed them. I used to play with Marian and Marva when we were girls, up there at that huge house."

"Such a pretty place," Mr. Mitchell said. "I wonder what'll happen to it. Me and Tee was coming back from Norfolk yesterday and we drove to see it—just to look."

"To look?" Jo said, intrigued.

"Well, don't nothin' like that happen here in West Mills, you know," he said, almost defensively. "We just wanted to go drive up and see the yellow tape and all. It's still there." Jo thought this was awfully strange—going to look at a crime scene as if it were a monument. But they were in West Mills. People found their entertainment wherever they could. At some point, Jo, too, might ride by the property. It had been years. "Ted Temple was there. I guess he wanted to see, too."

"Oh?" Jo said. "That's odd."

"Yeah. I said to Tee, 'Who's that white man?' My eyes ain't good as hers. He was standin' on the porch, leanin' on one of them columns, hands in his pockets. Tee said, 'That's Ted Temple.'"

"Just him there?"

"Yeah, just him," Mr. Mitchell replied. "You know, it's one thing for him to be curious and go look at the scene like everybody else. But I thought it was kinda disrespectful of him to be all up on the porch like he was. I guess the yellow tape ain't mean nothin' to him."

"Apparently not."

"What he ought to be doin' is helping his daughter out. She's 'bout to let my kinfolks' house go to the county. If I had a daddy with money like the Temples got, I'd put differences aside. It's foolish. If I could, I'd buy it." He paused. "But I should probably hush my mouth."

"Savannah Russet's having financial troubles?"

"I shouldn't say," Mr. Mitchell said. But he already had.

En route back to her house, Jo thought about Lymp, Nate, and the saga of AnaFaye. And she decided she would speak to them about it. But what she'd found most surprising about her conversation with the Mitchells was the bit about Ted Temple being on the Harmons' property, standing casually on the porch. Mr. Temple's argument with Marian was said to have been quite energetic. Fingers pointing and spittle flying. Was he feeling guilt about their final exchange?

Like others, Jo had assumed Mr. Temple's argument with Marian might be inconsequential, a row between landlord and tenant. But maybe there was more to it.

SIXTEEN

TED

Theodore "Ted" Temple sat in his small office at the shopping center, thinking about the large wire transfer that would arrive in his bank account within the next month. It was his best attempt at keeping his mind off Dr. Marian Harmon.

Ted had been in his office the day the Harmons had been found dead. He had heard of it over the CB radio, which sat on the corner of his desk, next to the telephone, next to a snow globe he had bought when he and Marian ran off together for a weekend in Pennsylvania. He'd gotten one for Marian, too, but she'd dropped hers accidentally while unpacking it at home. Now, his snow globe sat on the ledge of his office's only window. Sunlight bouncing off it.

It was a good thing he had been alone when he'd heard the news of Marian's death. Had anyone seen him gasp, slide from his chair onto the floor, cry, hold his chest, and rip his shirt pocket in pursuit of a nitroglycerin tablet, they would've figured out that Dr. Marian Harmon had been much more to Ted than a monthly rent check for a commercial unit. He had loved Marian more than he loved any woman in the world.

But she had turned on him. And his mourning had its limits.

With the forthcoming deposit would come the self-respect Ted had been waiting on for a long time. It might even bring him more respect from people on the east side of West Mills—where he'd lived most of his life. If anyone bothered to ask him, he would tell them that it was respect he wanted most of all. The kind that came from decisions he made—not some handed-down respect.

Ted was finally selling the shopping center and the land on which it sat. He had always believed that someday it would be worth much more than his older brother had paid for it (may God rest Chip's soul). From the moment Ted inherited the commercial property in '70, and the other scattered properties around town, he wanted to ditch them. But then West Mills's population had started to grow. More and more Coast Guard families were moving to the area. It was only a matter of time before some developer wanted to use that space for a larger shopping mall or a gated community full of identical houses. Ted decided to hold out, wait a while.

Having little else to do, Ted watched the shopping center run itself, and he bided his time. Now his patience was about to pay off, so long as Jeff Darby, the man who'd made the offer on the property, didn't find any reason to pull out of the deal. Darby had already ordered more appraisals and assessments than anyone could imagine. He had permits to build a three-level indoor shopping mall. And he had investors galore. Ted imagined it would likely be an eyesore, but people would love it anyway.

But Darby was old-fashioned. One of the those good ol' boys. A third-generation Klansman—though people used that term less and less. If Darby got so much as a hair-thin notion that Ted had been having an affair with Marian or any other woman who wasn't white, the deal would be off. No question about it. Darby loved money, but he respected tradition far more. Marian had known that about him, and she had threatened to use it. And to combat Marian's threat, Ted had felt it necessary to come up with a plan. He would make his own threat that would, no doubt, send her packing back north. As much as the impulse made him cringe, he would have seen it through. Marian had left him no choice. But she, Marva, and Lazarus were killed before he had the chance. And though it disgusted him to think of it, he was glad he hadn't had to cause her any harm.

But with Marian gone, Ted had begun to worry almost none at all about anyone learning about their affair. If anyone had known about him and Marian, it would be out already. Even Savannah, who had been so close to Marva Harmon, seemed in the dark. Ted felt certain that if his daughter knew that he had been sleeping with a Black woman, she would have marched through the east-side streets calling him a hypocrite. And she would have certainly brought it up a couple of days ago when she'd become impatient with him at Aiken's.

Ted reached for the freshly baked oatmeal raisin cookies his housekeeper had given him before he left the house. He liked them with lots of cinnamon, no more than a few raisins per cookie. Just as he was about to bite into one, there was a knock at his office door. Probably his mother, he thought. But no, it couldn't be. His mother would have knocked then opened the door without waiting for an answer. At least once a week she dropped by the office on her way to or from some highly unnecessary errand. Any excuse to drive her brand-new, daffodil-yellow Ford Mustang. Ted couldn't understand why on earth an eighty-three-year-old needed that type of car, fresh off the assembly line. But they could afford it. She might as well have what she wanted, he thought. Cookie in hand, Ted opened the door.

"Hello," Ted said to the lady standing there. He had seen this tall, thin Black woman around a few times. If Ted was five nine, she was at least five eleven, and she wasn't even wearing any of those high-heeled shoes. He felt sure she wasn't a West Mills resident. A frequent visitor, he supposed.

"Mr. Ted Temple?" she said.

"That's me."

"I'm sorry to come without an appointment. I'm Josephine Wright." Her accent was similar to the one Marian had picked up from all her years in New York and New Jersey. Miss Wright didn't move to offer her hand. So, he did.

"It's no trouble. We ain't much the appointment-making types 'round here." He smiled, but she showed no interest in pleasantries. "Miss Wright, do you like oatmeal raisin? My housekeeper made them this morning. I—"

"No, thank you," she said sternly. "I'm here about Marian Harmon. She, Marva, and Laz were related to my fiancé. He was their brother."

"Olympus Seymore," Ted said, remembering that Marian had mentioned rumor of his engagement. Marian had heard of it from a patient's mother. And she found it laughable.

"What do you have against him?" Ted had asked Marian.

"His very existence reminds me of my mother's heartache."

"It's not his fault, though," Ted had offered.

"I know that, Theodore. Still."

A couple years ago, Marian had told Ted that she and Marva had grown up with Olympus's intended. Why Josephine Wright would want Olympus, Marian simply couldn't understand.

"Awful what happened to them," Ted said to Miss Wright. And though he knew the Harmons and Olympus had been estranged, he still said, "I hope he's doin' all right. I imagine it's hard. I lost my own brother years ago." He set the cookies back on his desk.

"They weren't close," Miss Wright said, with a hint of impatience. Ted could tell she wasn't one for beating around the bush. She wore a pair of denim jeans, a thick blue knitted sweater, and shiny black shoes. This reminded him of how Marian sometimes dressed under her white lab coat. Marian always looked elegant—even in a sweatsuit.

"You mentioned you're here about Dr. Harmon." He almost said *Marian.* "Does Olympus want to go in the clinic and get their personal effects?"

"I doubt that," Miss Wright said.

She said she had heard about the altercation he'd had with Marian at the shopping center a couple of weeks ago. He and Marian had been standing in between cars in the parking lot, having it out about her threat to expose him to Darby. Apparently, people saw them. But as far as he knew, no one had heard them. Otherwise, everyone in West Mills would know that he had said, "I'll be goddamned if I let you ruin me. You better tread lightly." And Sheriff Horton would have at least mentioned it when he called to tell Ted he'd lost a tenant and to ask him about the row with Marian.

Now this Wright woman was here, dredging up things that mattered not at all.

"Yes. Dr. Harmon and I had a disagreement. And I'm truly sorry our last words to each other had to be fraught."

"I'm told you were quite irritated, Mr. Temple. Finger-pointing and all."

"Let me put this to rest once and for all, Miss Wright." Ted wished he'd used a different euphemism. He went to his chair and sat before telling her the same lie he'd told Sheriff Horton. "See, she wanted me to do somethin' outside the terms of our lease agreement, and I refused. Simple as that. Things got a lil heated because she didn't wanna take no for an answer."

"I see." But Miss Wright's words were laced with leeriness. It made him nervous.

"I have that same argument with one tenant or another at least three, four times a year, ma'am." That at least was true. "It just comes with owning commercial property. We can't please everybody. So many structural things to consider when remodeling. Not to mention fire codes and so forth."

"Is that what Marian wanted? Remodeling?"

"Yes, ma'am," Ted said. Sheriff Horton believed his expla-nation. Ted's mother believed it. So should Miss Wright. "I can't even remember what exactly she was askin' for now. Somethin' to do with the waiting area."

Miss Wright appeared to be turning it all over in her head. So, to fill the silence, and to conceal any worry that might be showing, Ted began to tell Miss Wright about the numerous things his tenants had asked him to do over the years. One wanted a kitchen installed in their office. Another asked for a closet to be turned into a shower stall. He could tell she didn't care about any of it. But maybe if he doubled down on the lie, it would spread.

"We were under the impression it had been about something more serious," Miss Wright said. "Serious enough that you were questioned by Sheriff Horton the day after the Harmons' bodies were found. Not taken to the station, though, as my fiancé was."

"But I was questioned. Over an argument about remodeling. And I cooperated. Answered all the questions, just as Olympus did, I've heard."

"But are people accusing you of murdering them?" the woman shot back.

"Why *would* anyone accuse me? As I've said, we quarreled over renovations. Now, I'm sorry to hear Olympus is having a rough time in the community, but I—"

"Do you know if the man Marian was dating might be one of your tenants here in the shopping center?" Miss Wright asked, her head tilted to one side.

Holy shit! Does this woman know? Hold it together, Ted. Hold ya shit together.

"I really wouldn't know anything 'bout that, ma'am. I don't get into my tenants' personal lives. But I doubt it would be any one of the other tenants."

"And why is that?" Miss Wright inquired.

"Well," Ted said, wishing he'd said less, "like I said, I don't know for sure, but most of these merchants are women, and the men are all married." Miss Wright looked as though she wanted to say, *And?* "Who's to say the doctor was seeing anyone at all? With the clinic being so busy and so forth."

"Your daughter confirmed that Marian was seeing someone," Miss Wright said. "She was certain of it. Marva told her. But she wouldn't give me a name."

Jesus Christ. Ted unbuttoned his cardigan. It was as hot as blazes all of a sudden.

"As they say, you learn somethin' new every day." He sat on the corner of his desk to steady himself. He could feel his legs trembling beneath him. "You know Savannah well?"

"We've been in touch," Miss Wright said. "I hope she's not upset with me. I may have imposed on her. But since she was so close to Marva, I thought she'd know best."

"Know what best?"

"Who the Harmon sisters were dating," Miss Wright clarified.

"Oh." Savannah didn't know his secret, did she? Marian always swore she hadn't told her sister about him. But how could Ted know for sure? If Savannah knew about his hypocrisy, what was to stop her from telling anyone she wanted? Ted yearned so badly to know what Savannah had shared with Miss Wright. But probably best if he didn't pry. "Well, I hope she was helpful."

"She was. It seems there's a lot more going in this small town than I'd expected. Everyone's got a secret. Don't they, Mr. Temple?"

"I wouldn't know, to tell you the truth. I mind my business."

"Why were you on the Harmons' property yesterday?" Miss Wright asked.

The truth? The God's honest truth? Ted went there to say goodbye. He went there hoping to find an unlocked door so that he could go inside and smell the scent of the house. Maybe he'd wander around, locate her bedroom, and take a trinket: a bottle of perfume, a blouse from her chest of drawers, anything. Ted had been introduced to Marian in that house.

To Miss Wright, this lovesick wannabe detective—Ted couldn't blame her—he said, "I went to look at the property."

"Why?"

"To be perfectly honest with you, Miss Wright, I'm a businessman, as you can see. Real estate is my business."

"I see," she said.

"I don't mean any disrespect, ma'am. But aren't these questions best for the sheriff's department to be asking? Sounds like you're headin' an investigation of your own." He chuckled nervously. "With the drugs they found, and all, I imagine things'll be wrapping up soon."

Ted knew Marian took advantage of some of the patients' fears and their insurances. He'd heard from her that Marva had briefly been a wild one when she lived with Marian in New York, while Marian attended medical school. (He had decided not to ask for specifics.) And Ted knew that cigarettes weren't the only thing Lazarus rolled and smoked. But that tale about them being drug dealers was a steaming pile from a cow pasture. An atomic bomb could've gone off at the Harmons' and Horton wouldn't care.

Miss Wright went about telling Ted things he'd already heard: that the Harmons' case was being neglected (Ted hated this, too, but what was he going to do? Go to Horton and D.A. Boothe and interrogate them about three colored people's murders and risk outing himself?); that Olympus was catching hell from the folks on the west side; that Olympus hadn't received the same benefit of the doubt that others had from the sheriff's department. Miss Wright was pissed off to no end.

She explained that she'd lived in New York most of her life and that at least five or six times a year, people from her neighborhood were found murdered in their homes, or in alleys and the like. The police wrote whatever they wanted on those reports, she said. Suicides. Hit-and-runs. Overdoses from shooting up. You name it. Anything to get it over with. Anything to get a case closed and filed away. "They didn't care, Mr. Temple. Just another Black man, Black woman, Black boy, Black girl. And the killer walked around doing it over and over. Families suffering all the while."

"That's terrible," he said sincerely. "Small town like this, we don't get murders. Especially not three at once."

"But every once in a while, I also saw those families fight back, Mr. Temple," she continued, as though she hadn't heard his comment. "They'd do their *own* legwork and gather information the police hadn't even *tried* to find. Cases reopened, police chiefs proven lazy, racist. Or both. I've seen it done." Ted didn't know what to say. What he did know was that if Savannah knew about his affair with Marian, and if she had told Miss Wright, or was planning to, he would be finished. "I'm sorry to have intruded on your time," Miss Wright said.

"No problem, ma'am," Ted said. "No trouble at all."

But as he watched her walk back to the parking lot and get into her car, he knew she might be a lot of trouble.

Why were you on the Harmons' property yesterday? Miss Wright had inquired. To feel close to Marian Harmon, Ted would go there again.

SEVENTEEN

TED

In '65, not long before Jessie Earl Harmon passed away, Ted went—sent by Darby—to inquire about some land that Jessie Earl owned on the west side of the canal. Darby thought it would be perfect for a gated, forty- or fifty-home subdivision—for young white families only. He decided Ted would be a perfect intermediary—his gentle nature and all.

"This is my firstborn, Mr. Temple," Jessie Earl said. "Dr. Marian Harmon. I have another daughter. Marva's upstairs. She's a nurse. At least, I think she finished her schoolin'. But they don't tell me shit, so I don't rightly know."

"Pleased to meet you, Mr. Temple," Marian said. She wore a pantsuit—a dark shade of green. Her blouse was pink with a ruffled collar. Her shoulders were drawn back. He wondered if she'd been to finishing school.

She didn't seem to be wearing perfume, but Ted could smell the cocoa butter lotion. His housekeeper used it. In the winter, so did his mother.

"The pleasure's all mine," Ted replied. His own collar suddenly felt tight around his neck. Without thinking, he undid his top button, a nervous habit of his since boyhood. Marian was the most beautiful woman in all of North Carolina. Her beige skin appeared as smooth as porcelain. Her eyebrows were thinned. He imagined that was something women in the North did. Then, in an attempt to not make a fool of himself, Ted turned back to Jessie Earl and said, "Like I was saying, Jessie, I'm willing to pay a little over the value."

"Then why would he sell it?" Marian chimed in from behind her father.

"I beg your pardon?"

"If you're willing to pay more than what it's worth, it's probably best that he *not* sell just now. Right, Daddy?" Jessie Earl's eyes nearly lit up when he looked at Marian. Pure pride.

"Well, I just figured since he had no plans for it, and—"

"Maybe *I* have plans for it," Marian said. Ted felt a rush. This woman's nerve at once annoyed him and excited him. "In fact, I do. We won't be selling, Mr. Temple. But we thank you for your interest." Ted looked at Jessie Earl, waiting for him to say something. But the old man just stared off at nothing, smiling. Jessie Earl didn't seem to be his normal self. Ted knew the old man's health was failing, so this resigned posture, this demure tone he had assumed, made some sense. "Care to join me for a drink in the parlor?" Marian said. She called out to her sister to come and help Jessie Earl to his bedroom. He needed his rest, Marian told her.

A couple days later, Jessie Earl died. It was as if he had been waiting for Marian, Marva, and Laz to come home for a visit. As if he couldn't go without seeing them, having them in the house. It was the coroner's wife—she also ran the floral shop, and one of the motels—who broke the news to Ted at the post office.

"He was a nice colored man, wasn't he, Ted?"

"Yes, he was." Jessie Earl had been a nice person and had a head for business. It seemed to Ted that his elder daughter did, too.

He couldn't get Marian Harmon off his mind. He had to see her.

Less than a week after Jessie Earl's passing, Ted visited the Harmons—not for Darby. He was visiting for himself. They had not yet gone back north and were still receiving visits from grieving townspeople who had known and respected Jessie Earl.

"Nice of you to come again, Mr. Temple," Lazarus said, extending his hand. "My father thought highly of you."

"Well, thanks for sayin' that. He was a good person, your father." Ted took notice of Lazarus's firm handshake. Impressive. The mark of an honest man, Ted had always been taught. "Now, Lazarus, remind me. What is it you do in New Jersey? For work, I mean."

Lazarus took a quiet but deep breath, as if he were about to be baptized.

"I work for my sister," he said.

"I see. Doing what, may I ask?"

"Well, I guess you can say I'm her and Marva's bodyguard, and their driver, and the janitor." Ted chuckled, assuming it was a joke. But Lazarus didn't laugh. "I do other things, too, though. Important things, like reading those medical journals for Marian. Help to keep her up to date on—"

From behind Ted, a voice said, "Laz, will you go and see if Mr. and Mrs. Dunston want more water?" It was Marian. And though she had asked, it sounded more like an order.

Marva was standing next to her. Both were dressed in black, as if the funeral had been that day. Ted thought that was mighty old-fashioned of them. He hadn't seen a family continue to wear black after the funeral since he was a boy.

"Okay. I will in just a minute," Lazarus replied. "I'll just finish my conversation with—"

"Mr. Temple, I'm going to sit out on the porch for a bit," Marian cut in. "Join me?"

Marva, with whom Ted had never spoken, stepped forward and said, "And Laz and I will check on the Dunstons."

Outside on the porch, Ted smoked a cigarette. Marian stood with him.

"Hope I wasn't out of line, askin' your brother about his work," Ted said.

"No. He just tends to exaggerate his role. He's our driver and he cleans. That's all. My father always called Laz the runt. Incapable of asserting himself. The world would eat him alive if I didn't watch out for him. Helpless soul."

"I see." Lazarus didn't seem helpless. But what did Ted know? "Maybe he just needs a wife, a kid."

Marian scoffed, "He doesn't want that, sadly. Where's *your* family, Mr. Temple? Are your parents still alive?"

"My mother is," he said. "My father passed long ago."

"How?" she asked. He thought it an odd question, and his face must have given that away. "I'm a doctor. Remember?"

"I guess you can say he killed himself. He was a heavy drinker."

"In a way, I think mine did, too. Not from alcohol. But from stress. Guilt and worry."

"Oh. I've heard worryin' too much can take a toll on your heart. That's what my doctor tells me, at least. But you really believe a person can die from feeling guilty?"

"I do. Daddy wasn't perfect," Marian said. "Not that he should have been expected to be. After all, we are human. Aren't we, Ted?"

"That's true, Marian," he said, delighted they were now on a first-name basis. And he liked that she had taken the lead on that.

"His problem was that he regretted too much," Marian said. "Laz is the same—not that my brother has much to regret. And Marva loves to fantasize. But she won't act unless she's told. Me, I regret nothing. Life's too short for it."

"Why are you tellin' me this?" Ted hadn't intended to say that out loud. There was something exhilarating, thrilling, in her brown-with-a-drop-of-gray eyes. He had seen it a week earlier, when the two of them sat in Jessie Earl's parlor, each having a splash of brandy in short, thick, square-shaped glasses. Ted wondered if Marian knew that he was utterly taken by her. Her power, her assuredness. He was spellbound. And if he was right, Marian was, too.

"That's a good question, Ted. Grief, I suppose. I don't know."

"I was hopin' it was because you think I'm a nice guy or something."

"I don't know whether you're nice or not."

Later that night, Ted and Marian met at a hotel in Chesapeake. She chose the place and the time. And a couple days before she, Marva, and Lazarus were to return to New Jersey, Ted went to pay a late-morning visit. Their house being so far off from town provided the necessary discretion. He didn't go inside. Marian came out to his truck.

"Thought I'd invite you to ride to Norfolk with me," Ted said.

"Have you ever heard the word 'rendezvous,' Ted? We've had ours already."

"That's not what I'm after today. I've got errands. Wondered if we could use the travel time to discuss business, or whatever you'd like to talk about. I imagine you could use some fresh air. Change of scenery."

"I'm not selling any land to you, Mr. Temple," Marian said. "At least, not anytime soon."

"Don't start with that *Mr. Temple* stuff again."

She smiled, reached into the window, and tugged gently on his left earlobe. "We don't have any business to discuss, Ted."

"Fine," Ted said. To hell with Darby. "We'll talk about other things."

He drove to a park on a hill near the airport, and they looked out over the Norfolk skyline. They talked a little about their pasts.

"I forgot to ask if you have children," Marian asked.

"One. A daughter. But she's grown and moved away. Started a life of her own."

"Sounds like there's a story behind it," Marian said. But he got the impression she wasn't terribly interested in hearing it.

"I s'pose so, but I've made peace with it. She's alive and well. That's all that matters to me. I've got my own life to live. I'm not an old man yet." He motioned for her to slide closer to him, and for nearly an hour they kissed like teenagers.

EIGHTEEN

TED

One week before the Harmons were killed, Ted decided it was time that he tell Marian that he was selling the shopping center. He took her to their favorite hotel in Norfolk, the Holiday Inn on Military Highway. He bought champagne, grapes, crackers, and fancy cheeses whose names he didn't know how to pronounce.

She would be thrilled for him, he had assumed. Marian was an astute, if not crude, businesswoman. It was one of the many things about her that excited him. He was certain she would love the idea of him selling his homestead and setting his mother up in a small house of her own. Marian would approve of him moving to a smaller, easier-to-manage property in Nags Head or Virginia Beach—a home with a view of the sea. She loved beach houses, and Ted envisioned her coming to his every single weekend. It would be her house just as much as it would be his.

Since Marian supported her younger siblings, Ted knew she would understand his decision to give Savannah some money to put her sons through college. He might even help his daughter move away again—to some bigger city where she, Terrance, and Troy might fit in better, feel more accepted. Marian, being as practical as she was, would applaud him for that. Of this he was certain.

That night at the Holiday Inn, Ted and Marian had champagne, made love, ate the grapes, and made love again. The evening was going without a hitch. They lay on the bed, side by side, thighs touching. Even after the champagne, he could still taste the mint of Wrigley's in her mouth when they kissed.

"How'd that career talk thing you had today go?" Ted asked. He always wanted Marian to know that he listened to her, and she seemed to appreciate it.

"It didn't go quite as planned, but oh well," she said. "Tell me something good, handsome." She reached over and stroked his beard with a finger.

Ted told Marian his big news.

"You slimy son of a bitch," Marian said.

"What?" He was stunned. "Didn't think you'd respond this way at all." She was now sitting on the opposite bed. Ted wanted to touch her hand, make sure she understood the change was all for the best. But she stood up and stepped out of his reach. She put on her panties, her bra, then her slip.

"Oh, you didn't? You're selling the place where I earn a living right out from under me! And to Jeff *Darby*? He's a Klansman, Theodore!"

"That's crazy talk, Marian. It's 1976. There's no *Klan* anymore."

She sucked her teeth and released a sigh that bordered on a roar.

"You really believe that, don't you? My God!"

He knew well that it still existed, and that it always would.

"Marian, won't you just listen to me? Please."

"And for a million and a half? You're more of a fool than I thought!" She sat on the edge of the bed and told him that Darby's shopping mall would probably make ten times that amount in less than a decade, what with everyone who'd stop driving to Virginia to shop, and with people from all the neighboring cities coming. "You've been robbed, idiot!"

"Hey, you keep your voice down. People might complain," Ted said, standing.

"Shut up. There's no one else at this dump! And get away from me! Go stand over there." She pointed to the other bed in the room.

"Dump?" Ted stepped away. "You always said you liked it."

"Don't talk, Theodore. Just be quiet." Marian always called him by his given name when they were having an argument. Though they had met in '65, it was '71 when they began seeing each other seriously. In all those years, there had only been a few times that she'd called him Theodore. "I can barely stand to be in the same building with you right now."

"Marian, come on now. I don't see what's got you so ticked off." Marian rolled her eyes. The two of them sat silently for a minute. And when he tried to speak, to ask her to hear him out, she shushed him.

Marian asked when Darby was planning to clear the lot. Ted didn't know for sure. But he did know that Darby wanted the shopping center emptied out by July.

"I'm not moving Friendly Pediatrics by July," Marian said. "I have a lease, and it—"

"It's got a clause for situations like these," Ted said apologetically. He didn't enjoy bringing this to her attention. But there was no point in not mentioning it. "It's in all of my contracts, Marian. Just in case I had to sell someday."

Marian poured herself a glass of the champagne and gulped it down.

"You *do* know this spur-of-the-moment sale of yours will screw me, don't you?" She was hurt. He could see it in how she stared at him—stared through him. The sight ripped him to shreds.

"Listen, Marian." He told her about the plans he had: the beach house, and all that. "This is a *good* change, babe. It won't screw anyone—'specially not you." But he knew that wasn't entirely true. There weren't enough empty commercial spaces in town to accommodate them all. And Ted doubted many of their businesses would be suitable for the shopping mall Darby was going to build. Ted felt for them, he really did. And he had already decided that he would try, as best he could, to help most of them find new homes for their businesses. "You'll have a new spot in no time. A much better one. Maybe even on the *east* side."

"Because that's the pinnacle, isn't it, Theodore?" she retorted. "The *east* side."

"No. But that's what you used to want, when you first moved back." She grimaced. Something about reminding her of her former want seemed to embarrass her.

"I thought I did," she said.

Ted said that she could still have that, if that was what she wanted. He told her that he would do all he could. He knew a couple of potential spaces.

Marian shook her head. "I don't need your help with anything. Don't you know what I've accomplished over the past thirty years? I did it on my own. Me. Never think I *need* you for anything."

"Marian."

"Fuck you." She rarely swore.

"Now, Jesus Christ, Marian. Come on. You know I don't like when you get all *soap opera* on me."

"Fuck. You."

"Who *are* you?"

"How long have you known, Ted?"

"That's neither here nor there."

"Answer. My. Question."

"Will you stop this?"

She rose from her seat and started to get dressed.

"Just leave," she said. "I don't even want an answer anymore."

"You know what, goddamnit?" Ted said. "I'll be more than happy to leave." He had grown impatient, decided she was being a brat. "This is unbecoming behavior for someone of your stature, *Doctor*. And to be honest with ya, I am disappointed."

"Ha!" Marian scoffed.

"I take that back. I'm *embarrassed* for you."

"Excuse me?"

"I think—no, I *know* you're overreacting about this thing. I tried to talk it out with ya. Adult to adult. Businessman to businesswoman. Lover to lover. But no! I'm done, gal."

"Oh," Marian said. "Now I'm a *gal*. I was wondering when you'd reveal yourself."

"I didn't mean it that way and you know it!"

"Oh, I think you did. You're a bigot. Just like all the Temples before you. Adam Temple spoke to field mice better than he did the colored men who worked in his horse stables. And we won't even talk about that mother of yours."

"Now you wait just a goddamn minute!" Ted said. He had been lacing up his shoes but stopped. He rose to his feet.

"Pickaninnies," Marian said between clenched teeth. "She called us pickaninnies. We were just children, minding our business up-bridge, and she harassed us."

"That was over fifty years ago, Marian." Yes, in her younger days, his mother had a reputation for saying an unkind word or two to the help. But she had changed. He hadn't seen or heard her mistreat a colored person in decades. He would be lying if he said his mother was no longer prejudiced, but he wouldn't hear anyone speak poorly of her. Not to his face. "You've got to get past that. Leave her out of this. And you can call me a bigot all you want to. I know different. I've been *good* to you and your people. And you *know* I have. I—"

"Me and my people, huh?"

"Stop tryin' to twist my words! I'm not like that!"

"Tell that to your daughter and your grandsons! Tell *them* you're not a racist. I wonder if they'd agree. Maybe *I'll* tell them. Maybe I'll tell *everyone* that you don't have a single prejudiced bone in your body. We have to make sure Jeff Darby knows, don't we? You're a good man. Can't be a bigot with a colored doctor for his girlfriend. Isn't that what you all call us? Coloreds? Or do you call us nig—"

"Stop it, Marian! Stop it right now!"

"I think it's only right that people know you're not a racist, Theodore. And who better to tell them?"

"Now, Marian, you had better watch yourself. I don't take kindly to threats."

"Neither do I," Marian said. She stepped closer to him and poked him in the chest with her unpainted fingernail. "There's no way Darby will do business with you if he knows about us. He's not just any ol' Klansman, Theodore. He's their goddamn *leader* in this region. If I know it, how can you not?"

A chuckle. "Do you know his number right off the top of your head?"

"You wouldn't."

"I most certainly would," Marian said.

"Marian Harmon," Ted said, as if he were her parent, "now, there's a whole lot riding on this deal and I won't let you fuck it up. I—I'd sooner—"

"You'd sooner what, Theodore?"

Ted and Marian stood there before each other—together, yet, to Ted, they felt so far apart. Behind her sat the nearly empty champagne bottle. Marian was right about Jeff Darby; Ted knew what Jeff would probably do in such a situation.

"You, Mr. Temple, may leave now," Marian said. "I'll take care of the bill. Just get out."

"Things don't have to get ugly, Marian. We—"

"Stop talking. Just go. Now," she said.

Ted put on his coat—his mother had bought him the black wool peacoat for Christmas of '74—and grabbed his matching hat from the dresser.

"Good evening, Dr. Harmon," he said. Then he left.

TED SAT AT his desk, in his office, thinking about how much he missed Marian Harmon—the first woman with whom he'd been willing to share everything. His late wife, Ruthanne, as kind, loving, and beautiful as she was, had lacked Marian's fiery passion, her wit, her willingness to fight for and take whatever she wanted. Ted wanted the Harmons' killer to pay for robbing him of her. But Marian was gone. All the vengeance in the world couldn't reverse that. And there was so much else at stake now. His future. His reputation. His mother's reputation.

Somehow he would need to find out what Savannah knew. It wouldn't be easy. Would he have to confess his hypocrisy to the daughter he barely knew anymore? She might use it against him. Their recent talk had proven she had no interest in reconciling.

Having nothing else to do at the office except stare out the window at Friendly Pediatrics, Ted decided to go home. His mother would be there. And though he would not be able to confide in her his sorrows or his worries, he just wanted to feel safe. With his mother, he always felt safe.

NINETEEN

TED

At home, Ted sat on the large, screened-in, wraparound porch of his colonial mansion, having a half cup of black coffee. A perfect sixty-five degrees. Chilly, but not cold—just the way Ted liked his early-spring afternoons.

Wearing her burgundy velour athletic getup, and having a cup of hot water with a slice of lemon, Ted's mother sat across the small table from him, flipping through the January issue of *Better Homes and Gardens*. She was a couple of months behind in her reading, she had said when they'd sat down. Ted nearly asked how that was possible. She had absolutely nothing to do. Yes, she volunteered at the hospital's Visitors' Services desk, looking up patients' room numbers and pointing people to the elevators. And to get them over with, she did her two days consecutively. Aside from visiting her twin brother once a week at the nursing home and spending time with her girlfriends—they were all between the ages of seventy-eight and eighty-five—his mother was as free as a butterfly.

Looking out into the large, pine-lined yard, Ted thought how sad it was that Marian had never been able to sit with him on his own porch and enjoy a warm drink. He'd had her at the house a few times, when his mother had gone on one of her weekend group shopping or gambling trips. He had asked the few household workers to go home and not return to the property until Monday morning. Marian had slept with him in his bed. Those nights had been wonderful. It had been too cold for them to sit outside.

"Theodore Temple," his mother said. "If you rock that chair any faster, I am sure you'll go flyin' through the screen and into those bushes. Maybe that oughta be your last cup of coffee."

Ted hadn't realized what he was doing. *Maybe so.*

"Did you have your oats this morning, and did you take your medications?"

"Yes, Mama," Ted said with a sigh, and he waited for her to remind him that he hadn't joined her for one of her daily mile-long walks in months.

After a minute, she asked, "Still on edge about the doctor and her family? I believe we're safe over here. Those killers would've come to this side of the canal by now if they wanted to."

"On edge?" Ted said. "I don't believe I'm on edge, Mama."

"If you say so." Pinky raised, she took a sip of her hot water. "You're not feelin' guilty about not goin' to their service, are ya? Like I said, from what I heard from Sybil, the Harmons didn't even want a service in the first place." Sybil, the Temples' housekeeper, had attended the unwanted memorial.

"I've got no reason to feel guilty," Ted said.

"Good." She turned a page of her magazine and looked it over.

"I can't go to every tenant's wedding, funeral, anniversary party, and the like, Mama. Crosses the line."

"That's *precisely* what I told Sybil."

"I don't imagine I was welcome, anyway. With the little altercation we had in the parking lot, and all."

"Like I told you last week, I wouldn't worry about that one bit. Anybody with good sense knows landlords and tenants sometimes have disagreements. You remember when Jake Bardlo wanted you to replace the toilet in his store 'cause it wasn't the right shade of white he liked?"

"I do. He was crazy."

"Just as crazy as they come, son. Anyway, you've got absolutely nothin' to feel guilty about. I still intend to give that Horton fella a piece of my mind when I see him. How *dare* he even think of callin' here and asking you those questions. Like you're some kind of criminal. The nerve to involve people like us. And askin' about *my* whereabouts. The audacity."

"I know, Mama."

"My poor brother was in such a state that night," she said. "Did I tell you 'bout it, Ted? His mind went back to when we were children and he just begged me to stay and protect him from the ghosts. Lord Jesus."

"You told me, Mama."

"Those nurses up at the home don't know how to handle him when he gets like that. I couldn't leave him. Good thing they have those cots for family. Anyway, Horton oughta be ashamed. What was he thinking, son? Neither of us has ever needed an alibi a day in our *lives*. Why in hell would we want to start needin' one now? That was high-grade foolishness."

"Yeah," Ted said. "But he was just doin' his job, Mama. He didn't mean any harm by it."

"Well, I don't like it." Then she giggled. "Good thing Elena threw Newman out that night. You wouldn't have an alibi to speak of."

Newman, Ted's godson—the son of one of Ted's cousins—was thrown out by his wife at least twice a year for coming home smelling of perfume she didn't wear, or for having tucked away motel receipts at the bottom of a full wastepaper basket. And each time, Newman spent a few nights with the Temples while he and Elena sorted things out. His own parents wouldn't have him. They raised him better, they'd said.

Newman had been staying with the Temples for just under a week. And on the night the Harmons died, he had showered, eaten almost everything Sybil had cooked, cried his guilt out to Ted (again), helped himself to Ted's bar, and passed out on the couch. Ted had been so glad when the fellow went to sleep. His own mind was full of worry over Marian's threat. He had been unable to gauge how serious she had been about her intentions to expose him. When they argued in the parking lot, he got the impression that he was more worked up than she was. She might have been messing with him that night at the hotel.

In any case, after Newman had fallen asleep, Ted considered going to Marian's to try, just one more time, to reason with her. If that didn't work, he'd have to call on some people he knew—a group of men who would understand his predicament, men who would run her, her sister, and her brother out of town for good. And if she were lucky, they might even buy her property at fair market value. But not one penny over.

"And imagine you," his mother said after a couple of minutes flipping through her magazine, "shooting three people. Did you tell them you don't even know *how* to shoot?"

"Now, now, Mama," Ted said. "I ain't in the mood for teasin'."

"*I ain't in the mood for teasin', Mama*," she mocked. "Anyway, I hear Horton's closing the case soon. They know who did it."

This confused Ted, given his conversation with Miss Wright. "Yeah? Who?"

"Well, they don't know *who*, who. Only that it was over drugs. Probably folk from up north come to collect or something. Who knows what they got into all those years they were up there." Surely, a long rant about Savannah was on its way. Whenever the North was mentioned, Savannah's name was soon to follow.

"Oh, right," Ted said. "I heard about that." His mother was pondering something. He could tell by the way she'd tilted her head while gazing out at the gazebo in the distance.

"Curious thing, isn't it?" she asked.

"What is?"

"Three people that long in the tooth, with all that schoolin', involved in drugs. Shameful." Viv Conyers, an officer's mother, had told Ted's mother what had been found in the Harmons' home: pills in unmarked bottles and marijuana. His mother called them *dope plants*. "Viv said they had them in the bedroom windowsills just like they were any ol' houseplant. Now doesn't *that* beat all? I didn't even think the stuff grew in America. Did you know that, Theodore?" She didn't give him a chance to reply—not that he intended to. "Viv said they were *big*-time sellers. Viv thinks it was probably just the brother who was dealin' and that the sisters were just in the wrong place at the wrong time when the killer came. I bet all three of 'em were selling. Like a family business." Ted knew the people of West Mills could tell a good made-up story. But Jesus Christ. He wondered how long it would be before he was hearing that the Harmons were involved in Watergate. Viv Conyers's theory did have merit, though. "Ted, do you think Savannah—"

"No, Mama. Come on now."

"Don't act like it's not possible. Only God knows what she's mixed up in over on that side of the canal."

Ted sighed. "I don't think Savannah's mixed up in any drugs. She's got kids."

"What's that got to do with anything?"

"And I don't know about all the drug lord stuff."

"Why not? I mean—" She seemed to be deciding whether or not to say what was just on the tip of her tongue— something she might have said, without hesitation, ten years ago.

"Yes?"

"Never mind." She turned another page. "You just never know."

"Know what, Mama?"

"What people are up to. Are you sure, and I mean absolutely, positively certain, that you never saw anything strange about those Harmons? You saw them five days a week, just about."

The Harmons were definitely unique. Ted had always found it interesting that Marian, Marva, and Lazarus all lived together. Yes, Ted and his mother shared his homestead. But to Ted's mind, that was only because he had been widowed and moved back for help raising his newborn. Then Chip's death made him the estate's owner. Not the same as the Harmons in the least, he believed.

And Ted had always been perplexed by the fact that Marva and Lazarus deferred to Marian. Only a handful of times had he been in a room with all three of them at once: the day Jessie Earl Harmon had introduced them to Ted in '65; the day he visited their home shortly after their father's burial; the day he had shown them the office space Marian ended up renting for Friendly Pediatrics; the day they'd opened the clinic to patients. Ted had noticed that Marva and Lazarus replied to Marian with haste. It was as though even the simplest of questions had to be answered within a split second.

But now, wanting to protect the image of the woman he loved, Ted said, "Nothin' I can think of. Seemed like normal people to me. But you're right, Mama. You never know."

She shrugged, pushed her glasses up, and continued flipping through her magazine. She wasn't going to let it go.

"I *will* say, they didn't look like they were strung out on anything."

Marian was a picture of health for a sixty-year-old. She rarely ate sweets, and it was even rarer that she drank. Her insatiable appetite for money, however, was a different thing altogether. And she made no secret of it. Jessie Earl had taught her that, she'd once told Ted. Money is freedom, she'd said to him on multiple occasions. Ted understood. His father and his brother had believed the same thing. Eventually, he adopted that motto. But he also knew money could just as easily bring headache—maybe even heartache.

"Well, either way, it's all terrible, son."

"Yeah," Ted agreed.

"And where that empty space is concerned, I'm—"

"Empty space?" Did she know he'd been seeing Marian, that he'd fallen in love? It was said that mothers always know.

"Friendly Pediatrics, Ted," she said. "I'm glad you won't have to worry about filling the unit." She sounded too cheerful for such a discussion. "Jeff Darby's 'bout to make you a very rich man."

"Shhhh!" He nearly leapt from the rocking chair. "Mama! Sybil's in there."

"No, she's not. You think I'd talk our business out loud like that? I'm no fool. Why it's still so hush-hush is beyond me. Darby *is* still buying, isn't he?"

"Are you sure no one's inside?"

"Not a soul," she affirmed.

"He's still buying," Ted said. "He just wants to keep it quiet for now. There's a buyer's remorse period. He could change his mind."

"He won't have any remorse when there's a mall full of people spendin' their money. He's too greedy. I won't be shopping there."

"Yes, you will."

"You're right, I probably will," she said before laughing. "Do you think he'll have a burger-and-shakes shop in there? I'd go just for that. God knows I don't need any more clothes."

Ted thought about Marian's critique of the sale.

"You think I undersold?" he asked his mother. She said she believed the seller in cases like these always undersells, but he shouldn't worry about that. He'd have money enough to see him through the rest of his days.

"I'm impressed, Ted," she said. "You held out." She reminded him that business didn't come to him as naturally as it had his father and brother. Yet, he'd done well. "You ain't done too bad a job taking care of me, neither, son. Chip would've thrown me in the nursing home with my brother by now." She laughed and took a sip of her hot water.

"Yeah." Ted smiled at his mother. "Chip probably would've." But Ted could never. He remembered when he was a young child, about seven or eight years old, she'd set up little picnics out there in the yard for just the two of them. Sandwiches, cookies, and lemonade so cold he'd catch a brain freeze.

"You're my hero, son," she said.

"I appreciate that, Mama," he said. "I really do."

"Good," she said. "Now, I'm going to have myself a lil nod-off." Then she closed her eyes and leaned her head back.

You're my hero, son, his mother had said. But after all she'd done for him over the years, Ted thought it was the other way around.

TED WAS ALWAYS looking for a hero. From boyhood, Ted hung on his brother's every word, which meant he was also admiring their father. Adam Jr. was nicknamed Chip because their father, Adam Temple Sr., had told everyone, proudly, that Adam Jr. looked just like him—a chip off the old block.

Ted was born in 1913, three years after Chip. And despite Ted's efforts, the brothers never seemed to have much in common. As they grew older, Chip seemed perpetually annoyed by Ted's presence. For what reason, Ted never understood. No one did. Ted often wondered if his own gentle nature was an affront to Chip's rough, brutish personality. Whatever the reason, Ted felt abandoned, shunned by the men in his home. Even now, whenever Ted attended a town hall meeting and saw the umpteenth generation of Pennington brothers, or the umpteenth generation of Edgars brothers, he mourned his relationship with Chip—or the relationship he wished they'd had.

When Ted was eleven, maybe twelve, his father went from being an attentive, baseball-throwing dad to a womanizing alcoholic. Having made a medium-sized fortune from purchasing land rich with oil in Virginia, his investments in a few welding companies up and down the East Coast, and what his father had made off the backs of sharecroppers, Adam Sr. spent most of his days sitting in his study, poring over his ledgers—a spiked coffee in hand. His nights were spent out, mostly. With whom Adam shared his time, Ted never knew, precisely. His father came home in the early morning hours, just before he had to get up for school. And based on the arguments he heard his parents having at least once a week from the other end of the long hallway, Ted knew his mother was growing tired of turning a blind eye.

"I'm the man of this house, goddamnit!" his father yelled one morning. "And I give you everything you could ever want. Hell, you're damn near rich!" His father was nine years older than his mother, who was only sixteen when they married in 1909. Whether they had ever truly loved each other was anyone's guess. They were distant cousins—the triple great-grandchildren of a pair of sisters, if Ted remembered it correctly. One of the sisters had married and moved to North Carolina. The other had married and stayed in their home state of Missouri, which was where Ted's mother had been born and raised. In any case, as far back as Ted could remember, Adam seemed to have very little regard for his wife. "I can do whatever I want. And if you ask me again, I'll show you how much I hate being questioned like you're doin'."

"That sounds like a threat to me, Adam Temple," his mother shot back. "You remember what happened the last time you hit me, don't ya?" She had been her parents' only girl. She'd told Ted many times how, to her mother's dismay, her brothers had taught her how to fight, how to fish, how to do all sorts of things most girls couldn't. She had once given Adam a broken nose. And it was clear to Ted that he didn't want a repeat of that. So, when Ted peeped out into the hall, he was not surprised to see his father sliding his hands into his pockets and heading for one of the spare bedrooms.

Everyone on the east side of the canal knew about and talked about Adam Sr.'s behavior. The east-side ladies were always inviting Ted's mother to visit them, or to meet them at some shop to knit, to have tea, or to look at fabrics. Ted imagined it was their way of offering her a respite from her troubles at home. She thought so, too, she later told him. But when she realized that some of the ladies were using her as a source of entertainment, she withdrew from them and found company with people who showed true compassion, those who only wanted to know that she was all right.

"My life ain't nobody's weekly serial," she said to Ted one Sunday when he asked why she and one of the so-called friends hadn't greeted each other at the county fair.

His mother became more independent. With money she had inherited from an older brother's passing, she bought herself an automobile. Adam Sr. didn't seem to mind. It gave him an excuse to fire the driver, with whom Ted and Chip had become friendly.

Some days she picked Ted up from school, where she paid money for her boys to receive extra tutoring. It was important to her that they receive the best education possible, since she hadn't.

"I'm missing Jefferson," she said to Ted and Chip of her hometown in Missouri one day after telling them a story about one of her teachers. Ted was fourteen at the time. Chip was in his last year of high school. He had plans to attend

UNC Chapel Hill. "I wish I could go there and visit a lil more often," she added.

"What's stoppin' you?" Ted asked.

"I wouldn't go off and leave you here with Chip and your daddy for more than twenty-four hours. Never. You'd starve."

"If I've gotta watch over him, take him with ya," Chip said before announcing that he was going to play ball with friends. Then he left.

"I'm not a baby, Mama," Ted said to his mother. "I can fend for myself for a week."

She began to go on more weeklong trips to Jefferson, but Ted was often forced to join her. Sometimes he enjoyed them, but mostly he would have preferred to stay in West Mills. When Chip was gone to college and Ted was a junior in high school, his mother's jaunts to Jefferson became even more frequent. Ted knew the getaways were a perfect excuse for her to have time away from Adam, and he wasn't required to go along anymore. It had seemed to him that she felt he was safer without Chip around. Ted knew his mother loved them both. But he'd be lying if he pretended not to know he was her favorite.

In May of 1931, one month before Ted was to graduate from high school, Adam Sr. died. The stable hand, Tudor, found the body. By the way Adam was lying (on his side in fetal position), Tudor had thought he was asleep. But after an hour passed and Adam Sr. hadn't moved an inch, and there was no snoring, Tudor stepped close enough to see the bloody foam coming from Adam's mouth and nose, flask at his side. He was icebox-cold to the touch.

There was no autopsy. But on the certificate, the coroner wrote *myocardial infarction*. It had killed Adam's father, Laurent, and Adam's grandfather Louis. Even now, Ted wondered if it would have eventually taken Chip's life if the car accident hadn't. He also wondered if heart disease would someday call his own number.

"Somethin' told me to head back home," his mother kept saying the next morning between crying spells. She had returned from Jefferson City with her twin brother, Jimmy. "Just had a feelin' something wasn't right here." Later that day, when the last pie-bearing visitor was gone, she said, "He wasn't that great a husband. But he was good to you and Chip. I'll give him that."

"He'll be missed," Jimmy chimed in. Ted's uncle had been getting into a lot of trouble in Missouri: petty theft, initiating bar brawls, and the like. Ted's mother thought it was a perfect time for him to leave their hometown and start life anew.

Chip headed back to Chapel Hill the day after the service. He couldn't stand being in the house without his father, he'd said.

A week later, the reading of the will revealed that Adam had written his wife out of everything. Everything belonged to Chip. If Chip were to pass on without children, all would go to Ted. But his mother hadn't seemed surprised. And when Ted asked her if she'd already known, she confessed that Adam had long ago given her a large sum of money and acres of land to do with as she wished.

"I saved the money," she said. "I'll probably end up givin' it to my grandchildren someday—when you and Chip give me some."

Ted went to school in Chapel Hill as well. But by then Chip had dropped out. While Ted studied English education, Chip lived the life of a young, carefree, well-off bachelor. He traveled the country and sometimes went abroad. His mother was once again queen of the homestead. Her brothers and cousins—most of whom had despised Adam—visited more. And she made friends with different women there on the east side.

Having fallen in love with Chapel Hill, Ted stayed after getting his degree. He believed he could live there forever. In '41, while working as a high school English teacher, he met Ruthanne Savannah Hobbs, who lived in a quiet corner of Raleigh. She was an only child, raised in a house with only two rooms. Both of her parents were dead by the time she was seventeen.

Ruthanne had the bluest eyes he'd ever seen. And her hair was such a light shade of blonde, it nearly looked white. Ruthanne had to be the smartest lady in Chatham County, maybe even all of North Carolina, Ted often mused. Far more knowledgeable of the world than he, Chip, or his father had ever been. And she had the most infectious laugh. A devastating smile.

The two were inseparable. They got on wonderfully. But though Ted held great affection for Ruthanne, he never quite fell in love with her. Still, he loved her enough, he always told himself. He loved her enough.

"Your mother will think I've tried to trap you," Ruthanne said to him when, in late '42, they married at the courthouse in downtown Durham. Ted asked a classmate to serve as a witness.

"No, she won't," Ted told Ruthanne, but he knew she was right. "She'll be so glad to have a grandchild coming, she won't care 'bout us gettin' married this way."

Savannah was born in the summer of '43. One hour after her birth, Ted and Ruthanne looked at her and agreed that they would have at least one more. How could they not?

Savannah had, in just an hour's time, brought them so much joy.

But something went terribly wrong that night. And the following morning, the doctors and nurses swore they'd tried everything. But despite their efforts, Ruthanne died. A couple of days after the burial, Ted's mother and Chip brought the baby back to West Mills. Ted would tie up loose ends in Chapel Hill and be home in a couple of weeks. He didn't know what he would have done had it not been for his mother. Chip, surprisingly, was also an adoring uncle. The baby had more love than any child could ever need, Ted believed.

"You'll rotten her, Mama," Ted said one day when she was rocking Savannah after she was long asleep.

"As a grandmother, that's my God-given right," she replied.

Ted found work teaching in nearby Pasquotank County, and he enjoyed it. Returning to West Mills had been the right thing to do, for him and his daughter. Who will have your back the way your mother does? he often said.

Savannah grew like a weed. To Ted, it seemed as if she'd learned to crawl, walk, and run all in the same week. She was a good child, never giving them any real trouble to speak of. Always did exceptionally well with her studies, and she even gave other children a helping hand.

"She's just like Ruthanne," Ted had said to his mother one day as she dressed the baby for a town picnic.

"And like me," she replied.

"She's a lot like you, too, Mama."

As Savannah approached her teen years, she had an abundance of friends. She was invited to visit the homes of other east-side families. Some of them invited her along on summer trips. And there were boys, east-side boys Ted heard her speaking to her grandmother about constantly. So, it was a great shock to Ted when Savannah came to him, privately, in '61, and said, "Daddy, I have something to tell you. You can't tell Nana." He was sitting in the gazebo enjoying the early-October breeze. His mother was somewhere in the house— sitting near a window reading, no doubt. Savannah had one of her grandmother's shawls draped around her shoulders.

Savannah had met a young man from the west side of the canal, and she was in love.

Ted rested his forehead in the palm of his hand, and he took slow and steady breaths. His heart was trying to escape his body and sweat poured. This happened when he was upset. Sometimes it happened for no reason at all. Manage your stress, the doctor had told him.

"Savannah, don't do this. For the love of God, please don't. You can have any fella in the whole state of North Carolina." He wanted to scream, but his mother might hear and come running out. "Any *white* fella, baby girl. This will cause a lot of pain and trouble."

"All that might be true, but I love Fitz," she said, resolutely. "He's a good man and he loves me just as much as I love him, Daddy. More, even."

"How do you know that, Savannah?" Ted said. "Because he said so? Look behind you at this house. Look around. You have—"

"Daddy, stop it. Stop right there." She looked around to make sure they were still alone in the yard. "Fitz doesn't care about your money. He loves me for *me*. Just plain ol' me, Daddy." Fitz wanted to be a lawyer, she said. They would go north together where he might have a better chance of getting into a good college, then law school. She would go to college, too, she promised.

"I still want to be a doctor, Daddy," she said. "None of that's changed."

"Poor child," Ted said. As far as he was concerned, everything had already changed. "You're expecting, aren't you?"

"I knew you'd think that," she said. She was beginning to cry. "I knew that'd be the first thing you'd assume."

"Are ya?"

"No!"

"Then put an end to it. Now. Your life will be ruined. *Our* lives. Ruined. No matter whether that boy goes to law school, medical school, or if he scrubs floors. Ruin for us either way."

"If you think you'll be ruined because I love someone with different-colored skin than mine, I've got news for ya, Daddy. You're *already* ruined."

"I need to be alone, Savannah," he said, on the verge of tears. "Please leave me alone."

Savannah stormed off to the house. And the next day, Ted didn't get so much as a glimpse of her, though he knew she was home. If avoidance was an art form, Savannah had mastered it. Ted was not a religious man, but he prayed Savannah would think things through, remember the world they lived in, think of her future, think of her beau's future. But Ted decided that if Savannah didn't come to a decision he could live with, he might have to call in a favor.

Two days passed. Then Ted heard Savannah talking with his mother in the kitchen.

"Anytime a fellow that young follows an old girl like me around in the grocery store," his mother said, "just to ask if her granddaughter's seeing anyone, he's smitten. I think you oughta have dinner with him."

"Carl Dowd, Nana? You don't even like the Dowds."

"They're all right. Think about it. He's a handsome, smart fellow."

Savannah didn't say no. Ted felt a great sense of relief. Maybe he wouldn't have to have the west-side boy scared off or beaten up after all, he thought. But later that evening, Savannah stepped into the house with FitzAllen Russet, who introduced himself and declared his intentions. As respectful as the young man had been, Ted had a reputation to uphold. The family had a status to maintain. So, hearing his daughter announce that she and the fellow would be leaving town right away was, in a strange way, a gift. Ted would not have to feel guilty about having the fellow beaten. Ted knew his father and brother might have done things differently. And if he was honest with himself, his mother might have, too.

"I don't want no harm coming to my daughter," Ted said to Toliver Wolfe, who saw them off the property. "They're leavin' town. Make sure they go untouched." Ted handed Toliver one hundred dollars. "For your time and discretion."

"No problem at all, Ted," Toliver said.

Though Ted later learned where Savannah lived, and that she had become a mother and then a widow, it would be over a decade before the two would speak to each other again. Not long after she returned to West Mills, he'd seen her at Sutton's filling station. It was shortly after Christmas. Sutton was attending to Ted's tank when Savannah drove up on the other side of the pump. Her eldest son was next to her in the front seat, the younger one in the back. Ted was certain she hadn't noticed him. And he doubted she would recognize the truck he was driving.

"That'll be three dollars, Brother Temple," Sutton said. Ted had told Sutton on multiple occasions that he was not a member of the brotherhood. But each time, Sutton winked and smiled. "Say, looks like the two of ya got the same idea today." He gestured toward Savannah's car. "If you want me to stop serving her, I will. Plenty places she can get gas 'round here. I—"

"No, no," Ted said. "No need for that." He handed Sutton five dollars and bid him a good day. Ted started his engine and inched toward the road. But before he drove off the lot, he put the truck in reverse, stopped in front of Savannah's car, and rolled down his window.

"Did you get the card?" Ted called toward his daughter's car. Savannah's windows were all rolled up and she was talking to her sons. It was likely that she hadn't heard him. Sutton tapped on her window and pointed at Ted.

And in that moment, for the first time since the early sixties, Ted and his daughter made direct eye contact.

Savannah rolled down her window, and Ted heard her say to Sutton, "What did he say?"

"Something 'bout a card," Sutton said. "But he's right there. Maybe you oughta get out and ask him."

Ted could have been knocked over with a feather as he watched his daughter get out of the car with her sons and walk toward his truck. It was as if it were happening in slow motion. Or maybe they actually were moving slowly. Like deer. Unsure, untrusting, but curious. Savannah hadn't aged much, it seemed. She looked very much like her mother. If Ruthanne had been alive, he imagined she would give their grandsons every penny he had to his name.

"Good afternoon," Savannah said, Terrance and Troy at her sides. Though it was his first time meeting them, he'd known their names from the time they were born. Money couldn't buy everything, but it could buy a lot—especially information.

"Afternoon. Just wondered if you received the card I sent."

"We did," she said. "Terrance, Troy, this is Mr. Ted Temple. He's my father. Say hello." And they did. Ted remembered thinking how unimpressed they seemed by meeting their grandfather for the first time. He decided Savannah must have explained, to some degree, why they were estranged. While Ted would never expect the boys to think of him as a saint, he hoped they didn't see him as a monster.

JUST AS TED came back from his trip down Sad Memory Lane, his mother, still holding on to the copy of *Better Homes and Gardens*, snored and woke herself up from her nap.

"How long was I out?" she asked. He told her it hadn't been more than fifteen minutes. "Good. I don't want to ruin my night's sleep." She looked at her watch. "I'm goin' to the nursing home to see Jimmy. Come along with me. You need some cheerin' up, and you know Jimmy's crazy as a cornered bat."

Ted enjoyed visiting his uncle on occasion. Jimmy suffered from dementia, but if they caught him on a good day, he'd remember their names. He often mistook Ted for Chip, but Ted rolled with it.

Ted and his mother went inside to get their jackets and keys. Just as they were heading out the door, the telephone rang.

"I'll get it, Mama. Go on and start the Mustang. You're the driver today." And into the receiver, Ted said, "Temple residence."

"It's me. Savannah."

"H-hey," he stammered. "Surprised to hear from you. Everything all right?"

"We need to talk," she said.

"Okay."

She asked if she could meet him at his office at the shopping center. "Tomorrow around twelve thirty, if you can. It's my lunch break." She spoke amicably, it seemed to him. It reminded him of the days in the fifties when they'd reconcile after some minor argument. Like the time she wanted an impromptu sleepover and he'd tried to explain that some things require planning. Or that time she'd been upset that he brought home jelly beans when she'd asked for chocolate.

"I'll be there," he said. "May I ask what you want to talk about?"

"Marian Harmon."

Ted could barely swallow. "What about her?"

"Well, it's about me," she said. "The Harmons and me. Let's just talk tomorrow at your office. Okay?"

"All right then," Ted replied.

Ted didn't sleep a wink that night. He tried cold medicine. He tried warm milk. He tried cough syrup with warm milk. None of it worked.

"What's the matter, son?" his mother said to him in the kitchen. She had on the big, puffy, pink wool housecoat Sybil had bought her a year ago. He could die of heatstroke just from looking at it.

It was one o'clock in the morning. She took a glass from the cabinet and got water from the faucet. "You were already on edge—whether you believe so or not. But since you got that call, you've been on Jupiter or somewhere. Tell me what it is. Right now."

"Savannah wants to meet with me," he said. Then he leaned against the counter and waited for her objection.

"She'll ask for money," she said assuredly. "For the taxes on that ol' shack she's living in."

"Taxes?" Ted repeated.

Savannah knows, and she's goin' to hold it over my head for money.

"She'll be put out soon if she doesn't pay. I heard about it weeks ago. You really didn't know?"

"No, I didn't know," Ted said. "Why didn't you mention it?"

"I thought you knew and just weren't sayin' anything to *me* about it. Either way, Savannah's not ours to worry about anymore. Still, I knew this day would come. Was only a matter of time before she'd come crawlin' back askin' for something. You gon' help her?" she asked, drinking her glass of water straight down. Ted shrugged. "Well, if you do, loan it. Don't give it. And make her sign a promissory note. She's not a child. Don't think for one second that she's the old Savannah you lost fifteen, sixteen years ago. It'll never be right between her and us." She practically threw the glass into the sink. Had it not been so thick, it would almost certainly have shattered. "She turned her back on us. Chose others. She's lucky we even let her live in this town."

"Mama."

"I mean it. You're a grown man, and I won't presume to tell you how to deal with her. But be careful. She ain't family anymore."

But the next afternoon, when he opened the door and invited Savannah into his office, all he saw was how much she favored a younger version of his mother—something he hadn't noticed the other day at Aiken's. Savannah would always be family. And he believed that deep down, despite their years of estrangement, Savannah felt the same way on some small level. As if the tension in the room between Ted and his daughter wasn't enough to make him sweat, hearing about what happened at Marian's career talk, and why his grandsons had been invited, rendered Ted speechless for at least a minute. Then he managed, "Just so I'm clear, you want me to talk to Dale Boothe about gettin' you immunity, and in exchange you'll testify against Eunice Loving?"

"Yes," Savannah said.

They sat quietly for a moment. Never in a million years did he think this would be the nature of their first sit-down in over a decade. Ted didn't have the slightest clue who'd killed Marian, Marva, and Lazarus. But he was having a hard time imagining that Eunice Loving had done it. And since Savannah said Eunice's husband seemed to be in the dark, it couldn't have been him. Either way, if the Lovings had wanted Marian dead after all that nonsense at the so-called career talk, they would have killed her the very day it all happened, or the day after Eunice and Marian fussed at the clinic. And they probably wouldn't have killed Marva and Lazarus. Ted voiced all of this to his daughter.

"I just told you the whole story," Savannah said. "She begged me to stay out of it while she *handled* it. It *had* to be her."

"Okay, well, now let me ask you this."

"Jesus Christ!"

"Savannah, why didn't you just tell Brent the truth when he first asked? Why protect Eunice Loving if you thought she might be a killer?" But as the question left his lips, he realized just how angry Savannah must have been with Marian and Marva. Savannah had likely been just as furious as Eunice was. Or else, she simply had no room to judge anyone for anything, given the rumors about her taking pills and her having financial troubles. Either way, there was something she wasn't telling him. Eunice Loving had a target on her back, and his daughter was holding the bow and arrow.

Savannah swept her hair to the back of her head, and she looked at him as though she were about to lay all of her burdens at his feet. He would have gladly collected them and held them for her.

"I didn't come here to answer a thousand questions about why this and why that," Savannah said. "Will you or won't you talk to Dale Boothe?"

"I don't know, Savannah. I need to think this thing through a bit. Maybe you tell me why you're offerin' the Loving woman up all of a sudden. She do something to ya? Got somethin' on ya? Anything to do with that rumor about you and pills?"

Savannah snatched her pocketbook from his desk and said, "To hell with that stupid rumor. Do I look like some kind of addict to you? Look at me!" She looked healthy enough, but her behavior suggested something different. "I'm done answering questions. Will you call Boothe or not? Yes or no. Right now!"

Maybe I shoulda listened to Mama and refused the meeting.

"Well, if that's how it has to be, I have to say no."

"Fine. But just know this: I—" Her gaze landed on the window. Ted wondered if someone was standing outside of it. Then she walked over to it and picked up the snow globe. "Well, I'll be damned." She made her way back to him, globe in hand. "It's you. You were Marian's gentleman caller."

"What?" he asked. What happens in the dark always comes to the light, he'd heard his mother say to his father so many times. *Jesus, help me.* "I don't know what you're talkin' about."

"After the *shit* you gave me about Fitz. And all along . . ." Her voice trailed off.

"Savannah. I—"

"You had us escorted off your property as if I were some intruder! As if I hadn't grown up there, all because the man I loved was Black."

"It was different, Savannah." His mouth felt as though it were packed with cotton. "You two were too young to know who or what you wanted. I thought you'd—"

"When did you start seeing her, Dad?"

Ted looked down at the floor. "Savannah, none of that mat—"

"When? Had to be a long time ago because I saw the globe at their house not long after I moved back here. Yet you never came to me to tell me you were wrong. Never came to apologize for the way you treated Fitz and me. Never tried to get to know your grandsons. You're a fraud."

"Savannah."

"I doubt Nana knows." Tears were streaming down her cheeks. "My God, the wailing she did about me and Fitz. Jesus Christ, you'd have thought someone had died. You two are something else, Dad. I swear!"

"Baby girl, sit and let's talk about this." But what could he say?

"Don't *fucking* call me that. Don't you dare." She looked more sad than angry. He wanted to run to her and hold her. "And no, I don't think I want to talk about it." Calmer now, she sat her pocketbook back onto his desk and pointed to the telephone. "Just do us both a favor and make the call."

TWENTY

JO

The morning after Jo visited the Mitchells and Ted Temple, she poured herself a bowl of bran flakes but only ate one spoonful. Despite all the poking around she'd done, she was still coming up empty. Yes, she had learned quite a bit about the Harmons—things she would have never imagined about them when they were all children. But no one in West Mills seemed eager to have any of the Harmons dead.

It was perplexing to Jo. There was Marian's argument with Eunice on the same day as Marva's with Savannah, within hours of each other. She'd have to be a fool to believe that was a coincidence. And she'd be a double fool to believe Eunice's tale that her row with Marian had nothing to do with her son. Why would Angela Glasper say she heard the boy's name mentioned so many times if it hadn't?

Jo didn't know what to think about Savannah. Who threatens to kill someone just because they've given unsolicited parenting advice? Imagine the number of murders that would happen every year if every mother killed her critics.

As for Marian's dispute with Ted Temple, that ranked low on Jo's list of bewildering things. Landlords and tenants have disagreements. Jo had been in countless tiffs with her landlords and supers in New York. And Temple's being on the Harmons' property was, she had to admit, fairly typical for a man who made his living from buying and selling land.

Most baffling of all was the fact that Lazarus had been shot more times than his sisters—once in the head. But not a soul in West Mills had an unkind thing to say about him. Had Laz been a drug lord when the Harmons were living in the North? Had someone driven down to collect a debt or to respond to an offense?

Maybe Sheriff Horton, however lazy, was right in his presumption that it was all drug-related and not done by a local. There hadn't been any other shootings since the Harmons' deaths. The killer was likely gone with the wind.

Jo hurled the soggy cereal out the back door for the stray cats, tossed the bowl and spoon into the sink, and decided she would go over to Lymp's. She could use a nice long walk to clear her head. She thought he might want to come along.

"One minute you say you want to clear your mind, the next minute you talkin' about the murders again," Lymp said after sneezing. They were in his attic, where he'd been looking for an old photo album. He felt certain his mother once had a picture of Jessie Earl as a young man. Dust was everywhere and the air reeked of mustiness. "Don't take this the wrong way, babe, but you ain't a detective. Them guys do a lot more than ask questions."

"I never said I was a detective." She sneezed, too. "I'm just trying to help wash the mud from *your* name. Remember?"

"Okay, okay," he had said, gently pulling her closer to him. He kissed her cheek. "I don't mean to offend. You know I appreciate it a whole lot. This mess is all gon' be over soon, I believe. But that don't mean we'll know who killed them."

But I need the Harmons' killer to be found, Lymp. That way I'll know it wasn't you.

AFTER LUNCH, JO sat in her living room and skimmed the newspaper. The telephone rang. It was Lymp.

"Babe, whatever you doin', put it on hold. I'm on my way over. Got a surprise for ya. You still got any of that hazelnut coffee?"

"Lymp, honey, I'm not in the mood for surprises right now. Can it wait?"

"We'll see 'bout your mood after I show you the surprise. I'll be over there in five, six minutes. Hazelnut if you have any, please." And he hung up. Soon after, he arrived with a large manila envelope. He had wrapped a red ribbon around it.

"What's this?"

Lymp smiled, wide-eyed. "Open it, Josephine."

Inside were a few sheets of paper with indecipherable figures and symbols. There were two columns: FIRST TEST and SECOND TEST.

"Just flip to the last page. Sums it all up for us."

Lymp had sat for and passed a polygraph test. Percival had finally been able to get ahold of an old police academy classmate who called in some favors. Lymp had gone to the Bertie County's sheriff department to take the test. The questions were there on the report.

The papers slipped from Jo's fingers. Where they landed, she neither knew nor cared. Jo threw her arms around Lymp's neck. She held him tighter than she probably had in the entire

"I'm glad you had someone," Jo said.

"Yeah, for a while, I did. Anyway, at some point, we got tired of talking and laid down in that shade under a tree. Took our shirts off because, as I've said, it was as hot as hell. Eventually, we both dozed off, laying close to each other, me using his back as a pillow. Then, all of a sudden, I heard something and opened my eyes. Mr. Jessie Earl Harmon was standing there with a white lady."

"A white lady?" Jo asked.

"He sure was. And not just any white lady. A Pennington. You probably don't remember, but Mama worked in a couple of the Pennington households. There were a few. I knew a Pennington when I saw one. Well, she was trying to cover her face and she ran off, but Jessie Earl stood there looking at us. He spit on the ground, hard, and said, 'God hates sissies.'"

"That bastard," Jo said. "He had a mean streak. I saw it before."

"One hell of a mean streak in that man," Herschel agreed. "Anyway, he could've been killed on the spot if a gun-toting white man had seen him out at that canal bank with that Pennington lady. They were bold for being out there together like that. I don't know what they were drinking, but it must have been strong."

"Evidently."

"So, he said to us again, 'God hates sissies. Says so in the Bible.' And he recited verses. You know which ones I'm talking about."

"I do."

"Claude and I just sat there. Frozen. When Jessie Earl left, Claude was worried sick. He was so, so worried, Jo. It was sad to watch him cry and rock as he did. But I said, 'He'd be

three years they'd been seeing each other. They swayed from side to side.

"I'm so happy for you, honey," she managed to get out between gasps and sobs. "I'm so happy for *us*. And I'm so, so sorry if I made you feel that I didn't—"

"Hush that," he said. Jo wiped his tears with her thumbs. "You ain't got nothin' to be sorry about. You were tryin' to make sure you ain't in love with a psycho. Making sure you ain't gettin' mixed up with another jive turkey that's gon' disappoint you."

"Lymp, I—"

"I don't fault ya. Not one bit. I love you, Josephine Wright."

"I love you, too, honey," Jo said.

AFTER LYMP LEFT to go home to meet with the plumbers who were going to install his septic tank, Jo called Herschel.

"This is really good news, JoJo!" he cheered. "So what if he told a lie to keep his son from getting his ass beaten?"

"Or shot," Jo reminded him.

"What matters is that Lymp was telling *you* the truth all along," he said. "Well, let's *hope* he was."

"What do you mean? I saw the results with my own eyes."

"JoJo, those tests aren't always completely accurate. Sometimes people pass them and end up confessing to crimes a month later. You know that."

"No, I didn't know that, Herschel," Jo shot back. "Damn it!"

"Calm down. That's not something that happens all the time. Lymp's test results are probably just fine."

Jo didn't answer. Suddenly she was so upset she could push her refrigerator over on its side.

"I don't enjoy suggesting that you should still be suspicious of him. Just doing my job as your brother. You're a good judge of character. Always have been. Just like Mama. And I trust you. Like I said, those results are probably just fine. Jo, are you there? Hello?"

"I'm here," Jo said. She was crying again. "Herschel, I need to believe those documents I saw. I have to." Otherwise, she had no choice but to accept that it was all happening again. The bad luck. She grabbed a napkin from the table and blew her nose. "Lymp's a wonderful man, Hersch. He loves me, and I love him."

"Then I guess that's all that matters," Herschel said. "But for me, Jo, please keep an eye on that temper of his. Okay? He's still Jessie Earl Harmon's son. And that man was a special kind of evil. I hope he's bur—"

"Herschel," Jo said, confused. She dabbed her cheeks and upper lip. "Did he mistreat you or something? What aren't you telling me?"

"Nothing, Jo," he said. "I don't want to drudge up old—"

"Nothing, my foot. Talk to me, Herschel."

"Mama never wanted me to talk about it. But hell, she's gone." She pulled the receiver along with her to the kitchen's window seat, the long cord hovering just over the floor.

"What did Jessie Earl do, Hersch?"

"He ran us out of West Mills, Jo."

"Ran us out?"

"Do you remember my friend Claude Royce? Lived by the schoolhouse?" Jo didn't recall. "He was like me, and we were good friends. Close friends. He and I were sitting up-bridge one day. It was hot as blazes. I remember it well because we wanted to take our shirts off but didn't. It was on a

Friday toward the end of August. School hadn't long back in session from summer break. Well, you know didn't really have a real break the way young people now. We worked in the field when school was on sun recess. Isn't that funny, Jo? Making children work in the instead of inside learning."

"It was awful. I remember it," Jo said.

"Anyway, we'd just left the schoolhouse and were gl had two days off. One of us had the idea to stop an candy or something from Edgars's store. He couldn't sta coloreds, but he'd sell things to anyone. He ran the stor his brother ran the mill. Their mill is how the town name. Did you know that?"

"I didn't."

Herschel explained that the whole town—the east an sides—was once known as Pennington, North Carol was named for the wealthiest family there. But wh Edgars family arrived and built a mill on the west side canal, providing many jobs, the name of the whol slowly changed to West Mills.

"It never really made all that much sense to me," H said. "But it is what it is, I guess. Anyway, after Claud bought whatever it was we wanted, we felt like going we couldn't be seen. Needed some privacy, and there spot about a quarter of a mile up the canal, north, t like a little beach on the canal's bank. It was wood trees. Just what we needed. Like I said, shade and pr

"Were the two of you a couple?" Jo asked.

"Not exactly," Herschel said. "Claude and I had bond. I knew about him. He knew about me. We two young fellas who understood each other."

stupid to say anything. Did you see who that was he was with, getting ready to have a picnic with under the tree, just like she was his wife? One of those Pennington sisters. We don't have to worry about him, man.' "

"So, what happened?"

"That night, Jessie Earl came to our house and told—not asked—Mama to come outside so they could talk. You don't remember him coming to the house sort of late one night?"

"I was probably asleep."

"Yeah, I guess you would have been. Well, he and Mama were outside talking for no more than eight or ten minutes. And when she came back inside, I was standing there waiting. She looked at me and said, 'We have to leave. We start packin' in the morning.' And I said, 'I won't ever do that again, Mama. We were just lying there.' She told me that was for me and God to figure out. Jessie Earl had told her that if we left within a few days, he wouldn't tell a soul. Same went for Claude and his mother."

"He ran them off, too?" Jo asked. "Where'd they go?"

"Greenville. Or maybe it was Greensboro? One of those," Herschel said. "Then, I told Mama about Jessie Earl and the Pennington lady. She said, 'As long as you live, don't ever breathe a word of that. You hear me?' And we all left a couple of days later."

Jo remembered coming home from school that Monday and being told that they would be going north the following day. Her mother had instructed her to ask no questions. "You'll like the North," she'd said. "Things'll be better for the three of us up there. I don't want to hear no fuss."

"That son of a bitch," Jo said, and Herschel laughed. "Now, just a second. Why didn't you or Mama ever tell me about this? Once I was old enough to understand, I mean."

Herschel reminded Jo of a few things. First, their mother had instructed him to never speak of it. Herschel was a mama's boy. He hung on her every word, and he trusted her judgment.

Second, for her mother to tell the story, and to tell it truthfully, she would have had to speak about what Jessie Earl had reported to her. And that, she simply would never have done.

"And *third*?" Jo asked.

"*Third*," Herschel mocked. "You're relentless, little sister." If Jo had learned the truth behind their fleeing north, there was no question that she would have eventually made her way to West Mills and given Jessie Earl Harmon a piece of her mind.

"You're probably right."

"Probably?" Herschel laughed. "You may not remember, but you were a happy child before we moved north. You loved it in West Mills. It was paradise for you, JoJo."

"I'm sorry you were separated from Claude," Jo said. "If you want, I'll try to find him. Maybe I can ask—"

"Jo, stop. I shouldn't have brought it up. You aren't satisfied unless you're doing something. Just focus on your happiness with Lymp."

"Well, that's if this world will allow Lymp and me to be happy."

After ending the call, Jo sat still in the window seat, contemplating what Herschel had revealed about polygraphs not always being right. If the margin for error was so wide, what was the point of the test's existence? Jo believed Lymp and the official test results she'd held in her hands. She hoped she wasn't a fool for doing so.

Then there was the other bomb Herschel had dropped. Jo would have never guessed that Jessie Earl Harmon had been the reason her mother had moved them to New York nearly fifty years ago. She couldn't help but wonder what her life might have been like if they'd been able to stay in West Mills. She felt certain the city had taken years off her mother's life—probably her life, too.

"Poor Hersch," Jo said softly to herself. How a gay teen could survive in a small, southern town like West Mills without losing their mind, Jo couldn't fathom.

God hates sissies, Jessie Earl had said to Herschel. What an awful thing to say. Though Jessie Earl had managed to run them off, Jo imagined her mother stood up for Herschel, her only son. She probably—

Lord, have mercy, Jo thought. Given what Angela had told her about Eunice's son and what Lymp had suggested about him, and given Marian's cruelty—yes, Marian must have said something awful about La'Roy Loving. Of course Eunice would give Marian a piece of her mind for it. Wouldn't any mother?

Feeling overwhelmed by all the day's news—it wasn't even four o'clock yet—Jo made herself a cup of chamomile tea, sat back down in the window seat, and thought about her brother, La'Roy Loving, Claude Royce, and all the people, young and old, who had walked in their shoes. Jo felt powerless. She knew their suffering might never really end, living in a world so full of hate, a world so fearful of difference.

Jo set her cup in the window seat, pulled her knees to her chest, and looked out at the gray sky. She wished for sunlight, if only a few minutes of it. She made wishes for the Herschels, the La'Roys, and the Claudes of the world. She wished for continued peace for her and Lymp.

Jo also wished for closure regarding the Harmons' murders. Not just for Lymp. Not just for her. But for the whole town.

TWENTY-ONE

Jo

The next afternoon, just before one o'clock, Jo and Lymp were sitting out in her front yard. It was an unusually warm day for March—nearly seventy degrees—and they wanted to take full advantage of it. They had pulled three folding chairs from the guest room closet. Two for sitting on, the third for sitting their colas and the batch of doughnuts Jane Glasper had dropped off. She was trying out a new recipe. Peach lavender, she had called it.

Earlier that morning, during breakfast, Jo had asked Lymp if he wanted to buy some flowers and take them to the Harmons' property.

"A more private memorial," Jo had suggested. "Without all the fuss Reverend Stephens put on. You know what I mean?"

"Yeah, but not just yet," he had said after swallowing a mouthful of oatmeal. He had used so much honey that Jo could smell it when he spoke. "But soon. We can do that soon. For now, I kinda just want us to try to forget about all that."

"Do you think you can? We still don't know who—"

"Josephine." He was calm but firm. "If we could just have one week of pretendin' none of that awful stuff happened, just four, five days."

"Okay," she said.

Lymp had been through pure hell. Jo could understand why he'd want to forget it all. For her, it wouldn't be that easy. But for Lymp, she would try.

Angela Glasper drove by and tooted her horn. Jo and Lymp waved.

"Nice young lady," Jo remarked. "She seems well. I can't imagine—" But Jo caught herself before finishing the thought. *If we could just have one week of pretendin'*, Lymp had said. "You know, Lymp, whenever we got warmth like this in the winter, my mother would say the world was about to end." She took a sip from her cola.

"Mine, too," he replied. "And here we are. Folk say the year 2000 will really be it, but I don't know. By then, the rich folk will probably be livin' on another planet."

"I wouldn't doubt it." A loud belch escaped her throat and Lymp matched it. They laughed.

Lymp reached for the paper bag of peach lavender doughnuts and took one out. Jo could smell the ripe peach aroma coming from the round, golden pastries.

"Can you taste the lavender?" Jo asked.

"Damn if I know. It's pretty good, though." He held it out for her to take a bite, and she did.

"I'll tell her to turn the lavender up a few notches," Jo said, taking another doughnut from the bag.

Just then, Percival pulled into Jo's driveway. He was still in uniform but driving his own truck.

"I been calling your house, Lymp," he announced, still behind the wheel. "Got some news." He shut his motor off and made his way toward them. Jo cleared the third chair and invited him to sit. This news he carried wasn't good. She could hear the anguish in his voice. It reminded her of when a doctor told her and Herschel that their mother had less than a week to live.

"What's wrong?" Jo asked.

"Couple hours ago, Sheriff had his guys pick up Eunice Loving for shooting the Harmons."

"Say what?" Lymp exclaimed.

"Well, they picked her up on suspicion, I should say," Percival corrected. "Brought her in for more questioning."

"Let me guess," Jo said. "Marian did or said something terrible to Eunice's son, didn't she?"

"Yes, ma'am. She did more than that. How'd you know?"

"A hunch." Now wasn't the time for Lymp to learn what his father had done to her family. "I was hoping I was wrong."

"Well, she hasn't been arrested," Percival said. "Her lawyer got her released just before I headed over here."

Lymp held his hand out. "See, now I'm confused. Start from the beginnin'."

"So, Savannah Russet and her dad came in with their lawyer and District Attorney Boothe and Judge Wallace. They all went in the interviewing room and closed the door. When I saw Sheriff drop and close the blinds, I said to myself, 'Some shit's 'bout to go down.' Wolfe went in there for a lil while, though. Came out shakin' his head. Told me and Conyers what was goin' on. Hell, we were gon' find out, anyway."

"Then?" Jo nudged.

"Sheriff came out and told Wolfe and Conyers to go bring Eunice in. Savannah cut a deal."

"That means she did something wrong," Lymp said. "If she makin' deals. Right?"

"Right," Percival said. "Savannah said she had information about Eunice's dispute with Marian. Information she had the day Brent Wolfe questioned her. Said she had reason to believe Eunice killed the Harmons. But she wanted immunity for it because she lied to Brent."

"Jesus Christ, man," Lymp said. "If somebody like Eunice Loving killed 'em, maybe the world *is* comin' to an end."

Jo took him by the hand.

Percival shared the details of Savannah's statement, and all that happened when Marian invited her sons to the career talk. What made it worse to Jo's mind was that Eunice had been the one to put the whole thing in motion.

"What in the hell is *wrong* with people?" she said. "That poor child. He's just a *kid*."

"Now, here's what I want to know," Lymp said. "Why in the world is Savannah just now sayin' something?"

"That's the million-dollar question," Percival said. "She claims she's afraid of Eunice. All of a sudden. But I don't know."

"What was Eunice's response to all of this?" Jo asked.

"Eunice wouldn't say a word 'til her lawyer arrived. She—"

"If ya innocent, you say so," Lymp cut in. "You ain't got to wait on a lawyer to say that."

When Eunice's attorney arrived, she gave a statement confirming that she had solicited Marian's help with La'Roy and that she had no idea Marian had planned to use violence as the method.

"She said she ain't have nothing to do with their murders, though. Breezy and their son came and answered questions, too. Everything matched what they'd already told Wolfe. Horton and Boothe had to let Eunice go. Nothing concrete enough to hold her."

"Don't sound to me like a whole lot's changed, then," Lymp said.

"In a way, you're right," Percival said. "Eunice volunteered to sit for a polygraph. Who knows when that'll be. Savannah said she'll sit for one, too."

"Well, they didn't kill 'em, then," Lymp asserted.

"Time'll tell. Anyway, I wanted to come tell ya. Plus, I had to get outta there. Miss Hera Temple was in there talkin' some mess I didn't want to hear. The way she carried on . . . good God. I wanted to put her in a cell."

"Carrying on about what?" Jo asked.

"See, evidently Mr. Temple hadn't told her what was goin' on and somebody must've seen him and Savannah goin' in the station, and they called Miss Hera. She came in the door and said, 'What are y'all doing with my boy? Let me back there!' I didn't say anything to her because I already know she don't like us. I let one of the white guys deal with her."

"What was she saying?" Jo asked. She finished her pop and sat the bottle on the ground.

"Said something like, 'Whatever Savannah's gotten herself into with those Harmons has nothin' to do with Ted. He answered all Horton's questions and y'all are to leave him alone! We pay taxes and I'll have all your jobs!' Then Conyers said, 'Miss Hera, Ted and Savannah came here. Nobody brought them in. Maybe you oughta have a seat and calm yourself.' She told Conyers to shut up. Said, 'Savannah's the *least* of my concern. Got herself mixed up with those dope dealers. I wish Ted hadn't rented so much as a *broom* closet to that Harmon girl. In the old days, colored girls, colored *people*, stayed in their place. Knew what was off limits to them.'

Conyers tried to shush her, but she wouldn't let up. Said, 'In the old days, uppity types were dragged outta their houses in the middle of the night and dealt with!' "

"She sounds absolutely evil," Jo said, flabbergasted.

"Why you surprised?" Lymp asked. "I told you Hera Temple's a trip."

"I'd always heard folk say she was," Percival added. "But I saw it with my own eyes today. She thinks they're above the law. She was mad as hell 'cause somebody had asked her son for their whereabouts. Reminded us they're the Temples."

"What was his alibi, by the way?" Jo asked Percival. "If you know."

According to the statement Percival had read, Ted Temple was home with a guest. Mrs. Temple had spent the night at the nursing home with her brother, an Alzheimer's patient. Apparently, Mrs. Temple stayed overnight whenever the nurses needed help calming him down.

Jo understood. She would do the same for Herschel if it ever came to it.

"So what happens next, Percival?" Jo asked.

"Nothin' until somebody comes up with some evidence," Percival said. "Eunice got a charge, though. Class two misdemeanor for giving a false statement to Wolfe."

"And not even a slap on the wrist for Savannah," Jo said.

"A deal is a deal. Her record's still clean as a whistle."

Lymp scoffed, "Like I said, ain't nothin' changed." He patted Percival on the shoulder and thanked him for stopping by. "I got a headache. Gon' lay down a while."

"Lymp," Jo called out to him.

"I'm fine, Josephine." He went inside.

"He just wants it to be over," Jo said to Percival.

"Oh, I don't blame him," Percival said. Jo thanked him for the update. "No problem, Miss Jo. Lymp and Nate like family to me. You part of the family now, too."

"Do you think any of this will make your bosses take the case seriously? Do some real investigating?"

"To be honest, Miss Jo, I doubt it. They'll keep pretending to do something, but it'll all be for show. People like Horton, Boothe, and Wallace don't care who killed Black folk. And they especially don't care 'bout who killed people like Dr. Harmon. See, to folk like the sheriff and Miss Hera Temple, Dr. Harmon was a whole lot different from other Black folk 'round here with money. Her coming back here wantin' to do business on the east side set her apart from folk like the Mannings and the Baileys."

"The Baileys?"

"The folk who own the funeral homes."

"Oh, right," Jo said.

"Dr. Harmon demanded equality. The Mannings and Baileys follow an unspoken rule, Miss Jo, which is to stay out of white people's way. Dr. Harmon was brave."

"Yes," Jo said. "She was."

When Percival was gone, Jo went to her bedroom. Lymp was sitting in the chair in the corner, his head against the wall, eyes closed.

"You want aspirin?"

"Nah, babe. Thanks, though."

Jo sat near the foot of the bed. "What do you think about Percival's news?"

Lymp opened his eyes and said, "West Mills is full of surprises nowadays, seems like. I don't know what to say 'bout any of it. I just wish things would go back to normal." He rose from the chair, kissed her cheek, and lay across the bed. "Love ya."

"I love you, too, dear," Jo replied.

In the kitchen, Jo washed dishes, put them away, and sat at the table, thinking about the latest developments. What galled her most remained that Sheriff Horton, a person sworn to protect the community, shamelessly refused to do his job, and that Hera Temple had stood in a municipal building and praised the days when Black people were murdered in their own front yards. To Jo, both acts were criminal.

As Jo stood to leave the kitchen, she noticed the bag of Jane Glasper's doughnuts on the counter. She was about to throw them away. Neither she nor Lymp had loved them as much as they'd hoped. But she hated to waste them, given how hard Jane worked, and—

Where do you work, Jane? Jo had asked when she went to visit Angela.

Just over at the nursing home, doing this and that, Jane had replied.

Percival said Hera Temple was supposed to have been at the nursing home on the night of the Harmons' murders.

In the old days, they'd be dragged out in the middle of the night and dealt with! Hera Temple had reportedly shouted.

"No," Jo whispered to herself. "I must be crazy." But still, Jo ran to the living room where her pocketbook was. She had written the Glaspers' phone number in her address book.

"Glasper residence," Jane said after answering on the fourth ring.

"Jane, this is Jo Wright. I have a very important question for you."

"I'm listening."

"At the nursing home, do visitors have to sign in and out?"

"Say what?"

Jo repeated the question. "I wouldn't be asking if it weren't urgent, Jane. Please."

"Yeah," Jane said. "It wasn't always like that. They just started requirin' that 'bout a year ago. Somebody walked right in and robbed some patients' rooms one day during the activities hour. Ever since then, every soul that goes in *and* outta there has to sign that book. In and out. Why you askin'?"

TWENTY-TWO

EUNICE

Eunice felt relief when Breezy called to tell her he was coming home. He and La'Roy had been staying with Pep and Otis Lee ever since Eunice was forced to reveal the truth. Now that the cloud of suspicion over Eunice's head had rolled away, it was time for them to talk, move on, heal, Breezy said. And while Eunice was happy to hear this, she wished La'Roy was coming home, too.

According to Nova, who got the information from Percival's grandmother while doing her hair, Mrs. Hera Temple had been arrested for the Harmons' murders and taken to a mental hospital in Raleigh. Percival had received an anonymous tip from a citizen, urging him to verify Mrs. Temple's whereabouts on the night of the Harmons' murders. Mrs. Temple had not lied about spending the night with her brother at the nursing home. But she hadn't been there all night long. She had left, claiming to go and get her brother some of his favorite snacks from the twenty-four-hour gas station. The time she was away from the nursing home coincided with the time the coroner believed the Harmons to have been killed. In most cases, that wouldn't have been enough. But all it had taken was for officers to mention that evidence to Mrs. Temple. She did the rest of their work for them.

"That's why people shouldn't talk without a lawyer sitting next to 'em," Nova had said. "I still can't believe no one called and told you any of this, Eunice."

"Why'd she do it, Nova? That's what I want to know."

While parked at the shopping center, Mrs. Temple had heard the argument between Marian and her son. Mr. Temple had been so angry with Marian that he hadn't noticed his mother's bright yellow Mustang parked just six or seven feet away. When she realized that her son had been threatened and that Marian was prepared to expose their relationship, she did what any mother would do, she said to the officers. And when asked why she'd shot Lazarus in the head, and why she'd shot him and Marva at all, Mrs. Temple said, "All three of 'em had to go. They didn't know their place. Their daddy didn't, either. They had to go."

Moments later, Ted Temple, who had sat on their large, screened-in porch, surrounded by officers, shocked at his mother's admission, fell to the floor. The officers did all they could, and when the rescue squad arrived, they tried again. But he was gone. Mrs. Temple ran to him and held his head in her lap. Having wailed for several minutes, she looked at the officers and said "I'd do anything for my boys. You hear me? Anything for my babies." Then she began calling out for her eldest son. "Where's Chip? Chip! Come help me with your brother!"

Eunice couldn't help but feel sympathy for the old woman.

But she was more focused on her own son, who she hoped would forgive her. La'Roy's wounds needed more time to heal. Eunice understood that. And she would be patient. If it were up to Pep Loving, neither La'Roy nor Breezy would ever go back home to Eunice again. Pep had said as much to her over the phone before hanging up abruptly.

And while Eunice knew, without question, that her decision to solicit Marian Harmon had been the biggest mistake of her life, she blamed Savannah Russet for the current state of things. Eunice had not been overly surprised when the squad car pulled up in her driveway to take her to the station. The real shock was that they hadn't come sooner.

"Did that Temple girl really think you'd *kill* somebody? Over something like *that*?" Eunice's mother had said. "A good cursin' out, sure. But shootin' three whole people? That just tells ya what she thinks of us, deep down." But this was not to be confused with support for what Eunice had done, her mother made clear. "You know you were wrong, right? Gettin' somebody mixed up in private family business? And without even tellin' your husband? Eunice, you knew better. Maybe Breezy could've helped."

"I shouldn't have taken La'Roy at *all*, Ma," Eunice had replied. "I shouldn't have asked anyone to change my child." To this, her mother had shrugged. And her father had only said, "You meant well."

Her parents had left her house a couple of hours ago. They had brought Eunice a late lunch. They had been spending time at both Manning Grocery stores, making sure the employees Eunice appointed to lead were up to the job, keeping things in order.

Eunice walked to the living room and sat on the couch that faced the front door. There she would wait for Breezy. She wanted to apologize, again, for the pain she'd caused their son, who she now feared might never trust her again. Eunice wanted to atone for it all. And she said so to Breezy when he walked in. But she didn't cry this time. Where would she find more tears?

"I'm sorry, too, Eunice. I shouldn't have left you here the way I did. That was just plain wrong."

"Thank you," Eunice said.

"That don't mean I like all that happened. I know women don't tell their husbands every little thing. All married men know that 'bout their wives. But when it comes to our child, I'm supposed to know what you got goin'. I'm supposed to know, Eunice."

"I know," Eunice said. "I should have never gone to her. She was—"

"I don't fault you for wantin' to get him help," Breezy said. "You were just tryin' to protect him. You meant well. And I don't think you oughta be too hard on yourself 'bout that part. But damn, Eunice. You didn't even ask Marian Harmon what she was planning to do to our son. Mean as everybody said she was, you had to know it was gon' be some ol' crazy shit."

He sat next to her on the couch, but they did not touch. They were silent a minute.

"I'll spend more time with La'Roy," Breezy said. "But I ain't no damn wizard, Eunice. I can take him fishing and make him throw 'round a football all day. Won't make no difference. I don't like it one bit, but if he's gay, probably ain't nothing to be done about it."

"I know, Breezy. But I worry for him. This world is so cruel, and—"

"Cruel to all of us, though. La'Roy will find his way. He won't live with us forever. We can't watch over him always.

And if you worried 'bout what folk say and think, you might as well stop because you can't win with people. You could go 'round this whole west side and give everybody a nice gift. They'd thank you to your face and still talk shit about you when you leave. You know that as well as I do. I need some water."

The house had been miserably quiet since he and La'Roy had left. So, Eunice enjoyed the sound of Breezy in the kitchen, rummaging through the package of chocolate chip cookies.

"You think our baby will ever want to come home again?" Eunice asked. Breezy turned on the faucet, filled a glass, and gulped it down.

"Mama and Pop got him 'til he's ready," Breezy said. "But I think he'll be back sooner than later. They won't spoil him like we have."

"Think he'll ever forgive me?"

"You already know the answer to that, Eunice. La'Roy's a mama's boy. To the core. You just need to forgive *yourself*."

Eunice gave herself over to a near-violent sob. Breezy sat down and held her.

"I gotcha, Eunice," he said. He kissed the top of her head. "I gotcha."

TWENTY-THREE

SAVANNAH

Assistant Principal Pherebee called Savannah at Aiken's and asked her to come pick up her sons. They had been in a brawl with two other boys, and they were all suspended from school for the rest of the week. Assistant Principal Pherebee was sorry to have to do it, given all that had happened in the past couple of weeks. But policy is policy. Savannah understood, and she appreciated the compassion with which Assistant Principal Pherebee had delivered the news.

When Savannah told her boss that she would take the boys home, then return to work, she received no such kindness. Stewart said, "Maybe you should take some extended time off. Seems like you have quite a bit going on."

"I suppose I should just go ahead and take the day."

"Longer," he said.

"Stewart, are you firing me?"

"Well, I wouldn't call it a *firing*, exactly. I've never *fired* anyone in all my years of business. But I just wonder if Aiken's is still the right fit for you. Your moods have been up and down, and—"

"Right fit? My moods? I lost my best friend. I've been a good worker, Stewart Aiken. And you know it. This is the thanks I get? Because of what my grandmother's done, you'd take food from my children's mouths? Well, screw you."

"I think you should go now," Stewart said.

"Oh, I'm going all right." And having felt she'd been more polite than the occasion called for, Savannah shouted, "Fuck you, this store, and this whole shit town!"

Thank God her father had covered her tax debt. Thank God he'd insisted she take more money. For extra cushion, he'd said. In a last will and testament drawn up not long after Savannah's uncle Chip had died, her father had willed everything to her grandmother. Savannah imagined he would have updated it if he'd had the chance. With her grandmother in a mental institution—Savannah doubted there was anything insane about the old woman except her beliefs—and with some big developer pulling out of a deal to buy the shopping center, there was no telling what would happen to his assets. Surely, had she attended the funeral, the whole east side of town would have been looking at her and thinking the same thing. That was one of the reasons Savannah chose to pay her respects privately, alone at the chapel on the morning of the service. The other reason had more to do with the wailing she knew she'd succumb to, for the father who had once given her a life most girls could only dream of. She wailed for the old Ted Temple—the one who had loved her unconditionally.

"What was the fight about, guys?" Savannah asked on their way from the school to her house. "And I don't want to hear any of that 'people say you take pills' crap." Oh, what she would do for one of those calming pills. But she knew that if she had one, she might fall deeper in love with them than she had ever been.

Neither of the boys spoke. Terrance looked out the window. Troy dug around in his backpack for God knew what.

"I want an answer right now," Savannah said.

"They got in our faces and started sayin' stuff," Troy said.

"What did we say you'd do if that happened?" Savannah asked. Terrance sucked his teeth. "What's that supposed to mean, young man?" No reply. Savannah pulled over onto the road's shoulder. "I know a lot's been going on the past few weeks, but I need you two to keep it together!"

"Why do we have to keep it together when people are talkin' shit about us and you?" Terrance said. "You're not the one being called a snitch's kid! You're not the one being called a pill popper's kid! And now your grandma is a murderer. Fuck all this!"

"Hey!" Savannah shouted. Then she remembered that just one hour ago she had said *fuck* at least four times while clearing out her locker at Aiken's. Terrance was entitled to one.

"You just do shit, and me and Troy are the ones who have to pay for it," Terrance said. "And then you blame it all on somebody else. We're not dumb, Mom!" His face was burgundy with anger. Or was that sadness? "Everyone at school is sayin' you're prejudiced and that you accused Mrs. Loving of murder to cover for your grandma because y'all are white and she's Black."

"They don't know what the hell they're talking about," Savannah said. "I had no idea she—"

"That didn't stop you from going and telling the police you thought Mrs. Loving did it. What if somebody lied to the cops about me and Troy, just because we're Black? How would that make you feel?" Tears ran down his face faster than he could wipe them. "Is that what you are now? A prejudiced white lady like your grandma?"

Savannah reached out to touch him, but he snatched his hand away. She looked in the rearview mirror at Troy. He was not crying, but he looked at her as though she were a stranger, a taxi driver giving them a lift. She put the car in drive, merged back onto the road, and drove home.

Savannah had done a lot of lying. She had lied to herself about her dependence on the Valium and to her sons about having used them. Savannah had lied to Brent Wolfe when asked about her quarrel with Marva. And she had lied to herself about being different from the Temples, different from the white people on the east side of the canal. After all, what had she done when the going got tough? She had leaned on what she knew would work. Fitz would be ashamed of her. She knew because she was ashamed of herself.

It was time for her to tell some truths. Her children deserved that much. So, later that night, Savannah asked Terrance and Troy to come out from behind their closed doors, and she asked them to join her at the kitchen table.

"I have made some very bad mistakes," Savannah admitted to them. "And I haven't been honest about everything. I misused a medication."

"So, you're an addict?" Troy asked.

"I don't really know," Savannah replied. "I haven't had a pill in weeks. But maybe I am still an addict. What I can tell you is that I don't plan to take any more of them. I can tell you that much. If I hadn't been on those things, I probably would've never even left you at the Harmons' that day. I wasn't myself. And I'm sorry I put you two in the position to be used by Marian."

"Did Dr. Harmon really think beating La'Roy up would change him?" Troy asked.

Savannah shrugged. "I guess she did, honey. I really don't know. Either way, she was wrong to involve the two of you." She saw Troy's face soften—but only a little. "Would you like to ask anything else? Anything at all."

"Why'd you lie on Mrs. Loving?" Terrance asked. "Did you really think she killed them?"

Deep, deep down, not really, she wanted to say. *But she insulted you two, which insulted me. I wanted to win the fight.*

Instead, she said, "I wouldn't say I lied, sweetheart. But I exercised poor judgment. Very poor judgment."

Terrance asked what would happen to her grandmother. Do people her age get sent to regular prison? Would she get the electric chair?

"She'll probably be where she is for the rest of her life," Savannah said.

"In the hospital?"

"Yeah." He looked perplexed, and she understood why. But she was fresh out of explanations. Tapped. "Now, back to your rooms. You two are still grounded for the fighting. I've got lots of chores planned for you."

As the boys left the kitchen, she heard Terrance say the chores were probably better than the shit they'd been dealing with from the other kids at school. And Troy agreed.

"Guys," she called out to them. "Maybe we'll move back to New York. A fresh start."

The boys looked at each other, then at her. Whether or not they liked the idea, she couldn't be sure. Savannah wasn't even sure if she liked the idea.

"She don't mean it," Terrance said to his brother.

"Maybe I do," Savannah said, thinking about the five thousand dollars her father had given her. "Who knows?"

TWENTY-FOUR

Jo

Despite the many invitations Jo and Lymp had received from Reverend Stephens and others to come to Shiloh Baptist to be prayed over, they both declined. Back in New York, Jo had once received similar overtures after her divorces. They were well-meaning, but intrusive.

"I didn't go to church before Marian and them got killed, and I ain't about to start goin' now," Lymp had said. "They need to pray for themselves for treatin' me like they did, and for Hera Temple's soul, and for this town." Jo could not have agreed more.

Jo spent the morning cleaning out her refrigerator, getting rid of anything that might go bad while she and Lymp went to New York for a week to visit Herschel. Lymp was at his own house doing the same. They were set to leave the following morning.

Jo was wringing out the rag, preparing to wipe the fridge's top shelf, when the telephone rang. It was Herschel.

"Are you sure he's not going to be uncomfortable, staying here in the apartment with two old sissies?" Herschel joked.

"You know I hate when you use that word, you jive turkey," Jo said. "Lymp will be fine. We've had a long discussion about it." They'd had more than one long discussion about his discomfort with gay men. "He understands that you and Dean are part of the package deal. If he loves me, he has to love you. That's all there is to it."

"Good. Tell him he shouldn't worry. We're into older men." Jo and Herschel laughed. "What's the news on Hera Temple's case? Is Lymp planning to attend any of the hearings?"

"No. He's ready to move on. We're driving over to the Harmons' property today." Lymp wanted to go visit his father's house once more before its new owners came and did God knows what to the place. Marian had willed the property to the children of some distant cousin on her mother's side. Lymp didn't know who they were or where they were from. "He wants to lay out some flowers in the yard. He says he'll never set foot there again."

"That's probably for the best," Herschel said. "You know how I feel about staying away from places that cause pain."

"Yes, I do," Jo said. "But I'll figure out some way to get you down here for a visit. I want you to see my house, Herschel."

"Well, you know, they have these fabulous contraptions called cameras, and they spit out these lovely little things called photographs." They shared a laugh and said they'd see each other soon.

Lymp was supposed to pick Jo up at eleven o'clock. They would stop by Manning Grocery to buy a handful of whatever flowers they had available, go to the Harmon property for a brief vigil, and then go to the Elks Lodge for lunch. It was eleven twenty and Lymp wasn't there. She called, but the line was busy. She waited a few minutes and tried again. Still busy. She would just walk over to his house, and they could leave from there.

Jo knocked on Lymp's door and waited half a minute before entering. He probably wouldn't have heard her knocking anyway. The television's volume was turned up high, and the sounds of a Tide commercial bounced around the room.

"Lymp!" she called as she walked in. He was nowhere in sight. But as she neared his bedroom, she heard sobbing. Lymp was sitting on the edge of his bed, crying like an abandoned child. He covered his face with his hands.

"Oh, honey," Jo said, wrapping her arms around him.

"I was supposed to look out for those three, Josephine," Lymp said. "But what did I do? I talked shit 'bout 'em. And that ol' woman killed my people. Shot 'em dead in my father's house." He had to gasp for breath. "I let 'em all down. Them and Jessie Earl."

"You've done no such thing, love. I'd say it was the exact opposite."

Jo reflected on what Herschel had told her about Jessie Earl, the man who had caused her family such anguish. Jo hadn't told Lymp any of it. He thought so highly of his father, and she didn't want to take that away from him. Eventually, she would tell him the truth. But not today.

Jo took hold of Lymp's hands, gave them a quick tug, and asked him to stand.

"You have me now, Olympus Seymore," Jo reminded him. "We've got each other. And I'm so happy about that."

ACKNOWLEDGMENTS

I'd first like to thank my readers. Your kind emails and DMs mean a lot to me. And I'm incredibly grateful to booksellers and Bookstagrammers. Your support is such a gift.

To my agent, PJ Mark of Janklow & Nesbit: You continue to do so much for me. You're always willing to answer my questions or offer feedback. Please know that I appreciate it.

To my editor, Daniel Loedel, and assistant editors Ragavendra Maripudi and Olivia Oriaku: thank you for your sharp attention to detail and your hard work. To Barbara Darko, Greg Villepique, Missy Lacock, and everyone at Bloomsbury Publishing: You all do so much behind the scenes to get writers' books out into the world. Thank you for all you do.

Many thanks to Liese Mayer, who saw this project in its earliest, messiest form and encouraged me to keep going.

My writing community is large and steadily growing. Shouts out to Regina Porter, Marcus Burke, Jason England, William Pei Shih, Derek Nnuro, Suzette Andrews, Zoë Ruiz, Monica West, Dawnie Walton, J. M. Holmes, Jade R. Jones, Grayson Morley, Connor White, C. Kevin Smith, Geoffrey Minter, Margot Livesey, Helen Phillips, Paul Harding, Robert Jones Jr., Maurice Carlos Ruffin, and Berend ter Borg, just to name some folks. Last, but certainly not least, I want to thank D. Cole Murphy, for whom I have immeasurable love, respect, and gratitude. You listened to me talk (incessantly) about this book for the past couple of years. What a patient, supportive, and loving human being you are.

A NOTE ON THE AUTHOR

DE'SHAWN CHARLES WINSLOW is the author of *In West Mills*, a Center for Fiction First Novel Prize winner, an American Book Award recipient, and a Willie Morris Award for Southern Fiction winner, and a finalist for the Los Angeles Times Book, Lambda Literary, and Publishing Triangle awards. He was born and raised in Elizabeth City, North Carolina, and graduated from the Iowa Writers' Workshop.